EVIL WALKS LIKE A MAN.

Sam looked around the house's interior one more time before following the long marks in the dirt. He stopped in his tracks when he saw the body of the dead Mexican lying sprawled in a dried puddle of dark blood, a machete only inches from his outstretched hand.

"It's only the start," he said, preparing himself.

Walking on, he saw the body of yet another man, this one lying ten yards away, also in a dried pool of blood. His head was missing. A few yards ahead, in the rear of the rock yard, he saw the table standing upended in the dirt, a naked, bullet-riddled body tied to it.

Hodding Siebert . . . , he concluded, seeing the grizzly handiwork of a monster.

LOOKOUT HILL

Ralph Cotton

BERKLEY
New York

BERKLEY
An imprint of Penguin Random House LLC
penguinrandomhouse.com

ISBN: 9780451238306

Signet mass-market edition / October 2012
Berkley mass-market edition / July 2023

Printed in the United States of America
5   7   9   11   13   12   10   8   6   4

For Mary Lynn . . . of course

PART 1

Chapter 1

—————

The Mexican Hill Country, Old Mexico

Arizona Territory Ranger Samuel Burrack rode up a long, slanted hillside above miles of smelting furnaces and mining encampments. When he'd reached a point where he could breathe without the acid odor of melted copper burning his nostrils, he stopped and pulled his bandanna down from the bridge of his nose.

Clean Mexican air . . . , he told himself, inhaling deeply, letting his lungs take their fill. Beneath him he felt the stallion chuff and blow and lift its muzzle to a cool passing breeze.

"You too, pard?" he said quietly, patting the big Appaloosa's withers with a gloved hand. He nudged the stallion forward, his right hand holding his Winchester rifle across his lap.

Fifty yards up the trail, he found the tracks he had lost earlier when he'd started crossing a hard rock ledge. Now that the ledge had given way to softer dirt and gravel, he saw the hoofprints of the two horses he'd been tracking all the way from the foot of the Sierra Madres. *For the last three days,* he reminded himself. Wanting a closer look, he stopped the stallion and stepped down from the saddle, rifle in hand.

Yep, it's them all right, he told himself, looking closer at the sets of prints. He had seen early on where a faulty nail head had broken off one of the shoes, leaving a shallow gap imprinted in the dirt. Soon that gap had filled with packed dirt. But crossing the rock ledge, the impacted dirt from the shoe must have broken loose. Now that the two horses had left the stone surface, he knew the empty nail hole would fill with dirt again. But that was all right, he thought; he was back on their trail.

He had come to know the hooves of these two horses. At a walk, one of them veered a little to the left over a short distance of twenty or so feet—the sign of a lazy hand on its reins. The other horse, the one with the broken nail head in its shoe, had a splayed right front hoof. With every step this animal took, the hoofprint turned a slight bit outward—hardly noticeable except to the sharpened tracker's eye.

Sam stood up from the prints and looked all around. He was not the gifted tracker that he would have liked to be, but he was still learning. Learning, with his fingers in the dirt. The only way to learn, as his captain would say. And his captain was right, he told himself, walking along, reins in hand, leading the stallion along the narrow trail.

Tracking required close attention to detail. Some men worked hard at learning it. Others didn't. Some men pinned on a badge thinking being gun-handy was all it took to be a good Ranger. But even though he'd only been a Ranger for a little over two years, he'd already seen that men who didn't learn sound tracking skills soon left the trail in defeat, or worse. Some of them left in a plank box.

He'd not only learned the particulars about these two horses, how they moved and what identifying marks they left behind—he'd also put more than just a little thought into the two men riding them. One was a quick-to-kill Missouri madman named Hodding "Hot Aces" Siebert. The folded wanted posters inside the flap of his bib-front shirt told the Ranger that Hodding Siebert had been outrunning the law for over three years. Siebert knew that getting caught left nothing of his future but a hard drop at the end of a hangman's rope.

Sam knew that with such a grim reckoning awaiting him, Hot Aces Siebert played out his life hard and fast. He took what he wanted when he wanted it, and heaven help the man who tried to stop him. But Siebert wasn't the first killer the Ranger had hunted down, nor did Sam have any intention of allowing him to be the last. So, while Siebert's murderous regard for the rest of the world gave Sam no cause for alarm, it did hold his attention.

Sam knew that in Siebert's three years of freedom from Yuma Penitentiary, the man and his various cohorts had robbed some nine banks, three trains and a dozen or more payrolls. At each robbery he'd left at least one dead man lying in his wake. In addition to the killings while in pursuit of his trade, Siebert was known for senseless indiscriminant killings all along the border country—an unpredictable lunatic with a gun. Especially when riding alone, left to his own devices, Sam told himself. Maybe riding with a partner would help keep him in check. He hoped so.

Real pieces of work, these two. . . . Sam shook his head a little, considering these men whose dark menacing life he'd committed himself to bringing to its bitter end.

It was his job, he reminded himself.

The second man was Texas outlaw and escaped convict Bobby Hugh Bellibar, another hard case with nothing to lose. Bellibar's crimes over the past years were so numerous and diverse he was certain the courts must've had a hard time deciding whether to list his heinous offenses alphabetically or in the order of their perpetration.

Sam stopped and looked out over a valley a few hundred feet below. A thin glittering river wound out of sight at the bottom of a steep hillside. He thought about the empty canteen he'd found along the trail three hours earlier. He'd known then that it wouldn't be long before they gravitated toward whatever water lay nearest them. And there it was, he told himself, Winchester in hand, leading the stallion behind him.

Twenty minutes later he came upon a lone horse standing to the side of the trail, its reins dangling loose to the dirt. The silvery gray dun stood dark with sweat and lathered in white foam. Upon seeing the Ranger, the animal shied away a few steps, favoring its right forehoof. *The horse with the outturned hoof,* he thought, not surprised that it would be the first horse to falter under the weight of its rider and the rigors of this steep, rocky trail.

He let Black Pot's reins drop from his hand, knowing the stallion would stay there. First checking for any sign of an ambush, Sam eased forward, his rifle hammer cocking under the pull of his thumb.

"Easy, boy," he murmured to the silver-gray dun, picking its reins up from the ground. He examined the animal's right forehoof, lifting it up between his crouched knees for a closer look. The horse chuffed and grumbled a little as Sam pressed with his thumbs and worked the horse's hoof around with his gloved hands.

"There's nothing wrong with you that a little rest and water won't cure," Sam said. "The water's not far, but you'll have to rest while you walk." As he spoke he loosened the cinch and dropped the saddle from the dun's back. "That'll help some," he added.

The horse looked at him, grumbling and scraping its good hoof on the ground as if in protest. Sam rubbed a hand along its withers.

"I know," he said as if the animal understood him, "but it's walk with us or spend the night here alone, feeding wolves."

The horse stared at him through caged eyes, but then it took a wary step closer and probed its frothy muzzle toward him.

"That's what I thought," Sam said. He chuckled to himself, rubbed the horse's muzzle and drew the tired animal over beside Black Pot. He stepped back up into his saddle. "Don't worry," he said to the sweaty dun. "We'll take it nice and easy down to the water."

On the same trail, miles ahead of the Ranger, Hodding Siebert lay prone on the gravelly stream bank, his face and the upper half of his body submerged in the cool rushing water. Bobby Hugh Bellibar stood beside him, holding the roan's reins loosely while the thirsty animal drank.

"Here's the hard truth of it, Bobby Hugh," Siebert said, his palms supporting him on the gravelly bank. "I'm not riding double the rest of the way to Copper Gully. Your horse gave out on you. We keep riding double, mine will do the same before we're off these hilltops."

"I hear you, Aces," Bobby replied.

"This is nothing personal against you, Bobby Hugh," Siebert said, "but when riding stock gets in short supply, every man has to fend for himself." He paused as if in reflection, then said, "If I had a dollar for every man I shot over a horse, or *thought* about shooting over a horse, I'd be rich as a pound cake."

"I understand," Bellibar said acceptingly. "Me too."

"So, figure something out before we leave here," Siebert said with resolve, and with that he lowered his face into the clear, cool water.

Bellibar watched him drink.

"I think I got it figured," he said as Siebert finally pushed himself up from beneath the water.

"Yeah, what's that?" Siebert said, water running down from his wet hair, his clothes.

"I'm taking your horse, Aces," Bellibar said flatly.

"You're talking out of your head, Bobby Hugh." Siebert gave a sharp grin and turned sidelong to where Bobby had stood watering the tired roan a moment earlier. But Bellibar wasn't there, and neither was the roan.

"Back here, Aces," Bellibar said, behind him.

"Right," said Siebert, getting the gist of it. He rolled over onto his back, his wet hair hanging in dripping points down his forehead. "I expect you think you've caught me at a disadvantage," he added, cocking his head slightly.

"Yep, that's how I make it," Bellibar said, the horse's reins in his left hand.

"You make it wrong, Bobby Hugh," said Siebert, the grin still there on his wet face. "Don't you think I already thought of this before I said anything about the horse?" He gave a dark, confident chuckle. "That's why I unloaded your Colt earlier while you were dozing against that big pine. You're jackpotted, pard. Now I kill you and take your power."

Take his power . . . this crazy bastard.

"You're bluffing," said Bellibar. "I heard that one before, tell a man his gun's not loaded, then gun him down when he makes a move to check it."

"Already heard that one, huh?" Siebert sighed, shaking his head a little.

"Yep," said Bellibar, "it might even have been you who told it to me."

"I wouldn't doubt it," said Siebert. He pushed himself up from the ground and stood with his feet spread shoulder-width apart. He wiped his left hand across his face, pushing his wet hair to the side. His right hand stayed poised near the tied-down holster on his hip. "Only this time it's a fact, Bobby Hugh," he added, in a stone serious tone of voice. "I've got your bullets in my pocket. Want to see them?"

"Nope," said Bellibar, his demeanor still confident, unwavering. "I believe you did it, you sneaking son of a bitch."

Siebert gave a short shrug. There was no sign of bluffing in his eyes.

"Like I said, Bobby Hugh," Siebert said quietly, "times like this it's every man for himself. You should have listened to me."

Bellibar could tell the older gunman was ready to make his play. He saw Siebert open and close his gun hand, getting ready.

"I did listen to you, Aces," he said. His expression softened a little. "That's why I took your Remington from your holster while you sucked water."

"Nice try, Bobby Hugh," said Siebert, "but I ain't falling for it—" As he spoke his right hand slapped against his empty holster and stopped him short. His eyes suddenly took on a look of desperation.

Now it was Bellibar's turn to give a wide, confident grin. He reached behind his back, taking his time, and grabbed Siebert's big Remington.

"See?" He wagged the gun back and forth in his hand. Looking down at it, he cocked it toward Siebert's chest and said, "I bet you didn't unload it, did you?"

"No, Bobby Hugh," Siebert said in defeat, "damn it to hell, I didn't unload it." In a flash he thought about the small Colt Pocket pistol he carried behind his back, shoved down into his belt under his shirttail. But it was too late.

Bellibar's hand bucked, once, twice, three times as he recocked and fired the big Remington. Each shot knocked Siebert farther out into the rushing water. The third shot flung him out of his right boot and sent him splashing into the thrust of the water's strong current. The freed boot spun three turns overhead, landing upright in the water and floating away.

"Nice action," Bellibar said. He smiled down at the smoking Remington, impressed, turning it back and forth in his hand.

He stepped forward into the water and took aim toward Hodding Siebert's bobbing head—Siebert thirty feet away and slipping farther downstream, blood trailing red, thinning in the water behind him.

But before he could squeeze the trigger, a sound from the sloping hillside behind Bellibar drew his attention. He turned quickly, the Remington up, cocked and ready.

"Who's there?" he called out, certain he'd heard something or someone up there among the trees and rock ledges. He looked back and forth on the steep hillside, knowing another stretch of this same trail switched back above him.

"*Quién hay . . . ?*" he called out, repeating himself in his border Spanish.

He waited, silent, his eyes searching every land stuck boulder, every rocky cut-ledge, every tall, clinging pine. Nothing. . . .

Beside him, the roan had taken advantage of the young gunman's cautious wait, drawing more water for itself. After another silent moment, Bellibar focused on the largest standing boulder. *That's where he would be if he were up there,* he thought.

"This man tried to kill me," he called out, hearing his echo roll off along the hills. "*Trató de matarme,*" he repeated in his imperfect Spanish. Still nothing. . . .

"Self-defense. *La defensa propia,* eh . . . ?" he called out, ready to level the Remington at the sight of anyone who appeared.

What the hell . . . ? Maybe he'd been mistaken, he thought, the ring of the big Remington still stuck inside his ears. Did it really matter? This was Mexico. Nobody cared if a couple of gringo outlaws threw down on each other.

He let the hammer down on the Remington and stuck it behind his gun belt. Beside him, the roan raised its dripping muzzle.

"Are you through?" he asked the horse in an impatient voice. Then he reached down, adjusted the horse's cinch more firmly and stepped up into the saddle. He turned the roan toward the trail and looked up along the hillside one last time. *Whoever's up there, this is your lucky day,* he thought—*the day Bobby Hugh Bellibar didn't kill you.* He smiled to himself, tapped his boots to the roan's sides and rode away.

Chapter 2

———

Huddled behind the boulder Bellibar had been watching so closely, an old Mexican by the name of Herjico Herrera wrapped his arms around his young granddaughter, Erlina, and her black-and-white-speckled goat, Felipe. He held one thin, weathered hand over the mouth of the girl and the other over the mouth of the goat. As the sound of the horse's hooves clacked across the rocky gravelly bank and faded out of hearing along the trail, the old man sighed in relief, lowered one hand from the girl's mouth and crossed himself. Behind him a donkey stood against the rock as quiet as a statue.

Erlina wiped her hand across her lips in exasperation.

"*Abuelo*, I am thirteen years old. You do not have to treat me like a child," she said.

"Thirteen is not grown-up. It is only old enough to get you into grown-up trouble," the old grandfather said in a harsh whisper. He stared warily in the direction the horseman had taken.

Felipe the goat wiggled his head until he freed himself from the old man's hand. Then the little goat shook his head and flicked his ears back and forth.

"And this pampered little devil," the old man added. "It is only by God's grace that this hombre did not come up and kill the three of us." He drew back a threatening hand toward the goat. But the goat lowered its knobby head, bleated out a warning and charged against the old man's hand. A cheap metal bell held around the goat's neck by a stripe of rawhide clacked vigorously.

Erlina giggled childlike behind her cupped hand, seeing the little goat appear to run in place, held in check by her grandfather's palm.

"Stop it, you little fool!" Herjico whispered harshly to the goat, knowing that removing his hand from its head would only invite it to charge again. "By the saints, I will have you for dinner!"

Erlina wrapped her arms around the goat's thin neck, pulling it back to keep it from charging her grandfather again. She hugged the goat to her lovingly.

"No, no, little Felipe," she said to the goat, clasping a hand over its twitching ears, "*mi abuelo* does not mean it. He would never eat you." She turned her dark eyes up to the old man. "Do you mean it, Grandfather?"

"No, I do not mean it," the old man said, standing, letting out a patient breath. "I would not eat little Felipe . . . not today anyway." He dusted the seat of his baggy peasant trousers and stared down at the trail winding out of sight away from the stream. "But tomorrow, who can say?" He reached back and took the donkey's rope in hand.

Erlina did not push the matter any further. She stood up, turned the goat loose and stared down at the stream bank.

"*Abuelo*," she asked, "is it now safe for me to take little Felipe down so he can drink?"

Her grandfather looked down at her and smiled to himself.

"Always, this worthless little goat is first with you," he said. He smiled and brushed a strand of raven black hair from her forehead. He noted how he no longer had to stoop down as far as he used to in order to touch her face. His granddaughter was quickly growing into a young woman while the years of his life slipped past him cloaked in inevitable silence.

"*Sí*, we can take the goat and the donkey down to drink, but we must be cautious," he said, putting aside his inner thoughts. "We do not know if the killer will return."

"But we must have water," the girl said. "Little Felipe, that is." She smiled.

"We will have water," said Herjico. "But I must first see to the dead."

"What will you do with his body, Grandfather?" she asked.

"I do not know, Erlina," he said, leading the sure-footed donkey behind him "but we must always respect the dead when they are placed in our hands."

They started walking down the rocky hillside, the feisty little goat bounding along in front of them.

"You have no shovel, no way to bury him," the young girl said. She walked a few feet in front of the old man.

Seeing her walk reminded him so much of her mother, his deceased daughter, Anna, that for a moment he thought that he had stepped back in time. He had to make a conscious effort to bring himself back to the present.

"I will pull him from the water and lay stones over him," the old man said.

"You will say the prayer for the dead over him?" the girl asked, half turning to him, the top of her thin cotton dress hanging loosely off of her bony shoulder.

"*Sí*, I will say a prayer over him, but not the prayer for the dead," the old man replied. "It is only a priest—a *sacerdote* of the mother church who can recite the prayer for the dead. For me to do so would not be *apropiado* in the eyes of God."

"With you, it is always God who is first," the girl said, referring to his mention of her and the little goat. "Like me and Felipe . . . ?" She left her question hanging playfully.

"*Sí*," her grandfather said with a tired smile, "for me, God is first."

"Like me and Felipe?" she asked again with a playful part smile.

"All right, if you must hear me say it, 'like you and Felipe,'" the old man said. He held up a seasoned finger for emphasis. "Except that one day soon you will become a woman, and you will outgrow this little goat. One must never outgrow God."

"I will never forget little Felipe," Erlina said with her child's laugh, hurrying on down the hillside behind Felipe.

"I did not say you will *forget* him, granddaughter," the old man said, lifting his voice for her to hear as she moved farther away. "I only said that you will outgrow him. . . ." His voice lowered to himself as he added, "As we outgrow so many things in our lives."

He smiled, shook his head and walked on down, watching her stop at the water's edge, the goat already standing in the water, its short tail swishing back and forth.

"While you drink I will wade downstream and search for the man's body," the old man said as he reached the water and turned loose of the donkey's rope. He stopped to roll up his trouser legs.

"Oh no, Grandfather! Look! It is him!" the girl cried out, pointing her finger toward the wounded gunman who dragged himself up along the other side of the stream, a hand clutched to his bleeding chest.

"Stay here!" the old man instructed, hurrying past her into the rushing water. "Keep the goat back out of my way."

Erlina watched her grandfather hurry across the stream, pull the man to his feet and loop his arm across his thin shoulders. The goat stood watching, its short tail swinging.

"Come back, Felipe," Erlina said, seeing the goat take a charging stance toward her grandfather as the old man helped the wounded gunman toward the stream bank. But the young goat wouldn't listen. Erlina had to step into the water and grab the animal by its thin neck to keep it from butting her grandfather's legs.

"Hel—help me," the wounded gunman rasped as the old man lowered him to the ground.

"Yes, we will help you. Now lie still," said Herjico, seeing the blood flowing from only one bullet hole in the gunman's chest. He remembered that he had heard the other man shoot three times. He crossed himself quickly, then stooped beside the gunman, ripped his wet shirt off and began tearing it into strips for bandages.

With the wounded man's shirt removed, the old Mexican could now see why he had only one bullet hole in his chest. The man wore a large metal medallion strung on a rawhide strip around his neck. One flattened bullet was stuck in an ornately embossed image of Jesus on the cross. The slug had welded itself to Jesus' feet. The other bullet had hit the cross, sliced off across Jesus' right hand and left a deep graze along the gunman's ribs.

"By witness of the holy saints!" the old man said, crossing himself again. "God has truly saved you from the mouth of hell on this day."

Siebert managed to grasp the old Mexican's forearm with a weak and bloody hand.

"Old man," he said in a pained voice, "God's got nothing to do with this. Get me plugged up . . . 'fore I bleed out."

"*Sí*, of course," the old Mexican said. "I will get you bandaged and take you somewhere for help."

"A doctor?" Siebert asked as the old man wadded a strip of wet cloth and pressed it to bleeding wound.

"No, there is not a doctor anywhere in these hills," the old Mexican said.

"No towns, then," Siebert said. "I've got men everywhere wanting me dead."

What he meant was *lawmen* who wanted him dead. The old Mexican understood.

"There is a healing woman nearby. I take you to her," said the old man.

"A healing woman?" Siebert asked.

"*Sí*," said the old Mexican, "a healing woman."

"I've heard of these so-called healing women in the hill country," Siebert said. "They're all witches."

"Some call them *brujas*, but it is not true." The old Mexican shrugged his thin shoulders. "She is a healing woman. She can heal your gunshot wounds, señor."

Siebert gave a dark, pained chuckle.

"Seen to by a witch . . . ?" he said. "Is that . . . what I've come to in life?"

"A healing woman," the old man corrected him. "And some say this woman is better than a doctor in matters like these." The old man added, "She is very quiet afterward about those she heals."

"Now you're . . . talking," Siebert said in a fading voice. Even in his weakened state, he managed to pull the hideout Colt from his belt. He brought the gun around and let it flop onto his leg. "Let's find this woman . . . get me fixed up."

Leaving his partner for dead, Bobby Hugh Bellibar had ridden hard, higher into the rocky Mexican hills.

Two hours had passed when he stopped to rest the tired animal. He watched from cover while a patrol of *rurales* in unmatched uniforms and peasant clothes rode past on the trail below him going in the opposite direction. He waited in silence until they rode out of sight before turning his horse from the cover of sagging pine branches back to the trail.

But as he turned his eyes to the trail ahead of him, he spotted two horsemen sitting on their horses, staring at him from a distance of thirty feet. Guns drawn and cocked at him, the two hard-looking riders sat grinning lazily.

"Do you see what I see, Paco?" the Texas gunman Saginaw Sparks said to the Mexican gunman seated beside him.

"What," said Paco Reyes, "a man who is hiding from the *rurales*? A man who has been caught off guard by two tough hombres and is wondering if this is to be his last day on earth?" His grin widened. "Perhaps a man who has not been paying attention to the things going on right under his—"

"So you do see him," said Saginaw, cutting a long story short. He was clearly a little put out with the Mexican's ramblings.

"*Sí*, I see him," Paco summed up. He raised his cocked Starr pistol a little toward Bellibar. "Now I think I kill him."

"Hold on, Paco," said Saginaw, "where's your manners? Never kill a sumbitch before you introduce yourself. That ain't the Texas way I was raised."

Paco let out a breath and relaxed a little in his saddle.

"Pay my Mexican pard here no mind, mister," Saginaw Sparks said to Bobby Bellibar. "He is what I've come to regard as violence-prone."

Bellibar let his free hand lower a little, hoping to get it nearer to his gun butt without being noticed.

"I know you, Saginaw Sparks," he said flatly to the hard-eyed gunman, pointing at Sparks with his left hand.

"Do you, now?" said Sparks, his grin fading a little. "Because if you *do,* you're bound to know I don't like a finger aimed at me when I don't know where it's been."

Bellibar lowered his left arm. His right hand had managed to ease a few inches closer to his holstered Colt. He could make a good grab from here when the time came—if the time came.

"I'm Bobby Hugh Bellibar," the young gunman said. "I was told by Wilton Marrs I'd be welcome in Lookout Hill, if ever I needed a place to lie low."

"It is called Colina de Mirador," Paco the Mexican corrected him, saying the name in Spanish.

"Only if I'm speaking Mex," Bellibar said with a hard stare. "Am I welcome there or not?"

"Well, now, that all depends, *Bobby Hugh Bellibar,*" Saginaw Sparks said in a mocking tone.

"On . . . ?" said Bellibar, almost welcoming the notion that he'd likely have to kill these two any second.

"On how much money you've got, of course," said Sparks, wagging his big Colt a little.

"That's a matter I'll talk to Marrs about," Bellibar said. He looked back and forth from one face to the other, judging which man he'd kill first once his hand made its plunge for his holstered Colt. He wished he had time to jerk Siebert's big Remington from behind his belt, see how it handled at this distance. But this wasn't the time to get playful, he decided.

"If you're going to talk to Marrs, you best talk loud," said Saginaw. "He's going to have to hear you all the way from hell."

Bellibar just stared.

"That's right," said Sparks. "He broke out with lead poison in a half dozen places—killed him deader than hell."

"Who shot him?" Bellibar asked. *Get them talking, wait for a slipup, then move quick. . . .*

The Mexican and the Texan looked at each other above their cocked and pointed guns.

Here it goes! Bellibar thought, seeing their eyes off him for a second. He started to jerk the Colt, but before he made his move Saginaw Sparks looked back at him and shrugged.

"We all shot him, more or less," he said. "Nobody liked him much, you might say."

"And if you are his amigo," said Paco, "nobody will like you much either, hombre. You see how that works?" He grinned and flashed a sidelong glance at Saginaw Sparks, the two with their eyes off him again.

"Yep, I think so," said Bellibar. This time he didn't hesitate. His hand went for his Colt as he spoke.

The two gunmen saw him make his move, but it was too late. Even with their guns drawn and cocked, Bellibar had them cold—so cold he fanned his shots, three shots left to right. The first shot knocked Sparks in a backward flip off his horse's rump. The second twisted the Mexican up out of his saddle like a corkscrew. The third shot went wild, Bellibar only needing it to keep his quick fanning rhythm going.

He stared at the two downed gunmen through a haze of rising gun smoke. Both of their spooked horses bolted away a few feet and stopped and stood piqued, ready to bolt again. He kept his left hand cupped above his Colt for a second, ready to fan the hammer again.

That was foolish, he told himself, but he smiled faintly in any case. He didn't give a damn. Sometimes *foolish* was the best hand in the game.

He saw Saginaw Sparks was still alive. He struggled in the dirt, turning onto his back, sitting up, gun in hand, his legs spread wide.

What have we here . . . ?

Blood covered the front of Sparks' shirt; a wide trickle of it ran down from his lips. He raised the gun and fired. The bullet sliced past Bellibar's shoulder.

This will do, Bellibar told himself. He shoved the Colt down into his holster and poised his hand near the big Remington behind his belt. Another bullet exploded toward him from Sparks' wobbling gun. It whistled past his head as he grabbed the Remington from his belt, raised it and fired.

The shot knocked Sparks into another backflip. He landed facedown in the dirt, the back of his head blown away, a mist of blood settling above him. The Remington's loud blast caused Bellibar's horse to spook and spin a full circle beneath him before he settled the animal with a firm hand on the reins. The other two horses bolted a few more feet, then settled again.

Bellibar turned the Remington in his hand, appraising it.

Pretty damn good, he had to admit. Not as smooth on the upswing as his Colt, but then he'd had it stuck down behind his belt—a rough draw to begin with. He twirled the big gun on his trigger finger and caught it with its barrel straight up; smoke still curled from it, leaving a silvery gray circle in the air. He looked over at the back of Sparks' open bloody skull.

Heavy, but hard hitting, he told himself, looking the Remington up and down. All right, then. He shoved the Remington back behind his belt and gigged his horse over to where the other two horses stood staring at him warily. He knew the *rurales* had to have heard the shooting, but it couldn't be helped.

"Easy, fellows," he said to the horses as he gathered their loose reins. "We're all friends here." He turned the animals beside him and led them over to the bodies on the ground.

Chapter 3

The Ranger had heard the shots in the distance on the trail ahead of him, but he kept Black Pot and the outlaw's tired horse at the same pace rather than pushing them any harder on the high, rocky terrain. A half hour had passed before he stopped both horses and looked down from the cover of pines onto the gravelly stream bank. Winchester rifle in hand, he nudged Black Pot forward, leading the outlaw's abandoned horse by its reins beside him.

"Keep it easy," he murmured to the side horse, drawing the reins taut to keep it from hurrying ahead to the water. He stopped a few feet short of some disturbed gravel. Stepping down from the saddle, he led the animals closer and recognized an assortment of foot- and hoofprints. He gave slack on the horses' reins and allowed them to step into the shallow water and drink while he examined the stream bank.

A donkey, a goat, he said to himself, his gloved fingertips touching the prints lightly. Then he detected a small human footprint and a larger print, both made by the flat imprint of a sandal. A child and a grown-up, he deduced—both Mexican judging by the flat rectangular sole of the sandal. He followed the prints back and forth with his eyes, trying to decipher what had taken place here. He stopped suddenly when he came upon a watery streak of blood and the imprint of a man lying prone in the pliable loam. He saw the imprint of one lathed riding boot, its heel dug into the bank, the other lying on its side.

There's the gunshots. . . .

Sam straightened to a stand and followed the prints with his eyes as the collection of unseen entities, both beast and human, appeared to have collected themselves on the stream bank and dissipated onto the hillside. He let the reins to the drinking horses fall from his hand and followed the prints a few feet onto the harder, rocky shelf leading away from the stream bank.

He stooped again when he found a half circle of sun-dried blood lining the single left boot heel. *Leaking blood,* he told himself. A few feet away he saw another half circle, this one lighter, only a trace. His eyes followed a single set of hoofprints moving back onto the trail, headed north into higher country. Then he looked back at the ground beneath his feet.

Someone had been shot here and someone had helped them up into the woods. But who? One of the outlaws, or some hapless traveler who had come upon them? A body would most naturally be lying somewhere in the wake of men like Siebert and Bellibar. He tried to work out the scenario at the stream bank more clearly in his mind. But before he could complete his thoughts on the matter, he heard the sound of several rifles cocking inside the surrounding pines.

On first instinct he would have flung himself to the ground and brought the Winchester up into play. But seeing the ragged, mismatched uniforms of *rurales* encircling him as they stepped into sight on the hillside, he froze and stood with his hand in place on his rifle stock. He reminded himself that if these men had wanted him dead, he wouldn't have heard their rifles cock—he would only have heard the blast of fire, then nothing else. He let out a tense breath and waited, seeing two mounted men step their horses into sight from behind the cover of a sunken boulder.

"You will lay down your rifle, *lawman*," a tense-looking man with a thick, drooping mustache demanded.

Good, they had recognized the badge on his chest, Sam thought. Sometimes that helped; other times it didn't. This time it appeared to have kept the bullets from flying long enough for him to explain himself. He slowly placed the Winchester on the ground at his feet and straightened up. Now would they ask him to lay down his sidearm?

No, he decided, hearing the thin man call out to him.

"Come forward with your hands raised, lawman," he demanded.

Sam held his hands chest high. He walked forward and stopped a few feet in front of the two mounted *rurales*.

"What brings you to our beautiful country?" the

thin Mexican asked in a mock welcoming tone, as if this were the first American lawman he'd ever encountered in the Mexican badlands.

"I'm Arizona Ranger Samuel Burrack, here in pursuit of wanted men, under the Matamoros Agreement, an agreement between our two governments," Sam said, as if reciting the words from some official document.

"We *know* about the Matamoros Agreement," said the other *rurale*, sounding offended. This one's face wore a fresh, clean shave beneath the thin, straight line of a mustache. A powerfully built man, clearly the leader, Sam told himself, noting polished black boots and a newer-looking uniform. "The agreement says that you must be prepared to explain to any *funcionario* such as I who you are searching for and why."

"I understand," said Sam. "I'm tracking two men. Their names are Bellibar and Siebert. They're wanted for murder and robbery. I have their posters inside my shirt." He made a slight gesture of his hand toward the bib of his shirt.

"Do not reach for anything, or I will be forced to shoot you dead," the thin *rurale* warned him.

Sam stopped. "I've identified myself. I've given you the men's names. I'm offering a look at their faces."

The clean-shaven *rurale* gave a flat grin and waved the notion aside.

"If I want to see ugly gringos," he said. "I have three cousins I visit in Ciudad El Paso." He chuckled at his obscure joke. The thin *rurale* joined in, the two nodding at each other as they laughed.

Sam only stared. They didn't know where to take this now that he'd presented himself with respect, knew the rules of the Matamoros Agreement and showed a willingness to cooperate. There was a slight opportunity for him here. He decided to take it while they both wondered what to do next.

"Am I being held, *Capitán* . . . ?" he asked the clean-shaven man, eyeing first the silver-braided epaulets on the shoulders of his officer's tunic, then staring straight into his black eyes.

The Ranger's look and demeanor summoned a no-nonsense response from the *rurale* officer.

"*Capitán* Fernando Goodlero," the man said, straightening in his saddle, his laughter suddenly silenced. "This is my *segundo*, Sergeant Lopez." He paused for a second as if pondering the Ranger's question, then said, "No, you are not being *held*." To Sergeant Lopez he said quietly, "Have the men stand down."

Lopez gave a nod and a hand gesture to the half circle of pointed guns. The guns slumped. He turned to the captain with a proud expression.

"You may lower your hands now, lawman," said the captain.

"It's Ranger, *Capitán*," Sam corrected him, "Arizona Ranger Sam Burrack." He lowered his hands but kept them clear of his holstered Colt.

The captain ignored his correction.

"Take your rifle and go, lawman," he said to the Ranger. "But be mindful that we are here. We are searching my province for rebels who have banded together to overthrow our emperor and his regime. But we also hunt outlaws when their paths cross ours. Unlike you *americano* lawmen, who think you are born with God's blessing to travel wherever you see fit, in my country, I keep my men where we belong, eh, Sergeant Lopez?"

"*Sí, Capitán*," said the skinny sergeant, staring coldly at the Ranger. "The difference is, we catch and kill the men we are looking for. We do not ride around in circles—"

"We wield the law as *we* see fit," said the captain, cutting his sergeant off. He raised a finger for emphasis. "When we come upon the kind of men you are hunting, we will execute them on the spot. This is how we deal with both gringo outlaws and *Mexicano* rebels here in my part of the province." He eyed Sam closely. "How do you treat *Mexicano* rebels and traitors?"

"Section four of the Matamoros Agreement makes it clear I'm to have no part in any political struggles, Captain," Sam said without hesitation.

"I am impressed, lawman," said the captain. He gave a tight smile. "I see you have actually *read* the agreement. Gringos have so little regard for my nation's laws they do not bother to learn them. Instead they take the word of some fool who also holds our law in disregard. Mexican *law* becomes no more than *rumor* to them."

Sam stared back and forth between the two.

"I know your nation's laws and I follow them to the best of my ability," he replied.

"Do you hear him, Sergeant Lopez?" The captain looked at the sergeant and shook his head slightly. "He follows our laws to the *best* of his *abilities*."

"*Sí*, I hear him, *Capitán*," the sergeant said in disgust. "They cannot help themselves, these gringos. They believe the world belongs to them. They do with it as they see fit."

The captain looked back down at Sam.

"To the best of your abilities, eh?" he said.

"That's all I've got for you, Captain Goochero," he said. His gun hand relaxed and moved nearer to his holstered gun butt. "That's all I've got for anybody." He let the captain and the sergeant see that he'd have no more of it. He sensed time ticking, widening the gap between himself and his prey. He came here to do a job, not to be put upon.

The two stared at him, both realizing the unquestionable reasoning, whether they agreed with his words or not.

"Are we through?" Sam asked bluntly.

The captain didn't reply. Instead he jerked his horse's reins, turned the animal and rode toward the rest of the waiting *rurales*.

The sergeant glared down at the Ranger.

"Go your own way, lawman, but be careful that you stay out of ours," he said in warning.

"I'll keep that in mind, Sergeant Lopez," Sam said. He watched the thin sergeant jerk his horse around and ride off behind the captain. Only when the two had formed their men up and ridden out of sight did Sam pick up his rifle and gather Black Pot and the silver-gray dun. Rifle in hand, he led the horses up among the rocks, following the tracks of the goat, the donkey and the footprints left by flat-soled sandals—one set of prints belonging to a small child.

Cause for concern? he asked himself. Yes, he believed it could be. A child thrown into the mix of things always demanded close attention. But he'd know more on the matter as the ascending path through the rocks revealed it to him. Looking down at the rocky ground beneath his feet, he saw the spot of blood and reasoned that it did not come from whoever wore the flat-soled sandals. That person's gait moved along at a straight and steadily pace. The bleeding came from the person atop the donkey.

It helped to know that.

He walked on, leading the horses, weaving his way another ten yards through unearthed boulders until the hoofprints and footprints began to fade across a flat, widening rock shelf. He kept close watch on the hard surface at his feet, yet even so, near the edge of the rock shelf, all signs of the prints seemed to vanish into thin air.

To his left, a steep path sloped downward fifty yards, then flattened onto a sheer rock wall. They obviously didn't go that way, unless they could fly, he reasoned. The ledge ended the same way on his right—a small path to nowhere. Whoever led this party didn't want to be followed. In terrain like this, he could search for days and never come up with so much as a hoof mark. By the same token, a person wise enough to leave no trail was also wise enough to leave sign for someone to follow if they felt they needed help.

Sam turned and looked out along the trail leading north, away from the water's edge—the single set of prints there. He had to either stay on that person while the tracks were fresh or search around blindly in the rock lands and take a chance on both men getting away.

All right.

It made sense to go after the one easiest to follow at this point. But he considered the small, flat-soled sandal prints and let out a breath. The one headed north would have to wait. He was going after the ones headed deeper into the rock lands.

"I hope you're leaving me something to go on," he murmured out across the hill country beneath him. He swung up into his saddle and turned both horses along the edge of the cliff to his right, toward the downhill path.

Near dark, Sens Priscilla, the healing woman, kindled the fire pit in the rocky front yard of her home—a part cave, part pine and stone structure clinging to the side of El Punto de Diablo. As she stoked the fire and sank a small covered kettle of water to boil in a bed of glowing embers, she felt the tiny black eyes of her sparrows watching from their perch along a short hitch rail. The birds stepped nervously in place and tipped their paper-thin wings in anticipation.

"Don't worry, little chippies," she said softly, her face shadowed inside the hood of a faded black robe. "When have I ever left you to the mercy of the night?"

The birds chirped even livelier and stared back as if understanding her words.

"*Don't tease us, Sens Priscilla,*" she said in a squeaky little voice. The birds chirped eagerly at the sound of her voice, recognizing the different tone.

Priscilla started to gather the sparrows into the warm, drooping sleeve of her robe for the night, but a sound from the pathway up the steep hillside stopped her. She froze for a moment and listened closely, as silent as death.

The scrape of an unshod hoof? Yes, so it is, she answered herself.

She turned toward the path, spread her hands slightly and let the baggy sleeves fall down over them. She continued to stand statuelike, her eyes closed, the catch of sparrows huddled and perched in a tense silent line behind her.

She focused all her senses toward the slow approach of hooves moving softly across rock, whisking past dried brush. She divined danger there, yet it was not danger immediate. It was danger impending—a dark omen of danger to come if left unrestrained. With that thought, she instinctively felt for the slim dagger tucked away inside her robe.

But when she heard the slightest clack of a small bell and watched the little goat walking into sight, her hand immediately eased back to her side, as if leading the way for the old man and his granddaughter, Erlina. Seeing them, Sens Priscilla almost let out a sigh of relief.

She caught herself as she saw the donkey walk into view. A man was sitting slumped atop the small animal's knobby back, the front of his half-naked chest covered with bandages and dried blood. She eyed the gun lying across his lap.

There is the danger and, with it, evil.

She stood perfectly still until the little goat walked up from the rocky trail, bounded the last few feet and stopped and nuzzled her knee.

When the old man and Erlina came closer, Sens Priscilla rubbed the goat's head and whispered, "What is it you bring me this day, little Felipe?"

The goat bleated and stared up at her.

"No, I do not blame *you*," Priscilla said. "You are just a skinny little goat." She brushed the animal aside gently. Then she stepped forward to make welcome these innocent ones who had delivered such danger and evil to her door.

Chapter 4

———

The sparrows disbursed from the hitch rail and disappeared into the rocky hillside as Herjico and Priscilla helped Hodding Siebert through the front door of the house back into the torchlit cave. They sat the wounded man down on a pallet of straw covered by a faded striped blanket. With the hideaway Colt dried firmly to his bloody hand, Siebert lay back on the pallet against the stone wall and looked all around.

"What kind of deal is this?" he asked in a weak and slurred voice. His head bobbed on his chest as he struggled to stay conscious.

Ignoring his question, Sens Priscilla turned to the old man and nodded toward the front yard.

"Bring me the hot water sitting in the fire bed, Herjico, *por favor*," she said. Then she lowered her voice just between the two of them and said, "Take Belleza from the barn and hide her, pronto. You know where to go."

"*Sí*, I know," said Herjico. Without another word, the old Mexican hurried away. No sooner had he left the cave than Priscilla stooped down beside the wounded gunman and reached out to take the Colt from his hand. Siebert's eyes had fallen almost shut, but he opened them quickly and in reflex swiped the barrel across her cheek.

Even though the blow was weakened by his loss of blood, Priscilla fell back onto the dirt floor with a hand to her cheek. She glared at him from within her hood.

"Huh-uh, witch," Siebert warned. "Don't be giving me no evil eye. And don't be trying to disarm me. I'm not giving this gun up. I let it dry to my hand just for that very reason. Anybody tries to unstick it . . . I'll know right off."

When he was finished talking, his eyes fell shut again. Priscilla rose to her feet, her hand against her cheek, inside the blackness of her hood.

"Do not worry, gunman," she said with bitter contempt, "no one is taking your gun from you. I only wish to move it aside so I can treat you."

"You're going to try to hex me?" Siebert said. His eyes opened dreamily. "Go ahead, then, witch," he said with a smile, recalling how Bellibar had slipped his Remington from his holster unawares while he'd lain drinking water. "Hex me so this gun never leaves my hand. It would be the best thing could ever happen to me. . . ." His words trailed.

"*Sí*, I will do it," said Sens Priscilla, going along with the man's delirium in order to quiet him down. Her tone turned soft, soothing, and fell almost to a whisper. "Now sleep, sleep deeper and deeper . . . and do not worry about the gun. No one can take it. A gun will always be a part of your hand, a part of your arm . . . as much a part of you as your own bone and blood."

A faint smile passed across Siebert's lips.

"Yeah, a part of my hand," he said dreamily, raising the bloodstained gun an inch and letting it fall back onto his lap. "I like that . . . keep going." His voice trailed away into sleep.

Out front, Erlina, the donkey and the little goat stood waiting. They all watched as Herjico hurried past them toward a plank and adobe barn, also built against the stony hillside.

"Where are you going, *Abuelo*?" Erlina called out.

"Never mind where I go," said the old man. "Wait here."

As he hurried past them, Little Felipe bleated, slung his head back and forth and darted forward trying to butt the old man's legs from behind. But Erlina saw what the goat planned to do. She caught him by his stubby horns and held him as he squirmed and bucked against her.

"No, no, Felipe," she said. "Our *abuelo* is busy. We must let him do what he needs to do."

Our abuelo? The old man shook his head as he hurried to the adobe barn, slipped inside and shut the door soundly. *Dear, dear Erlina,* he thought. The poor, simple child had now turned him into the grandfather of a goat.

Seeing the old man disappear into the barn, the little goat settled and twitched its short, stubby tail. Erlina released her grip on the animal and stood patting its skinny, coarse-coated back while she stared toward the barn.

"What is *Abuelo* doing in there, Felipe?" she asked idly.

In moments she saw her grandfather come out of the barn and hurry back to the fire a few feet from her and the two animals. He squatted down beside the fire and reached for the steaming kettle of water, using his wadded shirttail to protect his hand from the hot iron handle.

"Keep the foolish goat from under my feet," he said aloud, in spite of the tenderness her words and actions brought to his heart. "He will cause someone to fall and break their neck."

"No, *Abuelo*. Felipe loves everyone. He will tell you so," the young girl said, hugging the struggling goat's thin neck to her cheek as it tried to break free in order to butt the old Mexican. The goat bleated in protest. "See? Hear him?"

"I hear him," the old man said grudgingly. He cursed the little goat under his breath, yet he couldn't help smiling at his granddaughter and her sweet, childlike devotion to the little horned pest. It had been a mistake to allow her to make a pet of something that would someday have to be slaughtered and eaten. It had been foolish and cruel—but it was done now and there was no calling back the past to change anything.

As he stood with the water kettle in hand, he looked over at the little goat as it struggled in Erlina's arms.

"Hold him back," he said. "This water is hot. It would scald him if he caused me to spill it."

"I'm holding him, *Abuelo*," Erlina said, pressing her

cheek to the goat's thin neck as the animal stared dumbly after the old man.

Herjico hurried to the front door and stopped for a moment. He looked across the yard at the adobe barn, then back at Erlina.

"Take them both to the barn and find some grain for them," he called out. Then he stepped through the door, closed it behind himself and walked across the room to the open door leading down into the cave, hearing the sound of Priscilla's voice chanting softly.

As he approached quietly, he found the healing woman standing over the wounded gunman with her hands raised chest high. She continued chanting until the old Mexican announced himself by clearing his throat. Then she fell silent, lowered her hands and folded them in front of her as she turned and faced him.

"I—I have brought the hot water as you asked me to, Sens Priscilla," the old Mexican said. He held the kettle out slightly toward her, his shirttail wadded around the hot iron handle.

"Yes, thank you, Herjico," Priscilla said. When she didn't reach out for the kettle, the old Mexican set the kettle down on the dirt and stone floor.

"Did you do as I asked?" she said in a lowered tone.

"*Sí*, Sens Priscilla," Herjico replied, also in a guarded tone. "And I took the liberty of sending Erlina to feed the goat and the donkey in your barn," he said. "I hope this is all right with you. Perhaps I should have asked you first." He looked down at his feet.

Priscilla smiled, but with her face hidden in the hood the old Mexican didn't notice.

"You did not have to ask me, Herjico," she said. She paused, then said, "You and Eilina must be hungry too. There is food inside."

"But what about you, Sens Priscilla?" he asked.

"I have no need for food," she said absently, gazing down at the sleeping gunman.

"What are you saying, Sens Priscilla?" the old man asked, stepping forward with a look of dark concern. "Are you ill?"

"*Shhh.* It is nothing," said Priscilla. She appeared to collect herself and said, "Don't worry about me, Herjico. Feed yourselves while I clean this one up and examine his wounds."

"I do not like leaving you alone with this hombre, Sens Priscilla," Herjico said hesitantly.

She stared at him with a look that left no room for further discussion.

"*Sí*, Sens Priscilla, I will do as you say," the old Mexican said, his head bowed. He turned and left the cave as Priscilla turned back to the slumbering gunman and watched his eyes open slightly.

"You've got folks . . . dancing to your tune, don't you?" Siebert said sleepily.

"*Sí*," Priscilla said, going along with him. She stooped and set the small kettle down and lifted its lid in a gust of steam. "Now lie still while I get a clean washcloth."

Siebert watched her walk through the torchlit darkness to a large sea chest and lift its lid. She carried back a folded cloth in her hand, and he chuckled and closed his eyes.

"It ain't going to work, you know—this witching nonsense of yours." His eyed opened with determination as she knelt beside him, washcloth in hand. "Not on me, it ain't."

"I understand," she said. Once again her voice turned softer, soothing. "Now close your eyes and sleep . . . sleep. Let yourself feel nothing but warmth, peace . . . as sleep surrounds you."

As the gunman drifted away beneath her voice, she looked down at the gun in his hand, held in place by dried blood.

As she stood watching the gunman sleep, the old Mexican stole up quietly behind her.

He whispered in a trailing voice, "Is he . . . ?"

"No, Herjico," she whispered in reply, "he is only sleeping. Why are you not eating?"

"How could I eat," he said, "worrying about you alone with this one?"

"You need not worry about me," Priscilla said.

The old Mexican looked at the gun lying across Siebert's lap and started to venture forward, whispering, "Soon none of us will have to worry—"

"No, Herjico," she whispered, stopping him with a hand on his bony forearm. "We will not kill him. We will let him sleep."

"But, Sens Priscilla, why?" the old man pleaded. "There is nothing but trouble for us from this one. It would be easy to kill him now while he expects nothing."

Sens Priscilla didn't answer. There was no doubt in her mind that she or the old man either one could take the gun from him now and shoot him without him ever knowing it had left his hand. Yet she knew that was not the direction fate had chosen.

If only it were. . . .

In the night, Hodding Siebert awakened and stared into the flicker of torchlights lining the long cavern. It took him a moment to get his mental bearings and realize where he was. But when he looked at a small fire banked and burning low-flamed on the cave's dirt floor in front of him, he took a breath and raised his free hand to the clean bandage on his chest.

The floor of the witch's cave . . . the bruja. He pushed himself up onto his feet and looked over at the woman lying on a blanket across the fire from him. Rocking unsteadily, he caught himself with both hands on a chair back and stood wheezing loud enough that he woke the witch.

"What are you doing up?" she asked from within the darkness of the deep hood.

Siebert coughed deeply, red-faced with pain. He shook his head and leaned against the rough rock wall of the cave, the gun hanging from his hand. "How long have I been asleep?" he asked.

"Only through the night," Priscilla said. She sat up on the blanket and adjusted her face deeper into the hood. "You should be lying down."

Siebert stared at her. He wondered what power a man would take upon himself by killing a *bruja*.

"Don't tell me what to do, witch," he said menacingly. "I'm all right now." He patted his bandaged chest with his free hand. "Better than all right, I'm *damn good*, for a man shot in the chest." He still wore the big cross, and swung it back and forth on its chain. "You might say religion saved my life."

"You should not make mockery of such things," Priscilla said, watching the bullet-scarred cross come to a halt.

Siebert managed a weak but critical grin.

"Now I'm going to start taking religious advice from a witch?" he said.

Priscilla only stared at him.

He pushed himself from against the wall and stepped around the fire, feeling stronger after a night of sleep.

"Let's take a walk, Sens Priscilla," he said.

"How do you know my name?" Priscilla asked. Even as she asked she turned and walked ahead of him toward the door leading into the house.

"I heard a few things last night," Siebert said. "The old Mexican called you Sens Priscilla. You called him Herjico." He paused, looked down at the gun in his hand and said, "I see nobody took my gun, just like you said they wouldn't."

Priscilla stared straight ahead.

"How long have you lived up here, *Witch* Priscilla?" Siebert asked as they reached the door and stopped.

"I am a healing woman. I live here when it suits me, and I leave when I know it is time to go," she replied. "Something you should consider."

"Yeah, except I don't have a way to get around." Siebert grinned, feeling better, stronger, even with a throbbing pain deep inside his chest. "How do you get around?"

"I walk, of course," said Priscilla, "on these two feet God has given me, the same as God has given you."

"Do you really?" Siebert said in a skeptical tone.

"*Sí*, I do," said Priscilla, opening the door, stepping in ahead of him.

In the small room, Herjico stood up from a wooden table. The young girl was near her grandfather's side, the goat nestled up beside her. When the little goat saw Siebert enter the room, he lowered his knobby head and gave a bleat of warning. But before he could execute his charge, Erlina grabbed him around his thin neck and held him back.

"My, my," said Siebert with a dark grin. He raised his Colt and cocked it toward Little Felipe. "Breakfast on the hoof. Turn him loose, little darling. Hold your ears."

"No, no, señor!" cried Erlina.

"Stop it, you fool," said Priscilla. "Can't you see how much the goat means to her? It is her *cabra favorita*."

"Her *what*?" Siebert said above the sobbing of the child as her grandfather protectively pulled both her and the goat against his leg.

"Her *pet*, you fool," said Priscilla. "Perhaps *pet* is a word you can understand."

Siebert turned his Colt from the goat to Priscilla, putting the tip of the barrel up under her chin.

"Call me *fool* one more time, *witch*," he said, "see if you don't hear something *you* can understand."

"Señor, *por favor*!" Herjico cried out, the child sobbing,

the goat bleating, trying to pull free of Erlina's arms and make a charge. "Do not kill her! I beg you!"

"See? He begs me," Siebert said, grinning at Priscilla, close to her face. "I like that. Shows he's got respect for his betters."

Without fear, Priscilla reached a hand up and shoved the Colt away from her chin.

"Don't worry, Herjico. This one cannot kill me." She stared evenly into Siebert's eyes, almost daring him to try. "How can he kill one who was never born . . . one who can never die?"

"*Witch*, you've got a powerful opinion of yourself. I'll give you that," said Siebert. "Adios," he added. He put the tip of the barrel back under her chin; his hand tensed on the gun butt.

"No, no, *por favor*, señor!" Herjico shouted, pulling away from his granddaughter. "I brought you here to save your life. Do not repay me by murdering this woman." As he spoke he grabbed up a handful of dried field beans that lay soaking in a wooden bowl of water on the table. In his desperation, he flung the handful at Siebert, pelting him with them.

Erlina shrieked and squeezed the goat tightly against her chest. The beans struck Siebert's back and fell harmlessly to the floor around his bare feet. But Siebert's hand eased on his gun butt as a bean fell from his tangled hair and hit the floor. He turned from Priscilla to Herjico with a strange, bemused look.

"Did you just *bean* me, old man?" he said as if in disbelief.

Herjico clenched his jaw and jutted his chest, taking a stand. Water dripped from his fingertips.

"*Sí*, I *beaned* you, and I accept my fate for doing it," the old man said courageously.

"People—" Siebert shook his head. Another bean fell from his tangled hair. "It's hard to decide which one of you idiots to kill first." He swung the gun back toward Little Felipe and shrugged. "Back to breakfast, I guess."

Erlina screamed loud and long and squeezed the goat tighter.

Again Siebert took close aim at the goat, this time with no more regard for the young girl holding it. But before he pulled the trigger, the muffled sound of a horse nickering caused him to stop cold and listen intently in the direction of the barn.

"Where's that horse?" he said.

The old man and Priscilla looked at each other.

"I will not tell you," Priscilla said firmly.

"Nor will I," Herjico said.

"Suit yourselves, then," said Siebert. "Since this witch *can't die* and you ain't worth killing, this young lady will have to do." He looked at Erlina and gestured his gun hand toward the cave behind them. "Come on with me, little darling. We're going to go play a game every girl your age needs to learn." He grinned menacingly. "You can even bring your *pet* goat." He looked at the old man and said, "When I'm finished, you won't be able to tell which is which."

"*Dios santo*, no, señor!" the old Mexican shouted,

grabbing the girl and goat and holding them both tightly. "She is no more than a child!"

"Yeah, I know. . . ." Siebert grinned lewdly as he eyed Erlina up and down.

"Wait. I will tell you—"

"*Silencio*, Hejico!" Priscilla shouted. She started to spring toward the old Mexican, but a sharp blow from Siebert's gun barrel sent her sprawling on the floor. A trickle of blood ran from a nasty welt along her jawline.

The old Mexican gasped. Priscilla, struggling against unconsciousness, grasped at Siebert's leg. He kicked her soundly in her stomach with his bare foot. She fell into silence.

"Now, as you were saying, old man," he said, turning back to Herjico.

Chapter 5

In the hillside barn, Siebert stood with a hand on the small of Erlina's slender back while the old Mexican walked out through a rear door into another cavern. As soon as Herjico left, Siebert rubbed his hand up and down Erlina's back slowly, noting the firm rises of flesh pressing behind the front of her peasant's dress. The rings of her breasts showed through the gauzy fabric like dark budding roses. Siebert leaned close and breathed in the scent of the girl's long black hair.

"How old are you, honey?" he whispered, his eyes closed.

"I—I am ten years old," Erlina said, petrified, clinging to the little goat.

"Ten years old," Siebert whispered, knowing the girl was lying to save herself from him. "What a coincidence, so am I." He grinned and opened his eyes. His gripped her in case she tried to pull away.

The girl shivered in fear and revulsion. She almost looked around for Sens Priscilla for protection, even though Priscilla lay unconscious on the plank floor back at the house where they had left her.

"There's nobody here but you and me, honey," Siebert said, liking how he frightened her. Hell, she didn't have to worry. He had no time for some skinny kid like her. Looking around, Siebert noticed the donkey standing off by itself chewing contentedly on a mouthful of hay. Seeing the knobby-backed animal, Siebert shook his head.

This whole bunch is a mess. . . .

"If this witch woman's livestock looks as poor as the old man's, I might be better off walking," he commented out loud to himself.

A moment later he snapped his gaze toward the rear door as it flew open. The old man was struggling with a lead rope. Siebert heard a low, powerful nicker on the other side from the cave as the old Mexican pulled hard, then almost shot backward out the door.

"Belleza! *Por favor,*" said the old Mexican as if pleading with some strong-willed person on the end of the rope. "You must come with me, for Sens Priscilla's sake!"

Siebert shook his head in disgust. He shoved the little girl aside and walked toward the door.

"Yeah, *Belleza,*" he said in a scorching tone to an animal yet unseen, "get in here. If I take the rope, I'll yank your fool head off."

His words stopped short as he saw the tall, glistening black mare change her mind and lope through the open door, sending the old Mexican scurrying out of her way. Siebert had to jump back himself to keep from being trampled. The big mare circled the small barn, gracefully missed the little girl and came to a sudden halt less than five feet from Siebert, the lead rope dangling to the dirt floor. She blew out a hot, powerful breath, and Siebert felt the blast of it.

"Holy jumping monkeys!" he whispered in awe, taking another short step back, staggering at the sight of such power, such raw wild energy. "Now, *that* is some good-looking horse," he managed to say.

"No, señor, please," said the old Mexican. "Belleza is a mare. She does not like being called a horse."

"Belleza, huh?" Siebert said, his Colt hanging limply in his gun hand. "That means 'beauty,' right?"

"*Sí*, señor, it means 'beauty,'" said Herjico. He rubbed a weathered hand along the mare's withers in appreciation. "She is a rare beauty, no?"

The big mare chuffed deeply at the sound of her name. She shook out her raven mane and stared at Siebert. Another blast of hot breath hit his face.

"Yeah, she looks good," said Siebert, grudgingly. "But we'll have to see how she rides." He stared at the mare and said, "Right, Blackie?" He stepped forward and put out a cautious hand to touch the big mare's muzzle, but the big mare flipped her head to the side and stomped a hoof on the dirt.

"I think she does not like the name you call her, señor," the old Mexican said.

"I don't give a damn what she likes," said Siebert. "As long as she's between my knees, I'll call her what the hell suits me."

The mare stared at him menacingly. She scented the

blood on the gunman's chest and chuffed again. Then she lowered her head and scraped a front hoof in the dirt like a bull.

"Oh, señor," the old Mexican said in a wary whisper, "I think she does not like you."

"Now, that really hurts my feelings," Siebert chuckled with sarcasm. "Get her saddle and bridle. The sooner you dress her, the quicker I'll be out of here."

"*Sí*, right away, señor," said the old man, hurrying back through the door into the cavern. He wanted to get the gunman out of there before Priscilla awakened, knowing Priscilla would put up a struggle. She might not think she could die, but Herjico thought otherwise.

Siebert looked the big black mare over until the old Mexican came back through the door carrying a saddle with a bridle, bit and reins piled atop it.

"What the hell is this?" Siebert said, looking closely at the saddle.

"It is a sidesaddle, señor," said Herjico with a worried look on his face.

"Damn it, man. I can see it's a *sidesaddle*," Siebert said impatiently. "What's the idea trying to palm it off on me? Do I look like a woman to you?"

"Oh no, señor! You do not look like a woman!" the old Mexican said quickly. "And I am not trying to palm the saddle off on you. It is the only saddle on the place. It is the only saddle Sens Priscilla ever uses on Beauty."

Siebert looked at Herjico closely and decided he wasn't lying.

"Throw it aside, then," he said. "I'll just ride this big girl bareback 'til I get a proper saddle somewhere."

"You cannot ride her bareback, señor," Herjico said. "She will not allow it. She will only allow you to ride her sidesaddle."

"Yeah, we'll see about that," said Siebert. "Get her bridle on. I'll take it from there. She'll ride me any way I choose to ride. I've broken bigger animals than this—"

"But, señor, your wound," said Herjico, trying to keep any harm from coming to the big mare if he could. "Do not start yourself bleeding again. You must take it easy until you are well!"

Siebert touched his free hand to his bandaged chest. The old man was right. This was not the time to be wrestling with a headstrong riding mare.

"Damn it to hell," he cursed, "saddle her up. I'm through wasting time here. Just because she's wearing a *sidesaddle* doesn't mean I have to use it like a sidesaddle."

"*Sí . . . ?*" The old man looked a little puzzled, but he carried the saddle to the black mare and began preparing her for the trail.

Siebert looked at the hay-chewing donkey, then at the girl and the goat in disgust. A bean fell from his tangled hair and bounced off his bare foot. *Son of a bitch. . . .* He kicked the bean away and looked at the big, glistening black mare.

"Belleza, my gal, you and I are going to get along just fine, soon as you come to know your place and what's expected of you."

He yanked the reins from the old Mexican's hand and swung up across the sidesaddle rig as if it were a regular saddle. He scooted around, gun in hand and tried to make himself comfortable while the old Mexican watched with curiosity.

"Hell, this ain't going to get it. Not for long anyway," he said angrily. He sat awkwardly to his left, his right leg cocked over the hard edge of the leather side cantle, his left foot in the saddle's only stirrup. But it would have to do for the time being. He wasn't going to sit like a woman—*huh-uh*. He felt his face burn red with embarrassment just thinking about it. "What are you laughing at?" he said to the old Mexican, who stood looking at him stone-faced.

"Nothing, señor." The old Mexican shrugged. "I am not laughing, only watching, to make sure you are ready to go before I open the doors." He didn't mention to the gunman that he was leaving barefoot, hatless and without his gun belt. It was not his place to mention such things, he told himself. He only wanted this killer gone before Priscilla awoke.

"Well, now, old man," Siebert said with resolve in his voice and his eyes. He looked over at the girl and goat, then back at the old man with a cold stare. "You want to tell the girl to go on back to the house?"

"*Gracias.* I do." The old man swallowed a dry knot of fear in his throat. "Erlina," he said in a shaky tone, "take Little Felipe and go back to the house."

"But, *Abuelo*—" the girl started to protest.

"*Now*, my precious," he said, cutting her short. "Go, quickly, *por favor*."

The young girl read the urgency in her grandfather's voice and led the goat out the front door and toward the hillside house. Siebert sat atop the black mare with his Colt raised and cocked in his hand.

"Now you can open the doors for me," he said to the old man, staring intently at him.

The old man walked over to the barn doors and threw them both open wide. He turned and looked up at Siebert as the gunman stepped the black mare forward, stopped and looked down at him.

"Señor, I beg of you—" the old Mexican tried to say.

"Huh-uh, forget it, old man," Siebert said with finality, taking aim down at Herjico's bony chest. "Nobody beans me from behind and lives to tell it." The Colt Pocket roared in his hand, but the mare only flinched slightly beneath him. *Good gal. . . .*

The old man crumbled backward to the ground, a bullet through his heart. Siebert felt no power come to him from killing the old Mexican, only disappointment. He looked toward the house, then toward the trail. He tried adjusting himself in the sidesaddle, but gave up and sat leaning uncomfortably to his left. *Damn it.* He tried to shove the Colt down into his waist, but after three attempts he gave up and let the gun rest on his lap for the time being.

"Ride me out of here, *Beauty*," he said, tapping his bare feet to the mare's sides.

The big mare did not take the light tap as a signal to move slowly. She shot away from the barn so quickly Siebert had to clutch on to the sidesaddle with his free hand to keep from flying backward to the ground.

"*Damn*, you're fast on the takeoff, gal!" he said, managing to right himself in the awkward saddle.

As the mare crossed the rocky yard, Priscilla ran from the house, staggering, half-conscious, the long welt left from the pistol barrel leaking blood down her cheek. She ran toward the mare, her arms flailing in the air, screaming in a language Siebert had never heard before.

"Huh-uh, *witch woman*, she's all mine now," he said, gigging the mare hard with his bare heel as she tried to veer toward Priscilla. The witch shuddered to a jerking halt as two bullets from Siebert's Colt Pocket hammered and sliced through her chest.

The big mare reared and whinnied. She circled the yard and stopped beside the healing woman lying crumpled in the dirt. Siebert jerked the animal's reins and pulled it back a step, taking control.

Priscilla managed to push herself up onto an elbow.

"Look at you now, *witch*," Siebert said. "For a woman who can't die, your future doesn't look real promising." He grinned darkly and held the smoking Colt up in his hand.

The mare thrashed, trying to buck the man from her back. But Siebert held her in check, the steel bit in her mouth twisting her lips mercilessly to one side.

"Keep it up, I'll shoot you too," Siebert warned, pointing the barrel down at the mare's black withers.

"No, Beauty, no, *usted debe vivar!* You must live!" Priscilla rasped to the mare.

The big mare seemed to understand; she settled a little and whinnied under her breath.

"You best listen to her, *mare*," Siebert said, the pain in his wound intensifying. "It's the best advice you'll get all day." He laughed and looked back down at Priscilla in the dirt.

The healing woman lay whispering, as if chanting to the mare.

"How about one for the trail?" he said after listening curiously for a moment. Cocking the small Colt, he shot another blast of gunfire into Priscilla, sending her flat to the ground. The mare whinnied and screamed in grief and horror.

"Shut the hell up," Siebert commanded, waiting for just a second to feel what power he might gain from killing the healing woman. Nothing came to him right way, but it would; he knew it would.

He jerked the mare's reins with brutal force. The big animal continued whinnying but turned and raced away. Siebert laughed under his breath in spite of his throbbing wound. "You just need a strong hand, is all," he said, sitting awkwardly in the sidesaddle. As he rode away, he looked back and saw the girl and her goat race from the house, across the yard.

"Sens Priscilla! Sens Priscilla!" Siebert heard the child cry out as she ran. He wasn't going to waste a bullet on her, he told himself. He only shook his head and started to ride away.

"Damn it!" he exclaimed, realizing for the first time that he'd forgotten his hat, his remaining left boot and his gun belt. *This ain't like you, Aces,* he thought. *Get a grip on yourself. . . .* He turned the big mare and rode back toward the house.

Chapter 6

———

Riding in, Sam knew something was wrong. He'd heard the gunfire from a long way across a deep canyon, so he'd circled the house warily under cover of the sparse woods. Riding first to the open barn door, he'd seen the body of the old Mexican lying on the dirt floor—no doubt the flat soles of the larger sandals he'd first spotted at the water's edge. The donkey stood chewing a mouthful of hay in the corner of the barn. This was as far as the old man had made it.

What about the child? Sam asked himself as he'd looked around and saw the fresh hoofprints leaving the barn at a fast pace. The wounded outlaw had taken the donkey as far as he needed to in order to get help and a horse. Now, with a fresh mount beneath him, the donkey and its owner were of no more use to him.

"Hello, the house," the Ranger said quietly from just outside the open doorway. He waited for a second in anticipation. When he heard no answer, he repeated himself in Spanish, saying, *"Hola, la casa,"* and waited a moment longer.

Still no reply.

He'd seen a wide, dark bloodstain in the dirt, a blood trail leading away onto the rocky hillside. Yes, there had been big trouble here, he thought, stepping inside the open doorway, expecting anything. Yet nothing could prepare him for what he found.

His rifle barrel made a slow sweep left to right as he entered the house, his finger on the trigger, the hammer cocked. But he lowered the hammer when he saw the dark, dead eyes of the naked young girl staring up from the dirt floor. A wide puddle of blood was drying beneath her head. A deep, terrible gash ran across her slender throat.

My God.

He let the Winchester slump in his hand as he felt for the doorframe, managing to find it just in time to lean back and brace himself against it. Beside the girl lay half of a young goat's carcass, its rear carved away. Its picked-over hindquarter bones lay in front of the still-glowing hearth. Only then did the Ranger notice the lingering aroma of roast meat in the air.

He winced and forced his eyes back to the young girl, seeing the many dark bruises, cuts and burn marks running the length of her small, thin body. He looked at the rear door, which stood open a crack. He eyed the large pot of beans still soaking on the table, more beans strewn loosely on the floor. He no longer asked himself what kind of man would do this sort of thing. He no longer asked why. His job was to hunt him down, plain and simple.

As he stepped across the floor, rifle ready in hand,

he took a frayed blanket down from a wall peg, shook it out and spread it over the girl's body and the remains of the goat. Then he opened the rear door, gazing out along the shadowy tunnel in the flicker of torchlight still burning on the stone walls.

"*Hola*," he called out into the cavern. He stood listening to his echo repeat itself until it fell away in the darkness. Then he searched for a good throwing rock on the ground at his feet, found one and hurled it away.

He stood listening to the rock clatter, bounce and echo until it finally came to a silent halt. After a moment, he opened the front door and gazed out along the trail, seeing the fresh hoofprints reach out of sight onto the steep, jagged hillside. Whichever outlaw had been here couldn't have gotten over a half hour's head start. *But first things first . . .* There was burying to be done here, he reminded himself.

He let out a tight breath, walked to the barn and found a short-handled shovel. Outside, he scraped the hard ground free of rocks, cleared a large enough spot for two graves and began digging.

When he'd finished digging, he wiped his forehead with a wadded bandanna, carried the bodies to the spot in turn, wrapped them each in a blanket and laid them gently into their respective graves. Gathering rocks from the hillside, he piled a mound of them atop the shallow graves to protect the dead from the creatures of the wild. Using the shovel as a hammer, he pounded a simple cross into the ground between them—two planks bound together with a length of rope. When he'd finished every detail, he stood by the graves, took off his sombrero, held it to his chest and recited the Lord's Prayer to the high, rugged terrain.

"Amen," he said after a further moment of silence.

He put his sombrero on, took the reins to both horses and led them to the large circle of blood in the dirt. He followed the blood trail until it disappeared from his sight, just like the other blood trail he'd tried to follow from the water's edge. Looking all around at the steep hillsides and thin rock paths, he sighed and propped his rifle over his shoulder.

"This is good country for people who don't want to be found," he said to the horses. Then he stepped into his saddle, turned the horses back to the rocky yard and rode away, following fresh hoofprints along a winding trail.

In the middle of the night, Hodding Siebert sat atop the black mare at the edge of a cliff, staring down at a single candlelight burning in a window on the narrow canyon floor. He felt his stomach moan and growl, the meager meal of goat meat already leaving him on empty. Beneath him the big mare grumbled and pawed insistently, as she had all afternoon. *This hardheaded bitch. . . .*

The outlaw squirmed in the unyielding sidesaddle. His fingers opened and closed, adjusting around the handle of the Colt Pocket lying on his lap. He had strapped his empty gun belt on when he'd gone back to get his boot and his hat. But he didn't like the way the smaller pocket gun fit the large holster. He could use a larger gun, some bullets—maybe even a rifle.

His stomach growled again.

"Hear that, Accs?" he said aloud to himself. "You're riding down there, that's all there is to it." He jerked hard on the reins, backed the restless mare and turned her onto a thin path running down the cliff side.

At the bottom of the trail, he heard the yapping bark of a small dog coming from the direction of the house. He stopped the mare, slid down from the sidesaddle and stood stone still for a moment, hoping the yapping would stop. It didn't. Instead it came closer. He heard the dog barking through dry brush on its way toward him. An oil lamp came on in a window.

Son of a bitch!

The flickering light moved through the house like some fiery apparition. The yapping grew more intense; the sound of the small dog running grew louder, closer. Siebert quickly hitched the mare's reins around a stubby juniper. He stooped down and searched around on the ground for a rock, a stick, anything.

"Break that little son of a bitch's neck!" he growled.

Beside him the mare grew even more restless. She nickered loudly and jerked against the tied reins.

"Don't you start *too*!" Siebert warned her. Grabbing up a palm-sized rock, he saw a small whitish blur streaking through the darkness, headed straight for him. At the house, the front door opened; light spilled out onto a porch. "Come on, you little feist bastard!" he bellowed at the yapping dog. "I'll crush your damn little yapping brains—!"

His words stopped short as a huge mongrel shot through the air from his right, hit him at shoulder level and took him to the ground. As Siebert and a big, hairy wolflike creature rolled and tumbled back and forth, the little house dog bounced and jumped in place, yapping wildly. As Siebert beat the big dog's side with the pocket pistol, he saw the light from the porch move down onto the wild grass and come toward him swinging back and forth.

Atop the fallen outlaw, the big mongrel's fangs ripped and slashed at his shoulder, his face, the side of his head, his wounded chest. Siebert screamed loud and long; the mare reared and jerked at the reins until the juniper brush pulled free from the hard, dry ground. As she thrashed wildly, the bush swinging in the air, a shotgun exploded from behind the lamplight.

The little dog let out a yelp, as if the gunshot had actually hit him. The big dog froze in place with its wet jaws clamped around the side of Siebert's head. Silence fell instantly over the chaotic scene.

"Turn him loose, Big!" a voice commanded behind the cloud of looming gun smoke. The mongrel opened his jaws and let Siebert's head drop like a rock. But he stood panting, his big front paws planted on the mauled outlaw's chest, staring down at him with bloody drool swinging from his flews. A low growl persisted in the dog's throat.

Siebert groaned in pain and fell to the side, the pocket pistol still in hand. The little black-and-white-spotted feist sat down on its hindquarters and whined anxiously.

"Mother of God," Siebert moaned.

"*Deje caer su fusil! Sea rápido acerca de ello!*" said the voice in the flickering circle of lamplight.

"Wha-what?" said Siebert. "I mean, *No hablo Mexicano!*" He held up his bloody free hand between himself and the big dog as the dog's low, menacing growl grew louder.

"I said *drop your gun and be quick about it,*" the man repeated in English. "How come you don't speak *Mex*?" he asked, sounding suspicious.

"Because I'm not a Mex!" Siebert said quickly, gasping for breath against the weight of the big dog. "That's why I don't speak Mex. Please get this dog off me!"

"I won't tolerate thieving Mexes around here," the voice went on.

Siebert saw the shotgun barrels leveled down at him, one of them curling smoke.

"Jesus! This *is Mexico*!" Siebert reasoned. The growling grew more intense; the little dog joined in, springing up onto its tiny paws.

"All the more my concern," the voice said. "Mex or no Mex, drop the gun or I'll kill you where you sit."

Damn my hide!

His impulse was to turn the Colt toward the man and pull the trigger, but in a flash, it dawned on him that he couldn't remember if the little Colt was a five- or a six-shot—not only that, but he couldn't remember how many times he'd fired it. *Damn it! Damn it! Damn it to everlasting hell!*

Siebert let the Colt Pocket fall from his hand.

"There, it's dropped. What do you want from me?" he said, sounding like the one being put upon. "I only pulled it because your damn dogs were eating me alive."

At the sound of Siebert raising his voice, both dogs growled with renewed vigor.

"Get back, Big. Get back, Little," the man commanded the two dogs.

Big and Little, these sons a' bitches. . . .

With the big mongrel's weight off his chest, Siebert sat up, bloody from head to waist from dog bites, his shirt shredded down the front. His chest wound was throbbing. The big crucifix swung from its rawhide strip around his neck.

"Are you a man of faith, then?" the voice asked. The circling light came in closer. "I can see you're not a Mex."

"Mister, *faith* ain't even the word for it," Siebert said. "If it wasn't for this cross I wouldn't be sitting here."

"Oh . . . ?" The man seemed to consider it. "What are you doing coming around here unannounced, the middle of the night?"

Unannounced? Siebert looked around. He was over two hundred yards from the house, but he wasn't going to say anything. Instead he shook his lowered head.

"I don't know," he replied in defeat. "Just being plain stupid, I guess."

The man chuckled behind the flickering lamp as he opened the shotgun and slipped a fresh load in the empty barrel.

"Here that, boys?" he said to the growling dogs, snapping the shotgun shut. "Just stupid, he guesses." He tucked the shotgun under his arm and reached a hand down to Siebert. "Here, come on up from there. Let's go get you looked at." He clasped Siebert's hand

firmly and pulled. "Can you eat something, Mr. . . . ?"
He trailed his words.

"Howard, John Logan Howard, and, yes, I could eat
the ass-end out of a running wildcat—pardon my language," Siebert said, rising to his feet, dusting the seat
of his trousers.

"Dudley Bryant," said the man, introducing himself.
"Don't be saying nothing like a wildcat's ass in front of
the woman," he warned. "She can't see worth spit. But
she'll swing a broom handle on you if she hears black-
guarding of any kind."

"She'll hear none from me," Siebert assured the
man. "Can I pick up my gun now?"

"Yes, you can, brother Howard," the man said. "Big . . .
Little, both of yas get back," he commanded the growling dogs. "Let this man pick his gun up."

Brother Howard . . . ?

Siebert just looked at him. As he stood up from
grabbing his Colt, Dudley Bryant leaned in close to
him with the lamp and smiled at the gun from behind
a thick white mustache.

"Say, now, brother Howard," he said, "is that possibly an 1862 Navy Colt Conversion?"

"You're good, brother Dudley." said Siebert. "It is
that." As he spoke, he turned the gun back and forth in
his hand and held it between them, pointed loosely at
the ground. "This one has the custom Eagle handle
grip."

"The eagle holding the snake in its beak and talon?"
the man asked, looking excited at the prospect.

"Right you are again, brother Dudley," said Siebert,

impressed. "I think I'm in the presence of a man who knows his Colts."

The white mustache spread wide in a smile.

"May I, then?" he asked, his thick hand stretched out toward the pistol.

"Of course," said Siebert, handing him the Colt. "I'll hold your shotgun and lamp."

The two exchanged guns and Siebert took the lamp.

"My, my, brother Howard," said Dudley, looking the gun over good. "What I wouldn't give for a huckleberry like this." He turned the gun in his hand and held it out to Siebert.

Siebert took the gun and looked down at it, still holding the shotgun and lamp in his left hand.

"Addle-brained as it sounds, I can hardly ever remember if this gun is a five- or a six-shot," he said.

"That's not so addle-brained," said Dudley Bryant. "I've seen both, you know."

"My goodness, you are right again!" said Siebert. "Aren't you just *the one!*" He grinned and pulled the trigger. The bullet hit Dudley Bryant in the heart at a distance of two feet. Fire and smoke puffed on his shirt. He staggered backward, a stunned look on his face.

Siebert swung the shotgun toward the two dogs as they went into a fit of growling and barking. The big dog had crouched for a leap at him. But two fast blasts from the shotgun silenced both dogs at once.

He turned his face back and forth on the night air, searching for any power from the killing—nothing. Disappointed again, he walked toward the house, toward the sound of the black mare crying out in the night. When he found her, she stood nickering and thrashing against her reins, the juniper bush she was tied to stuck firmly between two rocks.

"Look at you now, idiot," Siebert said, stepping in to free up her reins. "You're damn lucky I even want to fool with you—the way you've treated me."

As he settled the mare and untangled its reins, he looked toward the house and saw a figure step out onto the porch.

"Dudley?" a woman called out in a shaken voice.

Siebert grinned to himself and said in a mock voice, "Dudley ain't talking."

"Well, who are you?" she asked. "I heard shooting. Where's the dogs? What's going on?"

"One thing at a time, ma'am," said Siebert, leading the mare toward the house, the lamp raised in his hand. "Your dogs nearly ate me alive. Dudley said you can't see much, but you're a fair hand with a needle and thread?"

"He's right, I am," the woman said. She paused and looked all around in the darkness. "I don't like this at all. Where is he anyway?"

"You'd better be good, ma'am," Siebert said menacingly. "I don't want you stitching an eye shut." He grinned.

"What are you talking about? Where's Dudley and the dogs?" the woman said to the night. "I don't like them being gone this way."

"You'll be with them soon enough, ma'am," said Siebert as man and animal swayed closer in the flickering glow of light.

Chapter 7

———

Siebert sat shirtless, clenching the edge of a wooden table with his left hand. Daphne Bryant rethreaded her needle and went back to sewing up a gruesome gash atop his left shoulder. In Siebert's right hand he held the small Colt Pocket. A cup of whiskey sat within close reach.

"Dudley brewed this himself, eh?" he asked, feeling tipsy. He'd been taking a swig every time Daphne finished running the needle and thread through another ripped and gaping bite wound.

"Yes, he did," Daphne said, paying close attention to her handiwork. She wore a pair of thick spectacles with a magnifying lens tied in front of one of them. She glanced up at Siebert with eyes that appeared to be the size of skillets. Her thick, frizzled hair stood out around her black, leathery face like a silver-white mesquite bush.

"Get ready to take another drink," she advised grimly.

"*Dammmmn!*" Siebert lamented painfully as the needle slid through his sore flesh and tightened down onto the coarse thread. He raised the wooden cup to his lips and threw his head back, pouring a long, fiery drink down his throat. "I love whiskey as much as the next fellow, but *dammmmmnn!*" he screamed again as the needle sank into him. He set the wooden cup down and wrapped his hand back around the pocket pistol.

"We're nearly finished," the woman said.

Siebert stared at her large, empty eyes.

"You can't see shit, can you, old Daphne?" he said drunkenly.

"I see well enough," the old woman said. Readying her bloody fingertips to take another plunge with the needle, she stopped and said, "You want to do this yourself?"

Siebert didn't answer. Instead he chuckled drunkenly under his breath and shook his swirling head.

"When this is over . . . *oh*, I swear to God . . . ," he said. Then he stiffened and said, "*Dammmnnn!*" again as the needle made another stab into his shoulder.

"We're stopping for a spell," Daphne said. She took off her spectacles and laid them in front of her. Her eyes seemed to shrink to the size of small berries. She folded her bloody fingers on the table. "You've killed Dudley, ain't you?" she asked. She'd also asked him the same question three other times since she'd started sewing his wounds.

"Hell no, I told you I didn't," Siebert said. "But I will if you keep crowding me about it."

"Okay, then, where's the dogs?" Daphne challenged matter-of-factly.

Siebert gave her a drunken stare. He reached over to the side of her head and clutched a handful of spongy silver-white hair.

"Do you think I'd do that, kill your man?" he asked.

"I don't see no dogs," she said with a shrug.

"You know, you're not a bad-looking old gal," Siebert said, appraising her in his whiskey lull. His eyes swerved; he caught himself and sat up stiffly. "Okay, listen to me." He jiggled her head, then turned her hair loose and placed his hand over hers. "I want you to feel something of mine." He picked her hand up and pulled it toward him.

"Huh-uh, I ain't that way," she said bluntly.

"Damn it, just feel it!" Siebert insisted. He jerked her weathered hand over and laid it on his bare chest. He squeezed it closed over the cross. "There, did that hurt any?"

"No, it didn't," said the old woman. She settled down with a slight sigh. "I'm careful what gets put in my hand, bad as my eyes are."

Siebert just stared at her.

"My point is," he said, "would a man wearing a cross kill your old man, your dogs either, far as that goes?"

"I'm not saying," Daphne replied curtly. "People carry a cross for all sorts of makeup—some for pure evil, just to catch folks unawares, I'm thinking."

"Jesus . . . ," said Siebert. "Let's get to sewing." He threw back a long drink, set the cup down and laid his hand over the pocket pistol.

Daphne's bloody fingers crawled across the tabletop and felt of his hand.

"Why do you keep your hand on this little thing all the time?" she asked.

Siebert grinned behind a warm whiskey glow.

"Because it's all I have right now," he said.

"Dudley's got a bigger one," she said.

"Really . . . ?" said Siebert. "Where's it at?"

"Back in the bedroom under a plank beneath the bed," the woman said. "We'll go get it when I'm finished here. There's a good liver dun horse in the barn too," she added.

"No fooling?" said Siebert. "Why are you telling me all this, Daphne?"

She paused for a moment before saying, "I'm hoping if I give you everything we've got, you won't kill us."

"Listen to you, old sweetheart," Siebert said affectionately. He cupped his hand over hers again. "God forbid if I were to harm a hair on your precious head— Dudley's either." He smiled and sighed. "Now get on with the sewing."

Even with the whiskey surging through his veins, he still felt every sharp sting of the needle sliding through his flesh, every draw of thread as the old woman tightened on it. But by the time the last stitch was looped and tied, he had fallen into a painful lull that kept him from being either asleep or awake. Twice in the night he either felt, or *thought* he'd felt, the old woman try to raise his hand from the pocket gun lying on the table. Both times he gripped the gun and gave a warning growl. Finally he turned half-closed eyes to the woman and saw her knobby hands folded on the tabletop.

"Are we through?" he asked.

"We've been through for a while," the old woman said. "It's near daylight. Do you want some coffee? I've got some boiling."

Barely awake, Siebert looked around at the ray of venturing sunlight stabbing slantwise through the front window. His wet eyes swam around the room to a coiled lariat hanging from a peg.

"Yeah, I want some," he said. His gaze moved back to the table and focused on a large Dance Brothers .44 revolver staring at him from the tabletop. Beside the big gun lay a large tin of ammunition. "Holy dogs," he whispered.

"I went and got it for you," said Daphne.

"Did you load it?" Siebert grinned, reaching for the pistol.

"I was afraid to," said the woman. "I was afraid you'd wake up and get the wrong notion."

"You should have been my ma," Siebert said. He picked up the big pistol and turned it in his hands. "What about that coffee?" he said stiffly, feeling the tightness of the fresh stitches all over his face, his head and his upper body.

The old woman went to a small hearth and poured coffee into a battered tin cup. Siebert stood up, loaded the revolver and spun it on his finger, liking the feel of it.

"All right," he said. He twirled the gun into his empty holster, drew it, reholstered it loosely and let his hand rest on the bone handles. "I need to see how it shoots."

Daphne set the cup of steaming coffee on the table. Siebert stuck the Colt Pocket down in front of his gun belt. He picked up the tin of ammunition and tucked it into the crook of his arm.

"Get on the table," he commanded.

Daphne stared at him through her thick spectacles. "Why?" she asked.

"Because I told you to," said Siebert, his palm resting on the butt of the small Colt, his fingers tapping idly.

"I never done nothing this crazy in my life," the old woman said. But she crawled up atop the table on all fours.

"You have now," said Siebert. "Lie on your back."

She stared questioningly at him through the spectacles, one lens covered by the magnifying glass.

"So I can tie you up," said Siebert, gesturing toward the lariat hanging on the wall. "I don't trust you anymore."

"Oh," she said as if she understood.

In the night, the boy had shaken his sleeping father as soon as he'd heard the sound of distant gunfire. Yet by the time his father was awake, the gunfire had seized. The night beyond the open windows of their small hillside adobe lay as silent as stone.

"I heard it, Papa," said the young man with determination when his father seemed skeptical. "By the saints, I heard it—this was *not* thunder."

His father stared at him and batted the clinging remnants of sleep from his eyes. He let out a long breath and looked around for his trousers even though they hung from the same peg where he'd hung his trousers for twenty years.

"Do you not believe me, Papa?" the young man asked.

"*Sí*, Julio, I believe you, my son," Umberto said. He

pulled the thin peasant trousers down from the peg and shook them for scorpions before stepping into them. "From the *gringos locos*, you say?"

"*Sí*, from the crazy *americanos*," said Julio. "The shot of a pistol and the double blasts of an *escopeta*."

"The *escopeta* is for wolves and coyotes," said Umberto. "The old gringo uses it too freely, I think. But the *pistola* is worrisome, especially in the night." He tied the strings of his trousers at the waist and picked up a machete from against the wall. "We go."

"*Sí*, we go," said Julio. Having anticipated his father's decision, he'd put on his sandals, his trousers and shirt, and thrown on a frayed poncho. A machete was hooked to his waistband, and a straw sombrero hung behind his shoulders from a string around his neck. "It is at times like this I wish we owned a horse."

"Oh?" said Umberto, eyeing him. "Why? So we could kill it on these dark high trails?"

Julio didn't answer.

"Besides, we travel across the rocks from here to the *gringos locos* quicker than any horse," Umberto said. "A horse must have a trail of some sort. We need no trail, nothing but a place to put a foot, a spot to clasp a hand, eh?"

"*Sí*, Papa," said Julio, wishing he had kept his mouth shut. A man did not speak of things he *wished for*. Wishing was for fools and wistful young girls. He kept a hand on the handle of his machete.

When they'd left the adobe, they did not walk down to the trail lying two hundred feet below. Instead they had moved right out the side door of the house and onto the steep, rocky hillside and negotiated the jagged terrain like driven, agile spiders.

They climbed silently upward and sidelong over boulder and spur and moved effortlessly down broken rock faces like two dark teardrops. At a steep, rocky ledge, Umberto made it a point to stop long enough for his son to look down at a sharp turn in the winding switchback trail that they both knew would have taken over an hour longer to reach were they relying on horse or donkey.

The two stared out across a steep wall of rock that rimmed the trails and hillsides in a half circle and stood high and vertical against the night sky.

"*Desea un caballo,* eh?" Umberto asked his son.

Julio gave a slight smile.

"No, Papa, I do not *want a horse,*" he said.

"*Qué?*" said Umberto, taunting his son a little. "I did not hear you."

"I said, 'No, Papa,'" said Julio. "No *caballo.*"

Umberto chuckled as they both took off their sandals and dusted the soles together before shoving them down into their waistbands.

"*Ahora el viaje comienza,*" Umberto said, standing.

"*Sí,* Papa," said Julio, "now the travel begins."

They stepped over the edge of the cliff and moved on.

It was silvery daylight when they had walked onto the hillside overlooking the Bryants' narrow home on the rocky valley floor. When they reached the bottom of the hillside and started across the stretch of brush and wild grass, they stopped at the sight of Dudley Bryant and both dogs, Big and Little, lying dead and bloody on the ground. No sooner had they come upon the gruesome sight than they ducked down quickly as the sound of rapid pistol fire erupted from the direction of the house.

A loud yell and a round of maniacal laughter arose behind the echoing gunfire. Both Umberto and his son let out a breath, realizing that this was just wild, random firing—at least no one was firing at them. Umberto gave a troubled look at the dead lying strewn on the ground beside them.

"That is not the old woman, Daphne," he whispered warily.

"No, it is not," said Julio. He rose into a crouch enough to duck-walk over to his father's side.

"Stay close to me," Umberto said. "We must see about the woman."

The two moved forward in a crouch as another round of gunfire erupted, then ended in a loud yell and another peel of laughter. During a reloading lull, they ran the last few yards and ducked for cover at the corner of the house. They both looked down curiously at long lines scraped in the dirt from the porch, around the corner and to the rear of the house. They stiffened as six more pistol shots erupted rapidly followed by a cackle of laughter as a man's voice called out, *"Yiiii-hiii!* I've never owned so many bullets in my *whole damned life!"*

"Quickly, follow me," Umberto said to his son. Realizing the pistol had once again been emptied in a wild, mindless shooting spree, he jerked the machete from his waist.

"No, Papa, wait!" said Julio, reaching for his father's arm. But he was too late.

Umberto stepped into sight from the front corner of the house and stood facing Hodding Siebert with his machete hanging at his side.

"Who the hell are you?" Siebert said, the Dance Brothers revolver lying empty, open and smoking, in the palm of his left hand. His right hand was full of bullets, ready to reload.

"Do not load that gun, hombre," Umberto warned.

Now that his father had made the unwise move, all Julio could do was follow suit. He stepped out from the corner of the house and stood beside his father, his bare feet spread apart, the machete in hand.

"The hell you say!" Siebert shouted, sticking bullet after bullet into the Dance as quickly as he could, some of them falling to the ground in his efforts.

Father and son charged forward, wielding the big glistening blades above their heads. But Siebert fell back three steps hurriedly, managing to get four bullets into the gun, then raise and fire it as the two made it dangerously close.

"Close, but no prize for second best!" Siebert shouted as four shots erupted almost as one. At his feet, the young Mexican writhed in pain, the machete gripped tightly, blood pumping hard from two bullet holes in his chest. Six feet behind the boy, his father lay dead, a brutal exit wound gaping on the back of his head, another on the back of his neck.

"Here, give me that," Siebert said. Clamping his boot down on Julio's wrist, he jerked the machete from his hand. "This might sting a little," he warned, raising the big blade high above his head.

Julio screamed, but he was silenced when the sharp blade came down and did its job.

Siebert turned loose of the sunken blade and walked away to the barn without a second look.

"If a man needs some practice, he can do worse than come here for it," he chuckled. He snatched up the reins to the black mare he'd hitched to a half-collapsed fence rail.

But his cheerfulness ended when he led the mare into the barn and saw a big liver-colored dun gelding lying dead on the floor.

"What the hell . . . ?" Siebert walked closer and looked down at the wide puddle of dark blood beneath the dun's neck; then his puzzled eyes went to the rays of sharp sunlight shining through several bullet holes in the barn wall. "I've shot the son of a bitch."

Beside him the mare scraped a hoof and chuffed.

"I dare you to say a *damned* word," Siebert warned her, giving a yank on her reins. He paused in consideration, and then a grin spread across his face. A worn California-style saddle was draped over a stall rail. "All right," he said, "at least I get a good saddle out of the deal."

Cursing his luck, Siebert carried the saddle over and dropped it at the mare's hooves. He removed the side-saddle, then pitched the California saddle atop the mare. But before he could fasten the cinch, the mare reached her head around, grabbed the saddle between her teeth and flung it to the floor.

Siebert bit his lip. He picked up the saddle, shook if off and pitched it back up on the mare. Almost before it landed on her back, the mare grabbed it, yanked it and threw it to the floor in a puff of dust once again.

Siebert drew the Colt Pocket from his waist, cocked it and pointed it at the mare as he picked up the saddle and shook it off.

"Do it again, see if don't stick a bullet through your brain."

The mare stood still as stone as he saddled her, gun in hand, cocked and pointed, and swung up onto the big comfortable saddle. Without a tap of Siebert's heels, the big mare walked out the door and milled, awaiting its rider's command.

"That's more like it," Siebert said. "Now show me some more of that speed." He nailed his single boot heel to the mare's side, the cocked Colt still in hand. But instead of running straight, the mare bunched up beneath him and cantered sideways a full thirty yards before Siebert could right her and finally turn her back toward the barn.

"I know I'm going to kill you," he hissed. "I just don't know when."

The mare chuffed and blew and shook her bowed head. Siebert almost lost his seat. But near the open barn door he managed to sit up straight, seeing the young Mexican stagger toward him, his whole front covered with blood, the machete blade sunken deep in the side of his neck.

"Why's this stuff *always* happening to me?" Siebert queried any and all universal sources. He raised the Colt with difficulty as the mare leaned dangerously to one side and bounced stiffly on to the barn.

PART 2

Chapter 8

Throughout the preceding afternoon the Ranger had traveled with the feeling of being watched—or being followed. Something like that, he'd told himself. But the fresh hoofprints he tracked ran clear and straight ahead of him on the dust-coated trail. There was no way the man he followed could have circled back on him, and there was no good reason for him to have done so. The man was on the run. His best interest was in pushing forward, not circling back, Sam reminded himself. Still, the feeling had been there, nesting somewhere between his mind and his gut.

Get rid of it, he'd told himself, making camp for the night, and he'd managed to push the feeling away. Yet, when his coffee had boiled and he'd eaten his food warmed over the flames of a small campfire, he had taken his blanket and rifle away from the firelight. He'd lightly slept the night in the cover of rock, one ear to the campsite, one to the trail behind him.

He'd risen before daylight and walked the trail back a hundred yards in the silver grainy birth of dawn.

Nothing, he'd told himself, warily examining the dirt at his feet and the rocky land surrounding him.

Let that be the end of it.

At the campsite he'd attended to and inspected Black Pot and the silvery gray dun, finding the dun's foreleg to be mending sufficiently without the weight of a rider on it. Then he'd cleared the campsite, stepped into his saddle and given another look along his back trail before tapping the stallion forward and riding on.

At midmorning he had followed the tracks down to the narrow canyon floor and stopped at the sight of the dead man and the two dead dogs lying in the stretch of wild grass. His eyes had searched around and seen no guns on the dead man or on the ground surrounding him. He'd stood breathing a sigh of regret in the hot, dry wind and looked off at the house in the distance.

He'd levered a round into his rifle chamber.

"Let's go," he said, taking the reins to both animals in hand and leading them forward, dreading what he might find waiting for him in the silent, windblown house.

When he neared the house, he crouched and moved to the cover of a broken wagon sitting on three wheels and a stack of rock. From there he watched, rifle ready in hand, as the creaking front door swung back and forth on the wind. After a moment he hitched the animals to the wagon and ventured forward.

"Hello, the house," he called out, standing at a hitch rail in front of the plank porch. He waited. After a moment he repeated in Spanish, *"Hola, la casa."*

Satisfied that no reply was coming, he stepped onto

the porch and stood to one side of the open doorway. On the floor he saw a wet, bloody cloth and a spilled pan of water. Scrapes, seeming to come from a table's legs, traveled across the floor and out the door at his feet. His eyes followed the scrapes down from the porch, off across the dirt and around the front corner of the house.

Sam looked around the house's interior one more time before following the long marks in the dirt. He stopped in his tracks when he saw the body of the dead Mexican lying sprawled in a dried puddle of dark blood, a machete only inches from his outstretched hand.

"It's only the start," he said, preparing himself.

Walking on, he saw the body of yet another man, this one lying ten yards away, also in a dried pool of blood. His head was missing. A few yards ahead, in the rear of the rock yard, he saw the table standing upended in the dirt, a naked, bullet-riddled body tied to it.

Hodding Siebert . . . , he concluded, seeing the grizzly handiwork of a monster.

"Aces, on his own," he added aloud, walking on closer to the dead woman hanging tied by her wrists to the table, as if crucified. He raised her bowed head with the tip of his rifle barrel and saw two gaping holes where her eyes had been. He shook his head slowly and let the woman's head sag over onto her shoulder.

Taking off his sombrero, letting it hang at his side, he looked all around and walked toward the barn. Again, he would need a shovel. Tracking a madman like Hodding Siebert, it might be wise to always carry a shovel.

Good idea.

He walked into the barn, looked around at the dead horse and the discarded saddle and the countless bullet holes in the wall. He shook his head again. Spotting a short-handled shovel lying in the dirt, he leaned his rifle against the wall and picked the shovel up to inspect it. *It'll do.*

Shovel in hand, he'd reached for the rifle when he heard a hammer cock from the direction of the open door behind him. He turned toward it, his hand going to the butt of his holstered Colt.

"No, señor," a tall Mexican said, standing in the doorway, his boots planted shoulder-width apart. He wore a long black riding duster and a dusty black sombrero, a faded red bandanna tied around his neck. In his right hand, a big Walker Colt was cocked and leveled at the Ranger. "For your own sake, keep both hands on the shovel."

Sam noted the stance. A familiar stance—a fighting stance, he reminded himself. He didn't put his right hand back on the shovel. Instead he froze it where it was, an inch away from grabbing his Colt if he needed to. But even as he readied himself for making such a move, he realized that if this man had wanted him dead, he would have been dead already. Nobody intent on killing him would have stepped in, caught him cold, then cocked the big Walker. *Huh-uh.* That wasn't how killing was done.

Cocking the big Walker gun in the open doorway was a warning, he decided, gazing squarely at the man.

"Quién es usted? Qué desea usted?" Sam said quickly,

still poised and ready even though this man had already taken the upper hand.

"Speak English," the tall Mexican said. "I am Juan Lupo." He gestured a sidelong nod toward the dead lying strew in the yard beyond the barn walls. "What I want is to know that you are not going to turn and start shooting."

Sam uncoiled a little, but only a little.

"You can't think I had anything to do with this," he said, hoping that the Territorial Ranger badge was visible on his chest behind the open lapel of his own black riding duster.

"No," said the Mexican, "I want to make sure you know that *I* had nothing to do with it."

Sam weighed his words, wanting to check, see is his instincts the night before had been right.

"I know you didn't do it, Juan Lupo," he said. "You were too busy dogging my trail last night. Besides, I would have heard you shooting, this close."

The Mexican gave him a curious look. "You knew I was following you? How?" he asked.

Sam saw the big Walker lower an inch.

"I have my ways," he said. Part of the tension had left the air. Now it was time to push a little. He calmly laid his hand on the butt of his Colt, not in a threatening way. "Just to keep this conversation civil, either you need to holster that six-shooter or I need to draw mine." He stared at the Mexican.

Juan Lupo nodded and lowered the big Walker to his side. But he made no attempt to slide the big saddle pistol into the belly holster strapped across his middle.

Fair enough.

Sam eased his Colt out of its holster and let it hang at his side in the same manner. *All is even*, he told himself.

The Mexican noted the Ranger's move but let it go.

"You're Ranger Samuel Burrack, the *Americano* lawman who's hunting outlaws along the hill country," said the Mexican.

The Ranger gave a wry half smile.

"I already knew that," he said. "The question is, what are you doing here, Juan Lupo?"

"Call me Juan, or call me Lupo, if you please, Ranger," the Mexican said. "As a bounty hunter I am also known as Juan Fácil."

"Easy John Lupo," said the Ranger, translating the name to English.

"Yes, *Easy John*," the tall Mexican said.

"A bounty hunter, huh?" the Ranger said, eyeing him up and down.

"Yes," said Juan Lupo. "Does that make us enemies?"

"No," said the Ranger. "But it does make me wonder why you were following me instead of tracking the man you're after."

"Because you have two horses, and I have none," Lupo said bluntly. He raised his big Walker Colt and slid it into his belly holster, a show of peace.

Sam just stared at him.

"Mine went in the hole last evening," said Lupo. "This hill country eats horses." He gave a half shrug. Then seeing the Ranger's flat stare, he said, "Don't think it, Ranger. Had I wanted to steal one of your horses, I would have done so and been gone."

Sam continued to stare evenly at him. "I have no horse for sale," he said.

"That works out well," said Easy John Lupo, "because I have no money—it was in my saddlebags and went over the edge with my horse."

"Go on," Sam encouraged him, letting him know there was more he needed to explain.

"I could tell you were after Siebert, probably Bellibar too," he said. "I came to offer an alliance— see if I can lend a hand in exchange for the loan of a horse."

"I usually work alone," Sam said.

"So do I," said Lupo. "But from the looks of this, the quicker we stop Siebert, the more lives we save."

Sam considered it.

"I know where he is going, Bellibar too," said Lupo. "It will save you much time."

"I know where they're headed," Sam said. "They're going to Barranca del Cobre—Copper Gully."

"No," said Lupo, shaking his head. "They will only go there as a place to rest and gather fresh horses. Then they will go on to Colina de Mirador."

"Lookout Hill," Sam translated. "I've heard of the place." He considered the bounty hunter's words for a moment longer, then asked him, "What is the price for a maniac like Hot Aces Siebert?"

"Two thousand five hundred in American dollars," Lupo said. "I'll share it. That's not to say fifty-fifty, but I'm willing to consider—"

"Save your dickering," Sam said, cutting him short. "I don't draw bounty."

"You mean . . . ?" Lupo's words trailed.

"I mean the bounty's all yours, far as I'm concerned," said Sam.

Lupo stopped and let that sink in.

"And I can use one of your horses?" he asked.

"That's right," Sam said. "You get the dun—Bellibar's horse. It's got a crooked front hoof. It's risky, but we've got no other choice."

"Risky?" Lupo just looked at him.

"Don't worry," Sam said. "It should be rested enough to get you to Copper Gully without hurting itself. You can change horses there."

"I didn't expect you be this agreeable," Lupo said, eyeing him almost with suspicion. "What are you asking in return?"

"Nothing." Sam tossed the short-handled shovel over onto the ground at Lupo's feet. "How's your digging?" he asked.

While Easy John Lupo dug graves in the hard ground, Sam reached out with a boot knife and cut the ropes holding Daphne Bryant's bullet-riddled remains to the tabletop. He carried her body out of the sun and wrapped it in one of three well-worn blankets he'd found inside the house. He laid the other two blankets over Black Pot's saddle and led the big stallion out to carry the bodies of Dudley Bryant and the two dead dogs to the rocky yard for burial.

Sam walked the big stallion over to the graves and

laid the old man and both dogs down beside the woman. Lupo stood in a shallow grave, sipping tepid water from a canteen. He'd removed his duster and his black sombrero and draped them over the California saddle he'd taken from the barn. He'd tied the red bandanna around his sweaty forehead.

"I was close behind you when you buried the old Mexican and young girl at the healing woman's hacienda," he said matter-of-factly.

"Oh?" Sam looked at him and took the canteen when Lupo offered it up to him. "Any sign of the healing woman after I left there?" he asked.

"No," said Lupo, "only the blood on the ground." He reflected for a moment. "The peasants call her Sens Priscilla. She always told them that she could not be killed, only changed into some other form."

"From all the blood I saw on the ground, I hope she's right," Sam said. "Sens Priscilla, huh?" He took a swig of water.

"Here she was Sens Priscilla," said Lupo. "But on your side of the border she is known as the Princess—to some she was Witch Annie." He took the canteen as the Ranger wiped his hand across his lips and handed it to him. "She was a Roma," he said, "a Gypsy."

"A Gypsy princess?" said Sam.

Lupo shrugged and said, "Who knows what she is, or *was*? She did more good than bad. What better can be said of anyone?"

"I agree," Sam said.

He wanted to ask Lupo more on the matter, but before had the opportunity, gunshots exploded from a stand of brush ten yards away. He dived to the ground and scrambled for cover as bullets whistled past him. Lupo ducked down, taking cover in the shallow grave, instinctively drawing the big Colt from his belly holster.

"Drop your rifle, gringo," one of the men called out before either the Ranger or Lupo could return fire, "or we will shoot you both."

Rurales, Sam told himself, having taken position in the dirt, flat on his stomach, his Winchester out, ready to fire. He saw three men stand in a crouch, each of them wearing the same ragtag mismatching uniforms he'd seen on Captain Goochero's men at their last confrontation.

"We didn't kill these people. I found them here," Sam shouted, knowing things had already gone too far. These men had fired on them too freely, and they wouldn't hesitate to do so again. But he had to try to stop things if he could.

"And we found you!" the voice called out.

Another round of shots whistled past Sam's head. He sighted on one of the three and fired the Winchester as they charged forward from the brush, shooting repeatedly. He heard one of the riders cry out in pain; he levered another round into the rifle chamber. They weren't interested in what had happened, only in drawing blood. He jerked the rifle back against his shoulder and took aim. *One down, two to go. . . .* But at the sound of Lupo's voice, he stopped and waited for a second.

"Hold your fire!" Easy John Lupo commanded from the direction of the barn. "This man is with me."

With him?

Sam saw Lupo stand straight up in the shallow grave, his Walker Colt pointed and cocked toward the lead *rurale* from less than twenty or thirty feet. The charging *rurale* slid to a sudden stop at the sight of Lupo and the big Walker Colt. His eyes widened in recognition as Lupo reached up and snatched the bandanna from his forehead.

"Do not make me tell you again," Lupo shouted in warning. "Drop your guns and raise your hands."

"Drop your guns, you imbeciles!" the lead *rurale* shouted over his shoulder. "It is *Coronel* Lupo!" His gun fell from his hand as if it had scalded him.

Coronel Lupo?

Sam looked down his rifle sights, ready for anything. He watched as Lupo pulled himself from the open grave and walked forward, his Colt still covering the lead *rurale*, who stood frozen with fear.

"Are you all right, Ranger?" Lupo asked over his shoulder.

"They're covered," said Sam calmly, a bead drawn on the lead *rurale*, just in case things took a bad turn for Lupo.

"Don't shoot us, Juan Lupo," the lead man said, shaking. "We did not know it is you!"

"You know it now," Lupo said firmly, his feet planted shoulder-width apart. He called past the lead *rurale* to the man standing a few yards behind him, his gun on the ground, his hands held chest high. "Get your wounded man up and bring him here, pronto," he demanded. Looking to the right in the brush, Lupo spotted three horses hitched to a standing rock. "Bring your horses with you," he called out.

The second *rurale* hurried to the fallen man and pulled him to his feet. Sam walked over beside Lupo, his Winchester still cocked and ready.

"A bounty hunter, huh?" he said. He eyed Lupo skeptically as the nearest *rurale* still stood frozen in place. Farther back, the other *rurale* walked forward leading the horse, his wounded companion's arm looped over his shoulder.

"Yes, a bounty hunter . . . among other things," Lupo said sidelong to him, keeping his dark eyes on the lead *rurale*.

Chapter 9

The Ranger backed away from Lupo as the three *rurales* approached. Lupo stared at them, the wounded man swaying in place, standing on his own now, a hand clasping his bloody shoulder. Both Sam and Lupo noted the Remington revolver in the wounded man's holster, but Sam wasn't going to mention it. This was Lupo's play. He kept his Winchester leveled and cocked.

The lead *rurale* tried to offer a smile, but it only looked stiff and nervous as he lowered his hands a little, keeping them spread in a show of peace.

Before Lupo could speak, the *rurale* rattled quickly in Spanish, *"Coronel Lupo! Mil disculpus, lenido nosotros conocido este hombre estuvo con usted—"*

"Speak English, hombre," Juan Lupo said, cutting him off.

Again Coronel Lupo, Sam thought, listening closely.

The *rurale* appeared stunned. He gave his two companions a baffled look, then took a breath and turned his eyes back to Juan Lupo.

"I offer a thousand apologies," he said in labored

English. "Had we known it is you with this one, we would never have fired at him. But we saw him loading a body onto a horse as we rode down to the valley and—"

"What are your names? Where is your *capitán* and the rest of his men?" Lupo demanded, cutting him off again.

The three looked at each other.

"I—I am Emilio Sanchez," said the nervous *rurale*. "This is Hector." His hand gestured to the other rider, then to the one with the Ranger's bullet in his shoulder. "This is Teto." The wounded man wobbled dangerously to one side, but caught himself at just the right moment. Watching him, Sam questioned how hurt he really was.

"Where are Goochero and the rest of his men?" Lupo asked again.

Emilio appeared to stall for a moment, then gestured back along the trail.

"The captain and the rest of the men are not far behind," he said.

"I see," said Lupo. "Then you three are scouting the trail?"

A look of sudden relief came upon the *rurale*'s face.

"*Sí*, that is correct," he said, "we are scouting the trail for the *capitán*." He looked at the one named Hector for support.

"That's right," Hector said. "We are trail scouts, the three of us."

"I see," said Lupo. He eyed them sharply. "I am glad

to hear that, because so many *rurales* decide to desert Goochero's provincial forces when they get this close to the *putas* and the mescal in Barranca del Cobre."

"*Sí*, it is true," said Emilio, working at hiding the guilty look on his face. "But that is not what we do. We are not interested in whores or mescal in Copper Gully, only in scouting the trail for our *capitán*." As he spoke his hands fell idly to his sides. Sam noted the move; so did Lupo.

"You, Hector," Lupo said, letting the big Walker Colt sag a little in his hand, "Bring those horses closer. I want to look at them."

Hector gave Emilio a guarded look before stepping forward with the horses.

"You heard him, Hector," Emilio said sharply. "Show him our horses."

Hector pulled the three horses forward by their reins and stepped all the way out of the brush.

Sam noted that Lupo had lowered his Colt. He was up to something, letting his guard down that way. The Ranger had seen that kind of move plenty of times, always by slick gunmen who wanted to put him off guard, make him think they had given up their edge. He had no idea why a man like Lupo would do this, but being Lupo's backup, he decided to play along. He lowered the butt of the Winchester three inches, and watched and listened.

"They are our regular horses," said Hector, even as he led the animals forward and stopped in front of Lupo.

"I will be the judge of that," Lupo said. He jerked the reins from the *rurale*'s hand. "Raise this one's front hoof. Show me the marking."

Hector's eyes slid to Emilio, then back to Lupo.

"Not all of our horses have marked hooves, *Coronel* Lupo," he said warily.

"But one out of these three better show a mark," Lupo warned. His dark eyes stabbed back at Hector like a dagger. "Now show me," he demanded.

"*Sí*," Hector said, "I will show you."

He backed up against one of the horses' rear legs, crouched and raised its dusty hoof between his knees. Lupo let his Colt point away from Emilio as he leaned in closer to Hector to inspect the animal for a hoof marking.

Here goes, Sam thought, seeing Emilio catch the move and let his right hand drift around toward the back of his belt.

"No mark on this one," Lupo said to Hector. "Show me another."

"*Sí, Coronel* Lupo," said Hector. He let the horse's hoof down and turned to the next animal. But instead of reaching down for the horse's hoof, he grabbed for a gun behind his back.

As fast as a rattler, Lupo's big Colt jammed into Hector's middle and exploded. The shot streaked comet-like through his belly and out his spine. Sam saw Emilio and the wounded Teto make their move at the same time. Going for Teto, the one visibly wearing a gun, Sam fired the Winchester and watched the man fly backward as the bullet's impact slammed his chest.

As soon as he fired, Sam levered a fresh round and swung the rifle barrel toward Emilio, but his help wasn't needed.

Lupo's big Walker Colt roared like some angry giant. Emilio turned a twisted backflip, leaving a red circle of mist in the air as he hit the ground facedown, as limp as a bundle of rags.

Sam watched Lupo swing the Walker from one downed *rurale* to the next, satisfying himself that each man was dead as the spooked horses tried to pull their reins free from his hand. Settling the animals, he let the gun hang down his side and turned to face Sam.

"Well . . . *bueno suerte* for us," he said flatly. "Now we have no shortage of horses."

"*Good luck for us . . . ?*" Sam only stared at him. "You set them up and killed them."

Lupo stopped cold as he saw the Ranger's smoking Winchester barrel pointed at him.

"Oh . . . ?" he said, as if disregarding the rifle. "And what did these cowards do? They slipped in on us, to ambush us, kill us and take what money we might have to pay for their spree in Copper Gully." As he spoke, he slid his Colt back into his belly holster and showed Sam his empty hands. "There, you see, I am unarmed now. I don't think you will shoot me, Ranger," he added, "not that it upsets you this much to kill these jackals."

"Don't bet your life on it, 'Colonel' Lupo," Sam said. "You've got about one second to start leveling with me."

Lupo let out a breath. He kept his hands chest high, still holding the three horses' reins.

"All right, it is true I hold the rank of colonel in the emperor's *federales*," he said. "But it is only an honorary commission bestowed upon me by *Generalissimo* Manuel Ortega for finding some missing gold, stolen from Mexico City." He gave a sight shrug as if to dismiss the matter. "Does that clear things up for you?"

"Some." The Ranger continued to stare at him, but he lowered the rifle butt from his shoulder to his waist. "I saw how these men acted when they recognized you. You didn't have to kill them. You could have shooed them away like pigeons."

"Yes," said Lupo, "and like pigeons they would have flown off somewhere and sooner or later let someone know they saw me here." He paused, then added, "A bounty hunter does not like for his comings and goings to be known." He gave the Ranger a look. "Neither does a lawman like yourself, eh?"

"Neither does a spy," Sam said bluntly.

"A spy?" said Lupo. "That is what you think I am now because I killed these deserters, these ambushers?"

"To be honest, Lupo," said Sam, "right now I don't know what you are." He gestured toward the three horses at Lupo's side. "Now that horses are more plentiful, I don't see much need in us riding together."

"All right, Ranger, you've got me," Lupo said. "Perhaps I am something other than a bounty hunter. Perhaps it is more accurate to say I am a special attaché serving the emperor of Mexico under *Generalissimo* Manuel Ortega."

"Special attaché . . . ?" Sam said with a skeptical

look. He was squeezing for an explanation, but he wasn't sure what he was getting for his trouble.

"All right, then, ambassador, if you like," Lupo said with a slight shrug. Seeing the unyielding look on Sam's face, he said "An envoy? A public servant?"

"I'm sticking with *spy*," said Sam.

"Have it your way," said Lupo. "But I can still show you the way to Colina de Mirador."

"Or I can still find Lookout Hill on my own," Sam replied, knowing his words were part bluff. Whatever Lupo was, he was worth riding with if he led them both to the killers they were looking for.

"While we stand here talking about it," Lupo said, sounding a little impatient, "Siebert and Bellibar ride farther from us. One good hard rain and it will be as if they never rode through these hills."

"I agree," said Sam. He let the Winchester droop in his hand and gestured back toward the open graves. "We can finish up here and talk about it on the trail," he said.

"Yes, that would be wise," Lupo said. Offering nothing more on the matter, he led the three horses over beside Black Pot and the silver-gray dun. Sam watched as he walked back to the half-dug graves and picked up the shovel. "Meanwhile, you can ask yourself how bad you really want the man who did all this killing, and his companion, Bellibar."

Bobby Hugh Bellibar had not wasted any time. When he'd shot Hodding "Hot Aces" Siebert and left him for dead, floating away downstream along a switchback hill trail, he'd ridden Siebert's roan almost nonstop to Copper Gully.

As soon as he arrived at the booming little mining town—a venture financed and overseen by the Pettigo-American Mining Company—he reined Siebert's roan and the other two dead outlaws' horses up to a row of iron hitch posts out in front of a ragged tent cantina.

Just when he started toward the cantina, four gun-shots exploded from inside the large tent. Bellibar stepped quickly aside, his hand going to the Reming-ton for assurance as a bloody gunman wearing a frayed red pin-striped suit staggered out through the tent fly. The man stood unsteadily, one hand clutching his chest where blood spurted and gushed from three bullet holes. With his other hand he tried in vain to raise a shiny double-action Colt Thunderer as he fired it repeatedly down at his side.

Bellibar watched as the man shot himself three times in the right foot before pitching face-forward onto the rocky ground. Severed toes bounced like pop-corn from his shot-open boot.

Bellibar grinned with perverse satisfaction.

"Bobby Hugh, this is your kind of town," he said aloud to himself as the three horses nickered in terror at the hitch post.

Two men filed out through the tent fly, the one in front carrying a smoking revolver in one hand, a short-handled blacksmith hammer in the other. He crouched over the bloody man on the ground, drew the hammer back and dealt him a hard blow to the base of his skull.

The body flopped once on the ground, then fell still as stone. The man with the blacksmith hammer stood ready to swing the big hammer again.

"Figure he's dead?" he said to the man behind him.

The second man stood holding a shotgun at port arms.

"If he's not, I want no part of him," he said.

"You're right," said the man with the big hammer. He dropped the hammer beside the body on the ground and wiped his palm on his trouser leg. "I'm obliged to you for catching him cheating. I hate a card cheat worse than anything."

"Whoa, now," said the man with the shotgun, "I never said he was a card cheat. I said that a red-striped suit was *hard to beat.*"

"Jesus . . . ," the other man said. He rounded a finger deep inside his ear. "I'm getting to where I can't hear worth a damn." He looked at the body on the ground, then back to the man with the shotgun. "He was a card cheat, though. I can see it in him, can't you?"

The shotgun holder considered it for a moment. "I'd have to say yes, he was a cheat," he said. "Let's not go blaming ourselves for this, Harvey. There's folks gets killed every day." He reached a thumb over the shotgun hammers and let them both down. "We need to clear out of here before Pettigo's mercenaries catch wind of this."

"Pettigo and his mercs don't give a blue damn about one dead gambler—" Harvey Moran said. Then he cut himself short and said, "Wait. What's this?" He stared at Bobby Hugh Bellibar, who stood watching, his hand resting on the Remington behind his gun belt. "What the hell you looking at?" he asked menacingly, the smoking Colt still in hand.

"Whatever suits me," Bellibar replied calmly, rapping his fingertips idly on the gun butt.

"Yeah?" Harvey took a step toward him, then stopped.

"Yeah," said Bellibar, not backing an inch. He'd heard four shots, meaning the man only had two shots left—*one*, if he kept his hammer resting on an empty chamber.

"Say, I know these two horses," said the man with the shotgun, eyeing the dead outlaws' horses standing next to Siebert's roan. "They belong to Saginaw Sparks and Paco, the Mex." His eyes cut from the horses back to Bellibar. "What're you doing with them?"

"Whatever suits me," Bellibar repeated. His fingers stopped tapping.

"Whatever suits you. . . ." A dark chuckle came from Moran, who stood loosening and tightening his grip on the Colt, realizing how short he was on bullets. "Is that your answer for everything, hombre?"

"Pretty much," said Bellibar. He gave a smug little grin that told Moran he knew how many shots he was facing and wasn't worried in the least. "Are you going to scold me for it?" he asked.

The man with the shotgun had also realized their situation, he himself not wearing his gun belt, owing to a fiery rash around his waist. He started to put his thumb back over the gun hammers.

"You're making the last mistake in your life," Bellibar said, his grin disappearing as easily as it had arrived.

The man's thumb moved away from the gun hammers; the shotgun slumped in his hand.

"I know Saginaw Sparks," he said in a cautious tone. "He'd never give up that horse long as he was alive."

"Ain't that the truth, though?" Bellibar said calmly.

A tense silence fell around the three. Inside the tent a guitar, a trumpet and an accordion spilled mariachi music tinto the dry evening air. After a moment Harvey Moran let out a tight breath.

"Well, well," he said, keeping cool in spite of his shortage of firepower. "Here we are, three ol' Anglo boys having ourselves a Mexican standoff . . . in Mexico, no less."

Bellibar just stared at him.

"I've got an idea," Moran offered Bellibar, trying not to stand down too easily. "You drag this dead fool away, hurry back here and Bad Sharlo and I will buy you a drink."

"Bad Sharlo Bering . . . ?" Bellibar cocked his head slightly. "I've heard of you."

"Yeah?" said Dering, his chest puffing a little. He and Moran looked almost relieved. But then Bellibar returned to the matter at hand.

"I've got a better idea," he said to Moran. "Drag him away yourselves, both of you hurry back here and buy me a drink."

"You've heard of Lookout Hill?" Moran asked, not letting the newcomer's words affect him.

"Yep," said Bellibar, "that's where I'm headed, looking to ride with the Cady brothers, Bert and Fletcher."

"That's who we ride for," Moran said bluntly. "What do you say now?"

"I say in that case, you can both hurry back and buy me *two* drinks," Bellibar said.

Bad Sharlo bristled; Moran stopped him with a look.

"Can't you see he's just scouring us both down?" He looked at Bellibar and said, "You're a crazy sumbitch, ain't you?"

"And then some," Bellibar replied with the same flat expression.

Chapter 10

———

At a makeshift bar, Bellibar and the two gunmen stood tossing back tequila from wooden cups. An empty bowl and a food-smeared spoon stood at Bellibar's elbow, flies circling above scraps of goat gristle and bean sauce. An hour earlier Bellibar had handed the reins to the roan and the other two horses to a Mexican stable boy. When the boy brought the horses back rested, watered and grained, he hitched them to the iron posts out in front of the tent cantina.

The boy's eyes grew wide as he crossed the dirt floor to the bar, watching two half-naked prostitutes roll and kick and brawl in the dirt beside an overturned table, their bare breasts bobbing and bouncing freely, glistening with sweat. Above the women's screams and curses, the mariachis played vigorously in a low swirl of cigar and pipe smoke.

"Don't try to tell me you two mullets live this good all the time," Bellibar said, raising his half-full cup of tequila as if in a toast.

"You ain't seen nothing," Moran replied above the

music, screaming and laughter. "Wait 'til tonight when everybody starts getting rowdy."

Bellibar turned to the young stable boy, who couldn't pull his eyes away from the two naked fighters. A shredded skirt rose in the air; onlookers hooted and whistled and clapped.

"Don't be watching them," Bellibar warned the boy, tapping his shoulder sharply with a gold coin. "It'll make your bed wet."

"I have no bed, señor," said the boy. He looked up long enough to take the coin and close his fist around it.

Bellibar grinned.

"Oh . . . in that case, have at it," he said, gesturing the boy toward the fighting women.

But instead of looking back toward the battling women, the boy slid a look past Moran and Bering and motioned for Bellibar to lean down closer to him.

"Yeah, what?" Bellibar said, stooping to ear level, in order to hear and be heard above the din of place.

"You said to tell you anything I hear about someone coming to town behind you?" the boy reminded him. He held his hand out to Bellibar.

"Yep, what have you got for me?" said Bellibar, fishing in his trouser pocket for another coin.

"The *soldados de mercenaries* from Pettigo Mining are in town."

Mercenary soldiers . . . Bellibar gave a cautious look toward the front of the tent.

"Where are they?" he asked quietly.

"They are at the *librea* barn. They will be coming here soon, señor," the boy said in a whisper. "Someone has told them what happened to the man in red, I think."

Bellibar handed him the coin.

"*Gracias*, kid," he said. He started to straighten up but stopped when he saw the boy had more to say.

"Should I also warn your amigos?" he asked, clasping the gold coins in his fist in a manner that implied more coins could be coming his way.

"Well, you see, kid," Bellibar said, "we're not what you call amigos. We're not even what you call *compañeros*, these fellows and me." He chuckled a little and added, "The fact is, I don't even know these plug-looking sons a' bitches. Never laid eyes on them until I arrived in town a few hours ago."

"I see," the boy said. He lowered his fist and his expectations, but asked anyway, "I will still warn them, if you want me to."

"I don't know. . . ." Bellibar clucked his cheek, seeming to struggle with the matter. "They're having such a good time. I hate to piss on their campfire." He fished another coin from his pocket and slipped it to the boy. "Why don't you ease out front and lead my horses around back for me—hitch them loose, *por favor*?"

"*Sí*, hitch them loose," the boy repeated, smiling at the third coin in his palm. "This I will do." He walked out the fly without turning another glance toward the female combatants.

"Damn, pard," Moran said to Bellibar, "you're palavering with that stable boy and missing all the fun." He nodded at a low cloud of dust in the center of the dirt floor where the two women had fought their way up onto their knees. The crowd remained seated, but they'd drawn their chairs in a circle around the women. Music still blared. Fists waved money in the air; wagers were made. A knife appeared as if out of nowhere in one woman's hand. The crowd roared. The other woman grabbed her wrist and the two grappled and fell back to the dirt.

"It's like this all the time?" Bellibar grinned.

"It never *stops!*" Bad Sharlo screamed with laughter.

"It's like dying, going to *Mejico* heaven!" said Moran, waving his cup, tequila slopping over the edge of it.

"All right, I'm going to live here from now on, that's all there is to it," Bellibar said in another toast. He licked his thumb, stuck it in a bowl of salt and put it in his mouth. He threw back a swig of tequila, stuck his thumb in the salt again and swallowed one more shot.

"I've got to choke a lizard," he said. "Don't let these gals stop fighting until I get back—I mean it." He pointed a finger and wagged it at the two gunmen as he moved away toward the rear of the tent.

"He's not such a bad sort, as it turns out," Moran said to Bad Sharlo, the two of them watching bleary-eyed as Bellibar left the tent.

In the town livery barn across the street and a block down from the ragged tent cantina, Dale Pettigo stood with five of his father's hired gunmen. He smoked a black cigar he held between the fingers of tan-colored riding gloves. A pale blond mustache drooped above his thin lips, and blond hair spiked out from under his wide, flat-crowned plainsman's hat. He wore a brown duster buttoned up to his throat, hiding a new tooled-leather holster tucked up under his left arm. A cutout slot in his duster allowed his right hand to slip inside and grasp the bone handles of a fully engraved Colt .45 if needed.

Ashes fell from the blunt tip of Dale Pettigo's cigar and landed on the body in the red pin-striped suit.

"No finely schooled accountant deserves to die this way," said a burly, red-faced gunman standing across the body from the young Pettigo.

Dale Pettigo raised sharp eyes to the man and said in a dry, critical voice, "How does a *finely schooled accountant* deserve to die, Denver? You tell all of us, for future reference."

Denver Jennings felt pressed; he slid red, bloodshot eyes over the other men gathered round the body. He gave a shrug, a rifle propped back over his broad shoulder.

"All's I'm saying is not like this." He nodded down at the bloody pin-striped suit, the ragged half-missing right foot. "He died too young."

"Harold Wartler was a simpering, milk sucking house dog who just had to run with the hounds now and then," Dale Pettigo concluded. He looked from one stoic face to another. "Save all your words of praise and condolences for my father. He thought the world of this fool—I didn't. I always thought he'd rub a man's leg, to be honest about it."

"I don't know what to make of that," said a rough-faced older gunman named Dodge Peterson. "But he liked playing the stage role of a rake and a gambler.

Look at him," he added in disgust to Denver Jennings. "A man wears a suit like that, how long should he *expect* to live?"

"It's a rake's garb he's wearing, and that's a fact of it," said a former Pinkerton agent named Gus "Shady" Quinn. "Rubbing a man's leg, I don't know. . . ."

"That was just a figure of speech," said Pettigo. "The poor bastard." He shook his head in disgust, staring down at the dead man's red-striped suit.

"What say you about the dear departed, Foot?" a former assassin named Newton Ridge asked a half-breed Cheyenne, Clayton "Cold Foot" Cain. Cold Foot stood a step back from the others, eyeing the body in the dirt more closely.

"He's dead," said the half-breed with finality, his deep voice sounding like a single clap of thunder from within a deep cave.

Pettigo and the men gave a dark chuckle under their breath, staring down at the body with the half-breed.

"Can't argue with Cold Foot," Pettigo said. He turned his head only an inch and spit in the dirt beside the dead man's bloody foot. "Damned degenerate. He couldn't just play the tables like any man might. He had to pretend himself to be some kind of slick-eyed gambling man." He paused, then added, "But that'll make no never mind to my father. He's going to want the men who did this swinging from a pole." He took the rifle from over his shoulder and levered a round into its chamber. "Let's get to it."

The men rallied around him and started toward the barn door. But they stopped at the sight of two more

Pettigo gunmen walking toward the barn, their rifles guiding Bobby Hugh Bellibar along in front of them.

"Hold up," said Dale Pettigo. "Let's see what Tiggs and the Russian have brought us."

When the guards arrived at the open barn doors, Leonard Tiggs, a squat, powerfully built Canadian, couldn't resist poking his gun barrel in Bellibar's back and sending him stumbling inside the barn.

"Here's one for you, boss," he said to Pettigo in a proud tone.

Bellibar instinctively turned facing Tiggs, his fists clenched, ready to do battle. But he froze at the sight of all the rifles and pistols cocking toward him.

"Easy, hombre," Pettigo warned him. He half turned and called out to the Mexican stable boy, "Hey, pissant, is this one of the hombres?"

The boy leaned a hay fork against a stall and hurried to the doorway. His eyes widened when he looked up and saw Bellibar staring down at him. He saw a trickle of blood at the corner of Bellibar's lips.

"Oh no, Señor Pettigo!" the boy said. "This is not one of the killers. This is a good man. He was just going into the cantina when the shooting started."

Dale Pettigo puffed on his cigar and turned his cold blue eyes to Tiggs.

"He was leaving the tent in one hell of a hurry, boss," Tiggs offered. He carried Bellibar's Colt and the big Remington shoved down behind his belt. Beside him, Cherzi the Russian carried Bellibar's rifle he'd pulled from his saddle boot. "His horse is tied out back there," said Tiggs. He jerked his head toward the stable boy. "He had the kid here leave them there for him, he claims."

Dale Pettigo's eyes went back to the stable boy. The rest of the gunmen stood gathered around Pettigo.

"Pissant . . . ?" Pettigo queried to the boy above his thick cigar.

"*Sí*, it is true that I took the horses there for him," said the boy. "But he is a good hombre, this man—not a killer."

Tiggs started to say something, but Pettigo stopped him with a raised hand. Then he turned his eyes to Bellibar.

"So you were just heading into the tent when our accountant got shot?" he asked, looking Bellibar up and down, noting his empty holster and the wrinkled oily spot on his shirt where the Remington had stood at his waist.

"Your *accountant* . . . ," Bellibar said, bemused.

"Answer Mr. Pettigo's question, saddle tramp," said Tiggs, giving Bellibar a sharp poke with his rifle barrel.

Bellibar stiffened and grunted but refused to show any pain from the blow. He stared at Pettigo, his jaw clenched, showing he wasn't going to answer under this kind of abusive treatment.

"That'll be enough of that, Tiggs," Pettigo warned the squat gunman. He looked back at Bellibar.

"Yeah, I was going inside," Bellibar replied now that his silent demand had been met. "I heard four shots, saw your *accountant* there stumble out with three bullets in his chest."

"What about his foot?" Pettigo asked.

"He couldn't get his Thunderer up," said Bellibar, "but that didn't keep him from pulling the trigger."

"He shot himself?" said Pettigo.

"Yep," said Bellibar, "over and over, the same foot." He stifled an evil little grin. "It was hard to tell which he would run out of first, bullets or toes—"

"Watch your mouth, saddle tramp," Tiggs warned, cutting him off. "That man was one of us."

"Oh?" said Bellibar. "So you own a suit like that?" He gestured over at the dead man on the dirt floor.

"Why, you lousy—" Tiggs gripped his rifle tight with both hands, keeping himself in check.

"Stand down, Tiggs," Dale Pettigo warned the powerful Canadian gunman. He turned back to Bellibar and asked, "What happened to the back of our man's head?"

"While he was still jerking, wiggling some, one of them smacked his head with a smithing hammer," said Bellibar, liking the way a couple of the men winced at the thought of it. "I hope I never hear such a terrible sound again in my life."

"But you went on inside and drank with the men who did it," Dale Pettigo reminded him.

"That I did," said Bellibar, "for the purpose of keeping them rounded up until some arm of authority, like yourselves here, come along." He paused and stared at Pettigo in silence for a moment, then said, "Can I be honest?"

"That's what *I'm* wondering," Pettigo countered. He blew a stream of cigar smoke beneath a raised and skeptical brow.

Bellibar ignored the veiled insult.

"The fact is," he said, "when I left the tent, I was on my way *here*, to warn you. This young man told me you were here."

"Is that true, pissant?" Pettigo asked the stable boy.

"*Sí*, it is," the boy replied.

"So, if I wanted to be a real turd, I could've told those mullets about you and sent them running," said Bellibar, "but I didn't." He stared at Pettigo, his jaw firmly set. "You want to know why?"

"Tell me," Pettigo said with a curious look.

Bellibar looked all around at the rough faces, at the drawn guns. This was his kind of place—his kind of people. He'd fit in here, given a little room to make space for himself. Sure, he might have to pistol-whip the Canadian, maybe maim one or two of the others, kill one if he had to. But that was only natural. He took a deep breath. *Here goes. . . .*

"Because I rode up here looking for gun work. I heard that Pettigo-American Mining needs some real *professionals* here in the hill country."

"*Professionals . . . ?*" Pettigo gave him another quick once-over and shook his head slowly. "Not hiring," he said bluntly.

"Not *hiring*?" Bellibar stared at him in disbelief.

"You heard me: I'm full up," Pettigo said. "I've got work for hire."

"Not even for a man who'll walk into that tent, no gun, knife or nothing else, and kill them two mullets for you, in, say . . . five minutes flat?"

The men chuffed, all except Pettigo. He stared at the seedy gunman through a rise of cigar smoke.

"Five minutes, huh?" he said.

"Yep, I'll say five," Bellibar replied. Thinking it over for a moment, he added, "Maybe six . . . but I doubt it." He looked all around, seeing both laughter and scorn in the eyes of the gunmen.

Pettigo looked at Tiggs and the Russian and asked, "Who's got the back of the tent covered?"

"We left Hayworth Benton there with his ten-gauge," said Tiggs. "Nobody's getting past him."

"Good," said Pettigo. He turned back to Bellibar and said, "Take as much as *ten* if you need it. I never like to rush a *professional* when he's working."

Chapter 11

Bobby Hugh Bellibar walked into the tent through the rear fly dusting his hands together. Bad Sharlo Bering and Harvey Moran turned to him with bloodshot eyes, each of them smoking brown dope-laced cigars. The two young women fought on, but one lay naked and prostrate on the dirt floor, a fallen knife inches from her hand. Only her toes and fingertips struggled to right herself back up onto her feet. Thick red welts crisscrossed her from where the other woman had broken a chair across her back. Now the other woman stood back with one of the broken chair legs in hand.

"Stay down, *puta*," she warned in a rasping voice. Blood ran down from her swollen right eye. A four-inch knife cut bled down her left side; teeth prints bled down her left thigh.

Looking over at the woman in passing, Bellibar clasped both hands together as if in regret.

"Please don't tell me I missed the best part," he said in a mock sorrowful voice.

"Sorry to say, but, yes, you did," said Moran. He

licked salt from the back of his hand. "But there wasn't as much cutting went on as you might think." He sighed a little. "Like everything else, these hill country gals are becoming more and more civilized. They've gotten a little too tame for my taste."

"And for my taster as well," said Bad Sharlo. He commented to Bellibar, "Damn, pard, what took you so long? I've never seen a lizard so huge it takes this long to choke it down."

Moran and Bellibar just stared at him.

Sharlo's drunken face turned painfully red as he caught what he'd said and tried to fix it.

"Not that I ever wanted to see one that huge," he said. "Or that I even want to see one, of *any size* . . . far as all that goes." He winced at what he'd said. "What I mean to say is—"

"*Jesus!* Let it go, Sharlo," said Moran in disgust. He shook his head and turned back to Bellibar. "What's happened to your guns?" he asked, gesturing a nod at Bellibar's empty holster and the place where he'd carried the big Remington behind his belt.

"Damn it all," said Bellibar, sounding disappointed with himself. "I must've left them both out back. Can I see yours?" He held out a hand.

"You can sure enough, pard," said Moran. He nodded, raised his black-handled Colt from its slim-jim holster and handed it over to Bellibar butt first.

"Fine-looking six-shooter," Bellibar commented, examining the gun.

"It's always done well by me," Moran said with a tequila slur to his voice.

"I bet," said Bellibar. He cocked the big Colt with a flat grin and shot the unsuspecting gunman squarely between the eyes.

The sound of the gunshot prompted a thunder of boots across the dirt floor. The music stopped cold. Chairs turned over; men crouched behind overturned tables and drew guns of their own.

"*My God!*" Sharlo Bering bellowed as his partner's warm brain matter splattered all over his face. His reflexes kicked in. He fell back a step, reaching for his own gun, as Bellibar swung the smoking Colt toward him and fired again.

Bellibar aimed for the same spot between Bering's eyes, thinking how impressive that would look to Pettigo and the others. But the shot fell short. The bullet sliced through Sharlo's throat just beneath his chin and blew out the side of his neck in a spray of blood and exposed tendons. Drinkers continued fleeing in every direction; the woman standing dropped her chair leg, ran wildly headlong into a thick tent post and crumpled to the ground.

At the bar the bleeding gunman managed to turn and hurl himself away from Bellibar as a third shot exploded from the Colt in Bellibar's hand. The bullet hit Sharlo low in his back. He stiffened but didn't let it stop him. He stumbled and scraped, half running, half falling, and managed to get out the front fly onto the dirt street. Along the street the sound of gunfire caused more running, more shouting, more leaping for cover.

"Here it is," said Dale Pettigo, him and his men standing across the dirt street watching as Bellibar leisurely followed the bleeding gunman, the Colt out at arm's length, smoking in his hand. Another shot exploded, hitting Bad Sharlo between his shoulder blades. He went down but kept crawling, his gun flying from his bloody hand.

"I got to admit, he's made a believer out of me," said Denver Jennings, one of the most respected and feared of all the Pettigo mercenaries.

"Yeah," said Newton Ridge, the former assassin, "Bad Sharlo Bering has never been known as a man to take lightly—Harvey Moran neither, to my knowledge."

"Do tell," Dale Pettigo murmured, watching closely as Bellibar took his time, stepped alongside the crawling gunman and finally planted a boot down on his bloody back, stopping him.

"What do you say, boss?" Denver Jennings asked. "Are we going to take him in, make him one of our own?" He gave a wry grin. "Take him home to meet your pa, so to speak?"

"We'll take him in," said Pettigo. "But he's not going to be one of us."

Jennings looked at him.

"I don't get it," he said.

"Never mind," said Pettigo. "I've got plans all my own for this one—something special I want him to do for us here."

From the middle of the empty dirt street, his boot keeping the badly wounded gunman crawling in place, Bellibar looked over at Pettigo and the mercenaries and called out, "Did anybody check the time on that?"

"He's a cocky son of a bitch. I'll give him that," Jennings said sidelong to Pettigo. They stared at Bellibar, who stood at ease in the street with his holster empty, Moran's smoking Colt aimed down at Sharlo's bloody back.

"Nobody, huh?" Bellibar called out. "I'm going to say *under five minutes*," he added, "unless somebody wants to correct me on it?" He gazed back and forth among the faces watching him, waiting for someone to challenge his timekeeping. When no one did, he looked back down at Bad Sharlo, who coughed and hacked and spit up a surge of dark blood. With Bellibar's boot on his back, Sharlo still tried to press forward in the dirt. "Let me ask this, then," Bellibar called out to the silent, staring gunmen. "Has anybody got a hammer?"

"He's a gone-crazy son of a bitch, this one," said Denver Jennings to Newton Ridge.

"Yeah, I noticed," said Ridge, the seasoned assassin. "But he did exactly what he said he would do." A thin trace of a smile came to his lips. "That's about all that counts in gun work."

Dale Pettigo saw Bellibar look toward him. A faint smile of satisfaction came to Pettigo's lips as he gave Bellibar a single nod.

Bellibar fired a final shot through the back of Bad Sharlo's head; the gunman slumped beneath his boot and stopped moving.

"Never kill a man's accountant," Bellibar said down to the dead gunman. With the black-handled Colt smoking in his hand, he turned and walked over to the others and stopped in front of Dale Pettigo.

"Mind your manners," Denver Jennings cautioned him, noting the big Colt in his hand.

But Bellibar ignored him and stared straight at Dale Pettigo.

"Well, boss," he said to Pettigo, "when do I start work?"

Pettigo looked back and forth as three miners carried Moran's body out of the cantina and flopped it down in the dirt beside Bad Sharlo.

"About five minutes ago," Pettigo said.

Bellibar nodded and turned to Leonard Tiggs, who stood a few feet away. Cherzi Persocovich the Russian stood at Tiggs' side.

"I'll be talking my shooting gear back," he said with finality.

Tiggs and the Russian both stiffened, seeing Bellibar's thumb go across the Colt's hammer, ready to cock it.

Tiggs shot a tight glance to Pettigo, who gave him a nod. Without another word he slid Bellibar's Colt and the big Remington from behind his belt and held them out to him, butt first. Bellibar looked almost disappointed that the Canadian hadn't given him a reason to kill him as he took his thumb from over Moran's gun hammer and shoved the smoking gun down in his belt.

When he'd taken both revolvers Tiggs had held out to him, he shoved his Colt down into its holster and the Remington behind his belt. He patted his waist and smiled at what he considered a nice growing assortment of firearms. Turning a cold stare to the Russian, Bellibar let his eyes tell the big man what he wanted.

Cherzi got his message instantly and handed him his rifle butt first without a word. Bellibar took it, checked it and cradled it in his left arm.

"All right, boss," he said to Pettigo, "what's gonna be my job today?"

"Same as everybody's job *every day*," said Pettigo, "killing the gunmen and thieves from Lookout Hill when they ride down and gather here to rob us."

Gunmen and thieves?

Bellibar thought about Paco Reyes and Saginaw Sparks, both of them tough hombres from Lookout Hill. *Ha!* He'd left them lying dead in the dirt. All right, he thought, feeling better about how things were shaping up for him. Lookout Hill was where he'd been headed—a place to lie low, get his trail clean and make plans. But looking around . . . this wasn't such a bad place either.

"Point me to the bunkhouse, boss," he said to Pettigo. "I'll stow my gear and start killing them right off."

"Huh-uh," said Pettigo. "You're not riding to the mines with us. I'm leaving you here to keep down trouble before it gets started."

The men looked at each other in surprise. Pettigo noticed the expression on their faces.

"That's right," he said. "This man is going to be the first town sheriff of Copper Gully."

"Town sheriff?" said Jennings, taken aback by Pettigo's announcement. "Jesus, boss, this is *Mexico*."

Pettigo gave his top gunman a bemused look. A tense silence fell over the men.

"Thank you, Denver," he said in a mock tone of

gratitude. "I'm obliged to you for telling me where I am—"

"That's not how I meant it, boss," Jennings cut in quickly, correcting himself. "I mean, is Mexico going to stand still for us appointing a town sheriff of Copper Gully?"

"Look around you, Denver," said Pettigo. "There was nothing left of Copper Gully when Pettigo-American Mining came here. This was no more than a dried-up hole left by the early Spaniards. We'll have the full say-so here, until we ever decide to leave."

"I understand, boss—" Jennings tried to say.

But Pettigo cut him short. "If I say there's a town sheriff here, then, by God, sir, there *is* a town sheriff here."

"Yes, boss," Jennings said submissively.

Pettigo continued, looking from one attentive face to the next as he spoke. "The Mexican government agreed to allow us to provide ourselves with whatever resources we need to conduct our business here. Had I appointed a man to administer the law in Copper Gully sooner, our accountant wouldn't be lying dead on a barn floor today." He turned his eyes from the rest of the men and fixed them on Bellibar.

"I've seen this man in action," he said. Then to Bellibar, "I trust you're you up to this assignment, Mr. . . . ?" His words trailed into a question.

"Mr. Hughes . . . Bob Hughes," said Bellibar. "And you're damn right. I'll whip this town into shape in no time—"

"Whoa, hold on, *Bob*," said Pettigo, doubting any

authenticity to the name. "This town doesn't require any *whipping into shape*. What I want is a man who keeps an eye on the trail in both directions, and keeps this town cleared of thieves and border trash. Am I making myself understood?"

"You are that, boss," said Bellibar. He stifled a grin. "Border trash, beware," he said. "The law has come to Copper Gully."

"Jesus . . . ," Denver Jennings said under his breath. He shook his head and turned toward the barn where they'd left their horses.

On the eleven-mile stretch of trail from Copper Cully to the Pettigo-American Mining facility, Dale Pettigo pulled his horse to the side, stopped it and stuck a fresh cigar in his mouth as the men filed past. Denver Jennings swung his horse right along beside him, and before Pettigo could fish a match from his pocket, Jennings struck one on his saddle horn and held it out to the tip of his boss' cigar. Pettigo puffed the cigar to life, let out a stream of smoke and watched as the last rider led Harold Wartler's body past him, strapped over a horse's back. Wartler's muddy low-cut town boots dangled down the horse's sides. His red pin-striped rear end pointed skyward across the saddle.

After another long puff on his cigar, Pettigo crossed his gloved hands on his saddle horn and relaxed for a moment. Jennings sat his horse in silence beside him and Pettigo let out a breath.

"All right, spit it out, Denver," he said.

"I'm not saying nothing, boss," his top gunman replied in an even tone.

"Either spit out what's stuck in your craw right now or keep your mouth shut about it," Pettigo said gruffly. As he spoke he took a silver case from inside his riding duster and handed a cigar to Jennings.

"Obliged, boss," Jennings said, taking the cigar. He bit the tip off and spit it away. "Speaking flat out? No holds barred?" he asked.

"Yep, just the two of us," said Pettigo. He heard a match flare beside him as he stared straight ahead.

Jennings puffed his cigar to life and let go a stream of smoke.

"All right, here it is, boss," he said. "Are you out of you mind, leaving a crazy son of a bitch like this Bob Hughes, or whatever his name is, overseeing Copper Gully?"

"I knew that's what it was," said Pettigo, staring straight ahead, out across the hilltops in the evening sunlight

"You said, *spit it out*. There it is," said Jennings.

"He won't cause any trouble," said Pettigo. "Tiggs and Cherzi will keep him on track. I want a man like him on our side. I just can't have him around the house, so to speak—nobody would feel safe in their sleep."

"Tiggs and Cherzi already hate him, boss—he hates them," said Jennings. "I can't see how this will work."

"Never underestimate the power of hatred," said Pettigo, drawing on the cigar and blowing out a stream of smoke. "Everything I did, I did for a reason."

"I'm trying to lean your way, boss. I just don't see it," Jennings said, shaking his head, unable to apply any level of rhyme or reason to his boss' actions.

"If you'll listen closely and allow me to enlighten you," said Pettigo, "I'll give you a lesson in business management *usually* reserved for those of us with fathers who can afford it." He gave a smug grin. "Would you like that?"

Arrogant little prick. . . . Jennings bit down hard on his cigar and kept his mouth shut.

"I would be nothing but grateful, boss," he managed to say.

"All right, answer me this," said Pettigo raising two gloved fingers, his cigar resting between them. "What problem most besets our entire operation here in the hill country?"

"Gunmen?" Jennings said as if uncertain.

"Come, now, Denver," said Pettigo, giving him a withering look.

"All right, *gunmen*," said Jennings with stronger conviction. "*Thieving* gunmen, from Lookout Hill," he amended.

"Precisely," said Pettigo.

"But in all likelihood," said Jennings, "that's where this so-called Bob Hughes was headed."

"Absolutely," Pettigo agreed. "No cold-blooded killer like him shows up here just to do some sightseeing."

"So you're thinking he came up to ride with the Lookout Hill boys, but we got to him first?" Jennings asked.

"I'm betting on it," said Pettigo. "The good thing

about men like Hughes is that they will kill anybody for a price, *anyone*. This one is a straight-up maniac. He'll draw the Lookout Hill boys to us like flies to an outhouse—keep us from running ourselves ragged searching the hills for them."

Jennings started to understand the gist of Pettigo's thinking. He smiled and puffed on his cigar.

"Another good thing about men like Hughes," said Pettigo, "once he's helped kill off his own kind, we throw him away like a worn-out sheep gut." He tapped a gloved finger to his forehead. "It's called *managing resources*." He added, "Instead of letting *resources* manage us." He lowered his finger and wagged it, making his point. "Therein lies the *management lesson* I referred to."

Jesus . . . that's what old man Pettigo paid good money for his son to learn?

"This is going to work out just fine, trust me," Pettigo said proudly. "We're operating in my arena now."

Denver Jennings stared at him through a waft of smoke. Pettigo was still an arrogant little prick, but at least now Jennings understood what he was up to.

The problem was, Dale Pettigo had just proven that he had no idea how men like this fellow—this so-called Bob Hughes—thought. This man was a murdering maniac and Jennings knew it. There was no school he'd ever heard of that could teach how to predict and understand how a maniac thinks, but there was nothing more he could say about it. When it came down to it, Jennings realized he was nothing himself but a hired gun.

He was better than most—smarter than most. *But there it is,* he told himself. A hired gun and nothing more. Dale Pettigo was an educated man. There was a point to which he would listen to what Jennings had to say on a matter like this. But now young Pettigo had gotten full of himself, thinking he had a plan to solve the problem they had with outlaws from Lookout Hill. He wasn't going to listen to anybody—Jennings knew it.

Yet he's the man who pays your wages, he reminded himself, and with that he turned his stare into an impressed gaze of wonderment.

"I don't know what to say, boss," he replied as if almost in awe.

Pettigo gave him a firm smile as he nudged his horse forward back onto the trail.

"Just say, 'Right you are, boss,'" he said.

"Right you are, boss," Jennings said, nudging his horse up beside him.

Chapter 12

For two full days the bloodstained bodies of Bad Sharlo Bering and Harvey Moran stood leaning, untied and unassisted, against two boards perched out in front of a small adobe building owned by Petigo-American Mining. On the third day, for reasons no one understood, Sharlo Bering's lifeless knees buckled; he went down, then pitched forward across the boardwalk just as two mine foremen's wives walked past.

From inside the building, Bellibar heard the thump of the body hit the boardwalk, followed by the women's screams. He ran out, shotgun in hand, Cherzi the Russian right behind him.

Hearing the screams, Leonard Tiggs came running from the tent cantina. But he slowed to a walk as he saw the prone body on the boardwalk and realized what had happened.

As a mercantile clerk and his wife ushered the two distraught women inside their store, Bellibar turned to the gathering crowd of townsfolk with his hands on a shotgun.

"All right, everybody get the hell out of here, else you'll be leaning on a board your damned selves."

Jesus! Tiggs grimaced at Cherzi, but the Russian didn't appear to think the new sheriff's words were too strong or offensive.

"Hughes," said Tiggs, "you can't talk to people that way!"

"What way?" Bellibar asked, facing Tiggs with a thumb over the shotgun hammers.

The powerful Canadian gunman just stared at the two of them, the Russian stepping over beside Bellibar with his thick hand wrapped around the butt of a Starr revolver. Damn! The job had gone to both of their heads.

"In case you've forgotten, *Leonard*," Bellibar said with a sour twist to his voice, "Pettigo named *me* sheriff. What I say goes. You're only here to do as I say. Keep poking your nose in how I run things, you might become owner of Mexican real estate, same as these two." He gestured toward the two ripening bodies, one still propped on the board in a swirl of flies, the other lying facedown on the rough plank boardwalk. A skinny cat reached its nose out and sniffed at Bering's purple ear.

Bellibar's threat didn't cause Tiggs to back off.

"I don't know how you did it, *Hughes*," he said. "You managed to get the drop on these two bummers, but I'll see it coming." He thumbed himself on the chest. "You won't get the drop on me."

"If I wanted it, I'd get it," Bellibar said flatly. "But I'm not going to stand here chewing a mouthful of bad

gristle with you. Take these two stinking bastards out
and bury them."

Tiggs bristled, but he kept his temper in check. Pettigo
had told him and the Russian to keep things under control. How would it look if he killed this fool, right here,
right now, only two days into the job? *Huh-uh*, he wasn't
letting that happen. He took a deep, calming breath.

"All right, *Sheriff Hughes*," he said. "We'll get them
buried." He turned to the Russian and motioned toward
the purple-blue body on the boardwalk. "Cherzi, get his
shoulders, I'll get his feet—"

"No," said Bellibar, cutting him off. "There was no
we in what I said. I told *you* to get them buried. I've got
other things I need Deputy Cherzi doing. Right, Deputy?" he said to the Russian.

"Is true," said Cherzi, his chin and chest held high.

"Oh, *Deputy*, is it now?" said Tiggs. He gave the Russian a searing stare. Then he turned his eyes back to
Bellibar. "What about me? Does that make me a deputy too?"

"I haven't decided yet," said Bellibar. "But you are
under consideration. Let's see how well you take
orders." He nodded at the bodies. "Drag them out of
here. Get their graves dug."

This son of a bitch!

Tiggs gritted his teeth in rage, but restrained himself. He had to keep control of himself until Dale Pettigo and the others rode back from the mines. Then
he'd unload on this man in more ways than one.

"Don't bury them until I come look at those graves,"
Bellibar said. "I better not catch you short-graving me."

He grinned. "It wouldn't do, having a coyote dragging a leg around town. The good folks of Copper Gully deserve better than that."

"Is true," the Russian repeated, staring blankly at Tiggs.

The enraged Canadian gunman still managed to keep control of himself. Staring hard at the Russian, he stooped and grabbed Bad Sharlo Bering by his boots. Bellibar and the Russian watched as he dragged the body and its accompanying swirl of flies toward an alley leading to a crumbling Spanish mission, where grave markers of both stone and wood dotted a rocky hillside.

In spite of the pain in Hodding "Hot Aces" Siebert's healing chest, he reached down, grabbed the stable boy by the front of his shirt and pulled him up to the side of the black mare to eye level. The boy squirmed and started to cry out, but he felt the Colt Pocket gun against the side of his head and froze. He stared bug-eyed into Siebert's crimson, angry face.

"What the hell were you smiling about, you little nit?" Siebert growled. "You see something funny about me, do you?"

"No, señor, *por favor!*" The boy said quickly. "I do not smile because something is funny about you! I smile at customers, my way of telling them *gracias* for coming to do business with me!"

"Don't fool with me, boy," Siebert warned.

"No, señor!" the stable boy said. "I would not fool with you! It is how I always greet people."

Siebert considered it while he cooled down a little.

He lowered the Colt Pocket pistol. There was only one shot left in the chamber and he had no ammunition that would fit the smaller caliber.

Better save this last shot, he advised himself.

"Be forewarned," he said to the boy, "I catch you laughing at me, I'll kill you and save somebody else having to do it." He dropped the boy to the ground beside the mare. Then he slid down from the saddle, slapped his legs a few times to get rid of the numbness and stretched his back, cupping a hand to his spine.

The stable boy only stared, afraid to speak, to move.

"What the hell is this?" said Siebert, stiffening suddenly, stunned at the sight of his stolen roan looking at him from over a stall rail. In the split second it took for his senses to recover, the big Dance Brothers .44 streaked up from his holster in his right hand. His left hand raised the Colt Pocket instinctively. He turned, half-crouched, looking all around as if someone lurked in the shadows.

"Where's the man who rides that horse?" he asked in a lowered voice.

"The horse belongs to the town sheriff, señor," the frightened boy said.

"The sheriff?" said Siebert, looking taken aback by the boy's information. "Where—where did he get it?"

"I do not know that, señor," the boy said. "The sheriff is new here. He is the first sheriff in Barranca del Cobre. He only become sheriff two days ago, after killing some very bad hombres."

"New sheriff, you say?" said Siebert, the wheels starting to turn in his head.

"*Sí*, he is a courageous lawman," the boy offered.

"What's this *courageous lawman's* name?" Siebert asked, his suspicion beginning to pique.

"He is Sheriff Hughes . . . Bob Hughes," the boy said. *Just right!*

Siebert kept himself from grinning. The name was too close to be a coincidence. Couple the name *Bob Hughes* with his stolen roan standing staring him in the face, there was a killing in the making here, no doubt about it.

"And just who were these bad hombres this courageous sheriff killed?" Siebert asked.

"Their names are Bad Sharlo Bering and Harvey Moran," the stable boy said.

"Oh my," Siebert said in a mock voice. "Now, those are some bad hombres." He chuckled to himself. "Boy, where do you suppose I would find the sheriff this time of day—church, I'm guessing, seeking divine guidance?"

"I don't know, señor," said the boy. "I only take care of horses for the barn owner." He shrugged. "If I looked for the sheriff, I would start at the cemetery on the hill beside the old mission."

"The cemetery?" Siebert asked.

"Yes," the boy said. "That is where he will go to bury the bad hombres I told you about." He pointed in a southwesterly direction.

"Well, of course he will," said Siebert, "and what a bright lad you are for knowing so much." His eyes glistened and shone with anticipation. "You take care of this mare," he said, fishing a gold coin from his vest pocket and flipping it to him. "I'll find the sheriff for myself. It just happens that him and I are pals from way back. So keep your mouth shut that I'm here if you see him first."

"Oh, I see," said the boy. "You want to surprise Sheriff Hughes, eh?"

"Oh yes," said Siebert with an evil grin, "I want to surprise him in the *worst* sort of way."

He turned and walked out of the barn in the direction the boy had pointed. When he stopped fifty yards from the cemetery, he saw someone digging a grave. He took cover beside an abandoned old adobe and watched for a moment, his hand on the Dance Brothers revolver. But seeing the man stand up and mop his brow with a bandanna, he realized it wasn't Bellibar.

"Damn it," he said under his breath. Yet before he could turn and slip away, his attitude took an upsurge as he spotted Bellibar walk into the cemetery and look down at the man digging. "That's more like it," he whispered with a dark chuckle, his hand raising the big Dance Brothers .44 from his holster.

He held the gun out with both hands, steadying his arms against the corner of the adobe.

"Adios, you gun-robbing, horse-stealing son of a bitch," he whispered to himself, taking close aim.

At the open grave, Bellibar felt cold gooseflesh run up both of his forearms. He almost shivered from the sensation. *What the hell?* He searched the hillside cemetery warily as he stepped around to the other side of the two graves, then looked off toward the abandoned adobe.

Having seen the look on Bellibar's face, Tiggs eyed him as he traded the long-handled scooping shovel for a sharp spade to stab and loosen the tight, hard earth.

"Something over there get you spooked?" Tiggs asked, nodding in the direction of the old adobe.

Bellibar shook the feeling and looked down at the sweaty Canadian gunman.

"Don't you worry about anything spooking me," he said, his hand resting on the Remington shoved down behind his gun belt. "You'd do better worrying 'bout getting this grave deep enough." He looked at the mound of fresh earth where Tiggs had already buried Bad Sharlo Bering. "I told you to wait up on burying until I got here so to check for myself."

Tiggs mopped his brow with the wet bandanna. His hat and coat lay on the ground at the graveside.

"I know how deep to dig a bloody grave," he huffed. He stabbed the spade into the bottom of the grave and loosened the dirt. "You should have seen the look on your face. You looked like a ghost just squeezed you by your apples." He stabbed the blade down again and rocked his foot back and forth. "I don't know why it's so important to you, getting these graves so deep. There's enough chickens and goats around here that no self-respecting coyote or *lobo* is going to bother digging up supper in a Mexican boneyard."

"Maybe I just wanted to see you sweat, Tiggs," Bellibar said with a taunting grin.

Tiggs rocked his foot on the spade, breaking up a

chunk of hard ground. He wasn't going to let this man get to him.

"Wait until Mr. Pettigo gets back, Hughes," he said over his shoulder, straightening and jerking the wet bandanna from his shirt pocket. "We'll see whose grave is the deep—" His words were cut short in mid-sentence.

From the corner of the abandoned adobe, Hodding Siebert had cocked the hammer, taken close aim, held his breath and started to squeeze the trigger on the big Dance Brothers .44. But at the last second he'd held his fire, staring with his mouth agape as the loud *twang* of the long-handled shovel echoed across the quiet hill-side.

"Holy dogs," he'd whispered in awe. He'd seen Bellibar grab the shovel, but he'd made nothing of it. He'd concentrated on making the shot as Bellibar straightened up and drew the shovel around. Then, as he'd taken aim, he saw the shovel streak though the air and land a solid blow on the back of the unsuspecting grave digger's head.

A full second passed as Siebert stared with a bemused look on his face. Finally he shook his head a little, snapping himself from a suspended state of mind. He let the gun hammer down and lowered the weapon, both hands still holding it. He watched as Bellibar kicked Tiggs' hat and coat into the grave and rolled Harvey Moran's body in atop him.

A slight smile came to Siebert's face.

"He's always on his game. I'll give him that," he

admitted quietly. He holstered the big revolver and watched Bellibar shovel steadily for a moment. Then he saw Bellibar stop, look down in surprise and kick at a bloody, grappling hand clawing up from the grave.

Siebert winced as he saw Bellibar crouch, swing the long-handled shovel straight up over his head, and bring it crashing straight down. Another *twang* echoed over the quiet hillside.

All right, then. . . .

Siebert hiked his gun belt and looked around. This wasn't the time to kill Bobby Hugh Bellibar—*Sheriff Bob Hughes,* or whatever this murdering fool was calling himself today. *No,* he decided, watching Bellibar go back to pitching shovelfuls of dirt into the grave, as if hurrying before anybody else tried to climb out. This was not the time to kill him. This was the time to see what his ol' *ex-pard* was up to.

Chapter 13

———————

It was late afternoon when Bobby Hugh Bellibar finished filling the grave and gave the ground a couple of
good solid whacks with the shovel, just for good measure. He wasn't going to gather rocks and pile them
atop the graves because . . . well, he just *wasn't going to.*
He shrugged. Stooping, he picked up the spade. Holding both earth-turning instruments in hand, he looked
around and smiled to himself in the cooling evening
breeze.

If anybody asked—and he was certain Dale Pettigo
would—as far as he was concerned he hadn't seen
Tiggs since he'd sent him off to bury the dead.

Good enough. . . . He turned and walked away, back
toward the main street of Copper Gully, toward the
building set up to be the sheriff's office, where he'd left
the Russian.

*Being Canadian, Tiggs must've just wandered away for
no reason,* he imagined himself telling Pettigo.

The fact was, he could tell Pettigo whatever he felt
like telling him, Bellibar decided, walking along. Who

was going to dispute him? He had won the Russian over to his side. Besides, what could Pettigo say? People disappeared all the time. They couldn't blame him for that. For all he knew, Tiggs might have gotten his feelings hurt not being left in charge.

Maybe he'd worked himself into a huff and ridden back to the mines. Anything from snakebite to a bandit attack could have befallen him along the eleven-mile stretch of rock trail, cactus and brush lying between Pettigo-American Mining and Copper Gully. He might have resented digging graves, big gunman that he was, Bellibar told himself, turning the shadowed corner of the abandoned adobe. He'd known men like that. If they couldn't be in charge, they wanted no part of the job.

His thoughts flat out left him as he walked past a dark open doorway and felt the side of his head explode. He fell to the ground on his cheek. In the swaying stupor that he knew came before blacking out, he stared straight ahead at ground level, seeing one rough boot and one worn-out Indian moccasin standing beside him.

"Son of a . . . ," he heard himself mumble, his words trailing away as a furry black silence slipped in and wrapped itself around him. In his unconscious state, he came to enough to imagine a gathering of Indian youths steadily pelting his back and the back of his head with rocks. His arms were up above his head, rocks hitting them too, but he couldn't lower them, nor could he make his hand reach for either his holstered Colt or the big Remington stuck down behind his gun belt.

But after a moment he realized through the swirling blackness that his hands weren't tied above his head at all, nor was he being pelted with rocks by a rowdy band of young Indians. He was being dragged along the rocky ground by his boots. All right, that made more sense, he decided in his unconscious state. With the puzzle solved, he relaxed back into the darkness and disappeared for a time as he bumped and slid mindlessly across the hard ground.

When he vaguely awoke again, he realized he was no longer being dragged by his heels. He was upright now, tied to a support post inside the livery barn, his hands pulled back, bound wrist to wrist by a length of rope. He raised his dazed head from his chest and steadied it enough to stare across the circle of lantern light in the center of the dark barn. In the stall behind him, he heard a large animal chuff and stomp a hoof.

On the other side of the flickering circle of light he saw Hodding "Hot Aces" Siebert sitting with one hip propped on the edge of a wooden tack table. Siebert looked up at him above a bowl, eating red beans with a flat wooden spoon. Siebert had retrieved his stolen roan from its stall; the horse stood beside him.

Saddled, ready to ride, Bellibar told himself as his head fell back to his chest and the darkness reclaimed him.

When Bellibar awoke again, he did so feeling a rough hand shake his head back and forth by his tangled hair. Bellibar opened his eyes and looked down at Siebert's mismatched footwear. In a muddled tone Bellibar said, "Are they . . . giving out moccasins in hell?"

Chewing beans, Siebert looked down at his foot, turned it back and forth. "Oh, this?" He chuckled a little. "I took it after you shot me out of my boot, found it whilst rummaging a place I came upon on my way here. I killed an old man and his woman . . . and two damned dogs who nearly ate me alive." He gestured at all the stitches in his face, the side of his head, at his chest beneath his shirt.

"I . . . know you're dead, Hot Aces. I . . . killed you," Bellibar said in a weak voice, shaking his throbbing head. The side of his skull housed a wild monkey beating on a metal drum with an iron hammer, or so it felt.

"I'll soon say the same of you." Siebert grinned, looking him up and down. A tin of whale oil sat on the table beside him. "I want you woke up good and clear, so you'll know when I take your power."

"There you go with your crazy talk," Bellibar said. "It always spills out of you, sooner or later." Staring down at his feet covered with straw, he noted he wore nothing but his sweat-stained long johns.

Siebert gave a slight shrug and scooped up another spoonful of red beans.

"*Crazy* says you," he replied. "But there's not a warrior folk in history who didn't believe when you kill a person you take his power. Mimbreno Apache . . . Chiricahua. Hell, the Romans, Hannibal, the Huns, all of them believed it—"

"Not trying to piss on your place in history, Aces," said Bellibar, cutting him off, "but you're none of those *warrior folk*. You're nothing but a bummer and a poltroon coward."

"Well . . ." Siebert spooned more beans, then said, "I expect like any other religion, taking power only works if you believe it works."

"Yeah?" said Bellibar. "What kind of power did you get killing the couple and their dogs?"

"Not much from the couple," said Siebert, "but a pair of Mexicans showed up. That helped. I got nothing from the dogs except a passing desire to scratch my neck, sniff my own behind." He gave a short, cackling laugh.

"You've always had that," Bellibar said somberly.

Siebert ignored him.

"I killed a witch," he said matter-of-factly, chewing beans as he spoke.

"A witch . . . ?" Bellibar said in a dreamy voice. "An honest-to-God witch?"

"She tried to say she was only a healing woman," Siebert said. "But a witch will lie, even if she doesn't have to. So, sure she denied it . . . but I saw right through her."

"Jesus . . . ," said Bellibar, his throbbing head sagging back down onto his chest.

Siebert pointed the wooden spoon at Bellibar and wagged it a little. "That was a damned *strange* feeling, killing a *bruja*. Didn't sense it right away, but now there's a part of me feels like she's still right here at my shoulder, watching everything I do." He gestured the spoon past Bellibar to the stall behind him. "That's her black mare standing behind you. The animal and the *bruja* both have stuck a hex on me."

From the stall, the black mare stared defiantly at

Siebert and tugged at the short length of rope that held her tied to the stall rail.

Stuck a spell on him? This crazy son of a bitch. . . .

"Let's stop palavering," Bellibar said. He strained against the ropes holding his wrists tied behind him. "Untie me and I will kill you deader than hell."

Siebert took a bite of beans, seemed to consider the offer as he chewed and swallowed.

"Sounds like a damned good deal," he said. "But I'll pass on it. I've got it in mind to set you afire, you and that damned black mare behind you—now that I got my roan back."

"Then stop sucking beans and get it done, you loco, witch-killing son of a bitch!" Bellibar shouted.

"Easy, Bobby Hugh," said Siebert. He gave a dark, evil grin. "The belief is, the more you torture a man, the stronger it makes his power when you take it from him."

"Oh?" said Bellibar. "Burning's not enough?"

Siebert considered the matter as he ate the rest of the beans and set the empty bowl down.

"In this case, I would say no," Siebert replied, picking up the tin of whale oil and standing, wiping a hand across his lips. "But I can see where too much power from you might cause a wild goose to fly sideways." He walked forward and pulled the top off the whale oil tin. He started to pour the oil down around Bellibar's feet.

"Let me ask you this," Bellibar said. "Why am I standing here in my undergarments?"

Siebert stopped and stood with the tin of oil in hand. A curious look came to his face.

"I don't really know why," he said. "It just seemed

right for some reason." He paused, then said, "Now let me ask you something. Why'd you bury that son of a bitch alive?"

"You saw that?" Bellibar said. He instinctively glanced around the dark barn, making sure they weren't being overheard.

"It was hard to miss," said Siebert. He chuckled. "Poor bastard grabbing for his life, you shovel-thumping him in the head. What did he do to you anyway?" He looked Bellibar up and down. "While we're at it, how'd you make sheriff here? I figured you'd head straight to Lookout Hill after jackpotting me."

Bellibar noted that Hot Aces hadn't yet gotten back to pouring the oil down around his feet. *A good sign?* He hoped so. He'd have to play this right to do himself any good.

"I didn't *jackpot* you, Aces," he said calmly. "Leastwise not until I saw you were out to jackpot me."

"You didn't know I was jackpotting you," said Siebert, "not at that time. I was drinking water. You robbed me of my gun." He patted the big Remington now standing in his holster.

"I figured you might have had something up your sleeve," Bellibar said quietly. "Turns out, I was right. You'd unloaded my gun."

Siebert gave him a strange look.

"Let me get this straight," he said. "You figured I *might* jackpot you, so that made it okay for you to jackpot me first?" He tapped a finger on his chest.

"Something like that," said Bellibar, "since it turned out I was right."

Siebert just stared at him for a moment trying to unravel the twists of the situation.

"I'm not saying I was all the way right," said Bellibar. "I'm only saying I wasn't all the way wrong either."

"Oh," Siebert said with sarcasm, "now I understand." He started to tip the oil tin and pour it. "Obliged to you for straightening it out for me."

"Anyway," said Bellibar, seeing the explanation was getting him nowhere, "I killed him because he was going to be riding up to the mines every three or four days, reporting what I was up to down here. I only buried him alive because he didn't die as quick as he should have."

"That's understandable." Siebert shrugged a shoulder. "Go on," he said, getting interested.

"As for me being made sheriff," Bellibar said, "Mr. Dale Pettigo himself put me in charge—said he wanted me here identifying outlaws, making sure they didn't start gathering up in Copper Gully to make a run at his mines." He stopped and stared at Siebert. "I figure the sooner I buried that no-dying son of a bitch, the quicker I'd start gathering those outlaws to make a run on his mines." He managed a tight grin. "I know it sounds too good to be true, but there it is."

Siebert shook his head; the oil tin slumped at his side.

"Jesus," he said, bewildered, "talk about leaving a wolf to guard a meat house." He scratched his chin. "Pettigo . . . You have to wonder how a man can be that stupid and still manage to get himself such a big cut of the pie in this world."

Bellibar took an easier breath, noting the oil tin was no longer in play.

"I don't know," he said. "Sometimes I think maybe . . ." He stopped and let his words fall away.

"*Maybe* what?" said Siebert.

"Nothing," said Bellibar. "You don't want to hear it."

"Yes, I do," said Siebert. "Now spit it out, else I'll dose you down and we'll get right on with it."

"Maybe they can be so stupid and still acquire so much because they always stick together somehow," he said.

"And ol' boys like us . . . ?" said Siebert, knowing there was more coming on the matter.

"Maybe ol' boys like us are too busy always trying to kill each other," Bellibar said. "Maybe if we all—"

"You stole my gun and shot me, Bobby Hugh," said Siebert, seeing where Bellibar was headed.

"Only because *you* unloaded my gun and was going to shoot me, Aces," Bellibar returned.

"Damn it," said Siebert, "I don't see how you—"

"Let's don't go through all that again, Aces," said Bellibar, cutting him off. "Yes, I shot you, but I didn't kill you."

"No," said Siebert, "that's because this big cross of mine saved my life." He whipped the crucifix out from behind his shirt and showed him the bullet-scarred bottom edge. "Deflected the bullet," he said, lifting his eyes to the barn rafters and the endless sky beyond.

Staring at him, Bellibar said, "Something like that has to give a man pause. Peculiar, wouldn't you say? All we went through, now here we are again, neither of us worse for wear. And now I'm dealt the kind of hand we both would give our eyeteeth for."

"I got to admit you've landed on a sure thing, Bobby Hugh," said Siebert.

"I know," said Bellibar. "Think about it. Instead of us going to Lookout Hill, hats in hand begging for work, we ride right up to them and say, 'How would you fellows feel about robbing Pettigo-American Mining with us?'"

"It is one fine position to be in. I'll give you that, Bobby Hugh," Siebert admitted, taking a step back, considering everything Bellibar had said.

"What time's it getting to be?" Bellibar asked, letting his head hang down for a moment.

Siebert looked all around and said, "I don't know . . . I make it to be two, maybe three in the morning," he said.

"Damn," said Bellibar in disbelief. He noted the darkness beyond the circle of lantern light. "How long was I knocked out?"

"A long while," Hot Aces Siebert said with a dark chuckle. "I hit you hard enough to kill any normal man. They say it's hard to kill an idiot."

Bellibar let the remark slip past him. He raised his face.

"It's not too early to get some breakfast," he said. "How long since you've seen a couple of Mexican eggs stare up at you from beside a roasted capon?"

"Breakfast, huh?" said Siebert, thinking about it.

"Yeah, why not?" said Bellibar. "I'd like to hear all about that *bruja* and her mare putting a hex on you."

"It's a hell of a story," said Siebert.

"Then what are we waiting for?" said Bellibar. "I'm already tasting capon and eggs—some pepper gravy hot enough to lift an anvil . . . ?"

Bellibar noticed Siebert waver. He waited, tensed, until Siebert reached over and stuck the cap back on the oil tin.

"I could eat something, that's a fact," Siebert said.

Chapter 14

Inside the ragged tent cantina, at a table near the rear canvas wall, Bobby Hugh Bellibar and Hot Aces Siebert sat drinking steaming hot chicory from earthen mugs. As suggested beforehand, they'd ordered *huevos y gallo asado*—eggs and roasted rooster—from a young prostitute wearing the same soiled white peasant gown she'd worked in the night before. As she'd turned to leave, Siebert grabbed her wrist.

"That capon better be fresh," he warned, giving her a sharp, deadly stare. "You would not want me sinking my teeth into a sour rooster."

"*Sí*, rooster *más fresco*," the girl said, looking frightened, eager to get away.

"*Bueno*," said Siebert, turning her wrist loose, "and get some clean clothes on. We're eating here."

"*Sí*, I will," she said, grateful that his rough hand unwrapped from around her wrist.

When the girl had left through the rear tent fly, Bellibar started to speak, but Siebert held up a hand, postponing him. The two sat in silence for a moment until out back, the majestic crow of a rooster transformed into a cry of pain.

"Fresh enough for you?" Bellibar asked.

Siebert gave a slim smile.

"Yep. Now go ahead," he said.

"All right," said Bellibar, taking up where he'd left off, "I figure Pettigo took me for a hard case as soon he laid eyes on me. I'd lit out the back of this tent in a hurry. The livery boy warned me Pettigo and his men were here, and he knew that two Lookout Hill boys had killed one of his men—turned out the man was his accountant, who liked walking the dark side, so to speak."

"And . . . ?" said Siebert.

"And out back of the tent I ran into two of Pettigo's men. To get off a tight spot, I killed the two Lookout Hill boys. Pettigo hired me, put me in charge here— leastwise that's what he wanted me to think." He grinned. "I think I scared him. He saw in my eyes I might just kill him for the hell of it, and he figured it better to hire me, get me on his side."

"Fear is a wonderful thing," Siebert said.

"Well said," Bellibar replied. He grinned. "So my job is to keep an eye on Copper Gully. I see anybody who might be Lookout Hill boys, *Bang!* I kill them flat-out. Keep them from gathering up in strength. Not a bad job, as jobs go," he added.

Siebert sipped his chicory.

"So, if you and I was to repartner up, we get with the Cady brothers, set up a raid on Pettigo-American and ride away with our saddlebags full."

"Every miner working there gets their pay in gold

coin," Bellibar said. "Instead of us taking a small cut riding for the Lookout Hill boys, we'll take a bold share for setting it up and getting them up from Copper Gully without me warning the Pettigos."

Siebert's expression turned sour.

"I see some things that could go wrong for us," he said. "How do we know the Cady brothers will take us in?"

Bellibar stared at him.

"Aside from me leading them through the front door," he said. "I know they're four men short. I've been killing them rabbits for a stew." He held up four fingers and lowered one each time he said a name.

"Harvey Moran . . . Bad Sharlo Bering, right here in this tent cantina," he said. "On the way up the trail after you and I had our falling-out, I killed Saginaw Sparks and a Mex he called Paco something or other." He waved the name away.

Siebert sipped his chicory and gave him a grim look.

"I've got to think about it," he said after a moment of somber reflection.

"*Think about it?*" said Bellibar. "What got into you all of a sudden? You were on this as soon as I spelled it out to you. Now you got to think about it?"

"Don't be crowding me," Siebert warned, raising a hand in caution.

"I'm not crowding you," Bellibar said. He sat staring at him curiously. Finally he said, "This is all about the hex you think the *bruja* put on you, isn't it?"

"I don't *think* it. I know it," said Siebert. "But no, it's not that."

"Yes, it is," said Bellibar, disgusted. "You superstitious, witch-killing son of a—" He stopped short. "I hand you the best deal you've had since Texas didn't hang you . . . you're afraid some dead *bruja* has hexed you?"

"That's it. Make mockery of things you don't understand," said Siebert. "You wasn't talking this way to me when I was ready to fire you up from the ankles." He clenched his jaw and snarled, "You're making me regret that I didn't kill you." His hand went under the table.

"The way you're acting, you're making *me* regret it too," said Bellibar. He let his hand drop under the table, his Colt now back in his holster, though Siebert had taken his big Remington back from him.

"So it looks like we're right back where we started," Siebert said tightly.

"Not because I want us to be," said Bellibar. "I've got us a deal better than any I've seen. All I want to do is go *do it*. I don't give a damn about witches, or black mares are any of that malarkey."

"It's not malarkey," said Siebert, his hand still under the tabletop, "and I won't have you making it worse by poking fun at it."

"Do not let me hear you cock that gun, else I will cut you in half at the waist," said Bellibar. "We can repartner up or shoot each other to pieces. Right about now I don't give a damn." He stared coldly at Siebert, but

Siebert's eyes streaked past him, to the stable boy who ran into the tent, out of breath, looking scared.

"Señor! There you are," the boy cried out to Siebert. "You must come quick. Your mare has disappeared!"

"Somebody *stole* her?" Siebert asked.

"No—I mean, yes! I mean, I don't know, señor!" the boy shouted. "She is gone—*ido!* She has vanished—*desaparecido!*"

"See?" said Siebert, rising quickly. "There's nothing natural about this, not by a long shot." He hurried to the front of the tent, the stable boy leading him. "This is what happens when you make a mockery," he said to Bellibar over his shoulder. Bellibar stood up and hurried along behind them to the barn, where he stood watching as the stable boy showed Siebert a donkey standing in the stall where the mare had been, the short length of rope around its bony neck. At the sight of the donkey, Siebert jumped back from the stall as if he'd seen a ghost.

"Oh my God!" he said in a low, trembling voice. "This is the hex working. The dead *bruja* turned the black mare into a donkey."

Listening, the frightened stable boy made the sign of the cross on his thin chest and stepped away from the stall.

"Jesus, listen to yourself, Aces," said Bellibar. "*Dead* witches don't change nothing to nothing . . . if they ever could in the first place."

"Don't make light of me, I swear to God, Bobby Hugh!" Siebert shouted, his hand clasping around the butt of his Remington.

"I'm not making light of you, Aces," Bellibar said with a note of disgust in his tone. He walked to the stall and lifted the latch.

"Don't go in there, Bobby Hugh," Siebert warned, his voice still carrying a tremor.

Bellibar stared at him as he walked inside, stepped over to the donkey and ran a hand along its bristly withers. He held his wet hand up for Siebert to see.

"It's lathered with sweat, Aces," he said. "This mallet head was rode here hard. Somebody swapped it for the black mare. From what I saw of the mare, I can't blame them."

"Yeah . . . ?" Siebert stepped forward warily; so did the stable boy. "If that's the case," he continued, "I'm saying it was the *bruja* who did it."

"Make up your mind, Aces," said Bellibar. "Either you killed her or you didn't. I can't take much more of—"

"All right, I killed her—she's dead!" said Siebert. "Dead and gone." He turned and stared at the stable boy. "This was all your fault, you little son of a bitch," he growled. He kicked his boot at the boy and drew his Remington, but the boy raced away as fast as a rabbit before Siebert could cock and fire.

Siebert stood looming in the grainy light of the lantern, his chest heaving for breath. His Remington slumped down at his side. After a long, silent moment he turned and faced Bellibar.

"Are you done with it?" Bellibar asked in a solemn tone of voice.

"I'm done with it," Siebert replied. "I don't know

what got into me and I won't be taunted about it," he said in a warning tone. "But it's over. Tell me how you want to play things. I'm right beside you."

"First, we go back and eat the breakfast we ordered," said Bellibar, glad to see Hot Aces had come to his senses. "Then I want you to meet the Russian. He works for Pettigo, but he likes this Mexican dope. Cross his palm with enough gold coin to keep him doping and he's on our side all the way."

"What about my mare?" Siebert asked.

"What about her?" Bellibar asked.

"I can't let her get stolen and rode off that way," said Siebert.

"You stole her, Aces," said Bellibar.

"Still . . . ," said Siebert.

"You were all set to burn her alive," Bellibar said. "You've got your roan back. If anybody needs a mount here, it's me. Besides, if whoever took her is any thief at all, they are long gone by now. The time you spend tracking them down, we could be getting ourselves ready to be rich men."

"All right, I'll let it go," said Siebert, settling it in his mind.

"Good," said Bellibar, getting tired of Siebert's craziness, wondering if he should go on and kill him when this was over. "Let's go eat, and then I'll take you to meet the Russian."

Inside the adobe building set up to be the office for the sheriff, Cherzi the Russian sat behind a battered oak desk he dragged all the way from the mercantile up the street. A large Colt lay broken apart atop the desk, placed on an oil-stained cleaning rag. Cherzi looked up from cleaning the gun barrel as Siebert and Bellibar walked through the door.

"Cherzi, this is a pal of mine, Hodding Siebert," Bellibar said to the stoic Russian. To Siebert he said, "Hot Aces, this is Cherzi something or other. I won't *try* to say his last name, nor should you."

"Is Cherzi Persocovich," the Russian said in stiff English. *"Is not something or other."*

"Yeah, right," Bellibar replied with a chuckle, "anywho, Hodding here will be working with us."

"Oh . . . ?" the Russian said to Bellibar, eyeing Hodding Siebert up and down. "Why you call him *Hot Aces*?"

Bellibar considered it with a bemused look on his face.

"Yeah, come to think of it," he said to Siebert, "why *does* everybody call you Hot Aces?"

"For the same reason everybody calls you Bobby Hugh," Siebert replied in a sharp tone.

"Because Bobby Hugh is my name," said Bellibar. He gave a slight shrug.

"Let's let it go, Bobby Hugh," said Siebert. "My pa was a gambling man, all right?"

"Fine by me," said Bellibar.

The Russian appeared to hurry up cleaning the big Colt and reassemble it.

"I have not seen Leonard Tiggs since yesterday afternoon when he went to bury the dead gunmen," he said.

"Neither have I," said Bellibar. "Maybe he couldn't wait any longer to run up to Pettigo, spill his guts about how we're doing things here."

Cherzi looked back and forth between the two of them as he loaded his clean Colt and spun the cylinder.

"His horse is in the corral behind the livery barn," said the Russian matter-of-factly. "I saw it this morning at daybreak when I walked past." He stared blankly at Bellibar.

"You don't say," said Bellibar. "Do you suppose something bad has happened to him?"

"Yes, I think something very *bad* has happened to him," said the Russian. He looked coolly back and forth between them, seeing Siebert's hand gripping the butt of the holstered Remington, Bellibar's hand on his Colt. He gave a short, flat smile and slipped his Colt down loosely into his belly holster. "But I don't give a damn-it-to-hell," he said. "If Tiggs is gone, maybe we can start making some the money you tell me about, eh?"

"You bet your life we can, Cherzi," said Bellibar. He grinned at Siebert and said, "I told you you're going to like this fellow, Aces."

Siebert started to say something in reply when the front door swung open and one of the morning bartenders from the tent cantina hurried in, wide-eyed and out of breath. All three gunmen swung toward him, their guns out of their holsters, cocked and poised.

"You ever rush up on me or my men again, Burns," Bellibar warned in harsh tone, "I'm going to go on and kill you . . . We'll call it suicide."

"Sheriff, I'm damned sorry," said Cletis Burns, his

hands chest high. "You said let you know if any gunmen ride in who might be Lookout Hill boys?"

"That's right," said Bellibar. "What have you got?"

"Billy Boyle is at the cantina. He's one of the Cady
brothers' meanest gunmen. I know because Dale Pettigo's mercenaries shooed him out of here about this
same time last year."

The Russian and the two gunmen looked at each
other.

"Obliged, Burns," Bellibar said to the bartender.
"Now go back there and act like nothing's going on.
We'll take care of it."

"This is how they do it, Sheriff," Burns said. "They
ease in here one, two, three at a time until they've got
enough to ride straight up the gully to the mines—"

"I said *obliged*. We've got it, Burns," Bellibar said in a
stronger tone. "Now get going before I pistol-whip the
living hell out of you."

The bartender gave him a puzzled look, but he
didn't test his luck. He turned and left almost at a run.
When he was gone, Bellibar gestured to Siebert and
the Russian.

"Was I too harsh?" he asked.

"Not too harsh," said the Russian.

"Not at all," said Siebert. "I always said a sheriff
needs to take a strong hand for the law."

"All right, then, pards," said Bellibar, "I expect it's
time we start turning all this talk into action."

As the early drinkers filed into the tent cantina and
lined the bar, a wiry gunman named Billy Boyle stood

pouring a shot of rye. He didn't see the Russian come in with his hat low on his forehead and take a chair at a table in the center of the dirt floor. Nor did he notice Hodding Siebert walk in through the rear door and take position at the far end of bar. Boyle was here to test the town's defenses. He had gone unnoticed, he thought—*so far, so good.*

But when he threw back his rye and set the shot glass down in front of him, as if from out of nowhere an empty feed sack came down over his head and tightened around him. He reached instinctively for his holstered Smith & Wesson, but he was too late. A hand reached out and snatched it from him as he struggled inside the feed sack.

"Up you go, Billy Boyle. You're under arrest," said a voice with a dark chuckle.

Another voice added, "Keep fighting us and I'll crack your skull open."

"I have his gun," said another in stiff English.

Uh-oh! Boyle recognized the Russian's voice from the year before. Pettigo's mercenaries had sworn they would kill him if he ever returned.

"I'm not fighting you. I swear I'm not!" he said, feeling hands lift him off his feet. "This is a mistake. I'm only passing through town. I'm not here looking for any trouble!"

He felt himself slung over a shoulder like a bag of seed and carried away, out the tent fly and down the dirt street.

In a moment he felt himself carried across a boardwalk, through a squeaking door and plopped down onto a wooden chair.

Even as someone jerked the sack from over him, he spit lint and said quickly, "I swear to God I haven't come here to . . ." His words trailed as he looked into the grim face of the Russian.

"Shut your face up," Cherzi said, holding Boyle's gun in his big hand.

Boyle stared at him in fear.

"Don't soil yourself, hombre," said Bellibar. "We're all out for the same thing here."

"Oh? What's that?" Boyle said, looking back and forth at them.

"Robbing the Pettigo-American Mining Company," said Bellibar. He grinned. But the gunman looked suspicious.

"Then why did you snatch me up like this?" he asked.

"To keep from having to kill you," said Bellibar. "We needed to talk to you. You wouldn't have come peaceful-like, would you?"

"No, probably not," said Boyle.

"Also we didn't want to tip our hand to anybody here, let them see what we're up to," Bellibar said. "I'm the new sheriff, Bobby Hugh Bellibar. These are my deputies, Aces Siebert and Cherzi something or other. We're the ones who's keeping all you thieves from Lookout Hill away from here."

Boyle relaxed a little and said, "Damn, I've heard of you, Bellibar, you too, Siebert. You two would steal a hot stove with no gloves on."

"This I would do too," the Russian said proudly.

"All right, then . . . what can I do for you, Sheriff?" Boyle said.

"You can ride up to Lookout Hill with me, keep me from getting shot until I can explain myself. Once I put things right with the Cadys," said Bellibar, "we'll all ride up this damn one-way gully and take what we want."

PART 3

Chapter 15

Juan Lupo and the Ranger sat atop a cliff overlooking a stretch of hilltops and high trails winding upward toward Lookout Hill. Both manhunters gazed down respectively, Sam through a long, battered telescope, Lupo through a shabby pair of binoculars. Watching three riders gallop up along the rocky winding trail, Sam got a good look at Hodding Siebert's face as the outlaw looked up and all around, warily.

"It's Aces Siebert," Sam said.

"Yes, I saw him too," Lupo said. "That is Billy Boyle leading them up."

"There's little doubt in my mind the rider beside him is Bobby Hugh Bellibar," Sam added. He shook his head, lowered the field lens and rubbed his eye. "Somehow these two maniacs managed to get back together."

"And found someone to lead them to the Cadys," Lupo said, lowering his binoculars.

"How far are we from the trail they're on?" Sam asked.

"By the time we ride back and over to pick up their

trail, they will have made it into the protection of Lookout Hill. We will never get into the Cadys' lair on our own. The trail is too well guarded. They see everything coming up the trail for miles. There's no other way up to them."

"What about by rope?" Sam said, gesturing toward a high-standing vertical wall of rock on the northern side of the steep hill.

Lupo didn't answer. Instead he scooted back from the edge of the cliff, stood up and dusted his trousers.

"We must wait until these men ride back down to Copper Gully," he said, nodding southwardly. "The trail they ride comes from there."

"Then we ride over to their trail and wait right there," Sam said. "Let's hope the Cadys want nothing to do with these two."

The Ranger still suspected that Lupo wasn't being entirely truthful about what he was up to out here. It was time to squeeze a little more information out of him.

"*Sí*, we could wait right there," Lupo said. He looked restlessly back in the direction of Copper Gully. "But if we go to Barranca del Cobre, they are sure to come there when they ride down from Lookout Hill."

Sure to come there?

Sam stared at him and said, "How do we know they'll even come down at all? These two could lie under the Cadys' protection for weeks."

"This is true," said Lupo, "but I think—"

"Get it out, Easy John," Sam said, cutting him off.

"I don't know what you mean," Lupo said innocently.

"Tell me what it is that's got you wanting to give up chasing these two riders to Copper Gully. For a bounty hunter, you're sure letting your prey slip out of your reach."

"No, you are wrong, Ranger," Lupo insisted. "You misread my intentions."

"If I'm misreading your intentions, I can *misread* them sitting right here. I don't have to ride to Copper Gully to do it." He paused, then said, "You're after something bigger than the reward on these two murdering saddle tramps. I don't know what it is, but I've seen the clock start ticking ever since we rode up this high trail." He gave a short, wry smile. "I'm curious to hear what it is." He remained seated on the rocky ground as he collapsed the telescope and appeared to make himself comfortable for the long stay.

Lupo looked back in the direction of Copper Gully for a moment, then looked back at the Ranger.

"All right, Ranger," said Lupo, "you are right. The clock is ticking . . . and there is more at stake than the reward on these two murdering *vagabundos*. But I cannot tell you everything. The people I work for would never forgive me."

"I'm sure they would, Easy John," Sam said. He picked up his rifle from against a rock and held it pointed loosely at the government agent. "Tell them I held a gun on you."

"Put your rifle away," said Lupo. "They would not accept that as a reason for me to reveal my mission."

"Your *mission* . . . ," Sam said. "Now we're getting somewhere." He let his rifle slump onto his lap.

Lupo took a deep breath and let it out in a sigh.

"I will tell you a story, Ranger Burrack," he said, "and you must believe it or disbelieve it, as you choose."

"Fair enough." Sam nodded and listened intently.

"Over a year ago, I tracked a wagonload of stolen gold to Fire River Valley and recovered it for my government. Instead of taking it directly back to Mexico City, I buried it in the desert to keep it from being stolen again. But when my government recovered it from the desert, the man they sent to lead the mission was not loyal to my emperor or to *Generalissimo* Manuel Ortega, whom I serve. His loyalties lie with corrupt Anglo commerce interests who extort my people and bleed my country's resources."

Politics. Be careful, Sam warned himself.

He sat watching, listening, knowing the truth was now coming out. *But how much?* He'd have to decide that for himself.

"Instead of taking all of the gold back to Mexico City, he diverted much of it to his *Americano* associates. The gold is in the custody of the Pettigo-American Mining Company. It sits in a wagon, under guard, in a building that no worker is allowed to enter."

"How reliable is your information?" Sam asked.

"I found this out from peasant mine workers who did not realize how valuable their information was to me. So the gold has not yet been moved to a new location. How reliable is it?" He gave a short shrug. "It explains why the Cadys are always dead set on robbing a payroll which is modest at best, from a mine whose defenses are next to impenetrable."

Sam considered it.

"If all you're telling me is true," he offered, "why not send a troop of *federales* up to Pettigo-American, retrieve the gold and be done with it?"

"If only it were that easy, Ranger," Lupo said. "It is a fragile relationship my government has with yours. My poor country needs the help of honest American commerce and business. But along with the honest Anglo businessmen comes a bad element. And I'm afraid the Pettigos are the very worst of that bad element. Yet, if a force of *federales* enter an American mining enterprise, it would have dire and far-reaching consequences. Other American business would give pause to coming here."

Sam gave him a curious gaze.

"So you weren't interested in tracking down Siebert and Bellibar, or even in getting up to Lookout Hill. Your only interest is Pettigo-American Mining."

"And recovering my country's gold without turning it into conflict between our governments," Lupo added.

"You were pulling me into this knowing that my being here can have nothing to do with political matters," Sam said.

"I am still trying to pull you into this, Ranger," said Lupo. "I have no choice."

"Your government sent you alone, to get in and out the best way you can?" Sam shook his head. "That sounds real shaky, Easy John."

"I had three valuable contacts established," said Lupo. "One was Wilton Marrs, a leader among the Cadys' Lookout Hill boys. But as we know, outlaws have a habit of killing each other for little or no reason. In Marrs' case, the Cadys saw that he was gaining too much respect among their men."

"You said *three* contacts," Sam said.

"The other two, Paco Reyes and Saginaw Sparks, were killed right after telling me the Cadys were getting ready to launch a large attack on the Pettigos," said Lupo. "But after our meeting, I heard shots on the trail ahead of me and found their bodies there."

"One of our boys?" Sam asked.

"Yes, Bellibar," said Lupo. "I saw him later, riding on the trail below me."

"Then you spotted me," said Sam. "You saw that I was on his trail. You started following me."

"It is true, Ranger," said Lupo. "I followed you until my horse came upon a bull rattler, spooked and fell over a cliff." He gave a slight smile. "Knowing you had a spare horse, I had to come announce myself."

"That's your whole story?" Sam asked.

"Yes, it is," said Lupo. "I hope you believe it's the truth, because I need your help—my country needs your help." He paused, then asked, "*Do* you believe it is the truth?"

Sam gave a slight shrug. It was as much truth as he'd ever get out of a spy like him, he decided.

"Will you help me, Ranger?" Lupo asked in a somber tone. "It will put me in your debt. Anything I can assist you with to make your job less difficult, you will have only to ask—"

Sam raised a hand, cutting him short, still considering the political complexion of this.

"I'm only after Bellibar and Siebert. Nothing has changed," he said, "But if my interest and yours work out to be the same, so much for coincidence." As he spoke, he stood up from the ground and dusted his trousers. "We'll leave these two running free for now, if that helps you make your plans. But get your plans laid fast. The *next* time I see these men is the *last* time I ever want to see them."

The Russian, Cherzi Persocovich, didn't see his two fellow mercenaries ride into town. The half-breed, Clayton "Cold Foot" Cain, and the former assassin, Newton Ridge, deliberately circled around behind the town and rode in from the same direction any gunman on the prowl would use if that person was riding down from Lookout Hill. When neither the Russian nor Leonard Tiggs, or the new man, Bob Hughes, confronted them, Ridge turned in his saddle to the half-breed as they walked their horses toward the tent cantina.

"If this was a test to see who's on their toes here, Tiggs and Cherzi failed by a long shot," he said.

"What about the new sheriff?" Cold Foot asked, staring straight ahead.

"The new sheriff . . . yeah, right," Ridge said cynically. He spit and ran a gloved hand across his lips. "Far as I'm concerned, this Bob Hughes is a broken wheel getting ready to slip its hub."

Cold Foot shook his head, still staring ahead along the dirt street.

"I don't know what that means," he said.

"It means, my half-redskin amigo, that he is not

going to last very long." He gave a knowing smile. "This would be a good time for you to borrow some money from him."

"I don't need to borrow any money from him," Cold Foot said flatly. "I have my own money."

The former assassin for hire stared at the stoic half-breed.

"Damn, Cold Foot, do I have to spell it out for you?" he said as if in disbelief.

Cold Foot stared straight ahead in silence.

"I'm saying if you were to borrow some money from Hughes, you wouldn't have to worry about ever paying it back. Denver Jennings said old man Pettigo hit the ceiling when he heard his son hired this lunatic to watch for Cady gunmen. The old man and Jennings sent us down here behind Dale Pettigo's back to check on things. Jennings gave me the go-ahead, said nobody would miss this Hughes if a couple of bullets ran through his ears. Said were it to happen, it might even get a mercenary like me a hundred-dollar pay bonus."

The half-breed stared ahead as they drew nearer to the hitch rail out in front of the tent cantina.

"So, now do you understand about not paying him back if you borrowed money from him?" Ridge asked. They reined their horses toward the hitch rail.

"I understand," said Cold Foot, without taking his eyes off the street ahead.

"Thank God!" said Ridge with a roll of his eyes.

"But I have my own money," the half-breed replied.

Son of a bitch!

Ridge managed to keep his cursing to himself, stopping and swinging down from his horse and spinning its reins around the rail. Beside him the half-breed did the same.

"Cold Foot," he said with clear deliberation, turning to the half-breed, "let me do all the talking. You hang back and keep me covered. Okay?"

The half-breed only nodded, adjusting his gun belt and a bandolier of ammunition slung over his shoulder. The two walked into the tent and saw the Russian standing at an empty bar with a cocked, sawed-off shotgun lying only inches from his right hand. Ridge gave the half-breed a wry grin and eased forward with his head lowered until he stopped right behind the Russian. He drew his Colt and stuck the tip of the barrel into the Russian's back.

"Got you, boy!" he whispered. "You were supposed to see us when we rode into town."

Cherzi Persocovich was stiff with fear until Newton Ridge stepped around in front of him and lowered his Colt back into his holster.

"You should have seen us, Cherzi boy," he said, chastising the Russian. Then he noted the Russian's glassy eyes, and he understood why they'd made it all the way to the cantina without ever being seen.

"Where's Tiggs?" he said. "Where's the new sheriff?"

The Russian only shrugged—he didn't know.

"This looks bad on you, Cherzi, *really* bad," said Ridge. He wagged a finger at the Russian. "You didn't see us coming and you should have."

Cherzi looked at the wagging finger near his chest,

then over at the half-breed, who only stood back, staring at him, revealing nothing.

"Take away from me your finger," Cherzi told Ridge firmly.

"Easy, Cherzi." Ridge chuckled and lowered his hand. "I'm only funning you a little."

"Is not funny," said Cherzi.

"Anyway," said Ridge, dropping the chuckling, "you should have seen us . . . but enough said." He turned to the waiting bartender and said, "Burns, set us up a bottle and a couple of glasses."

"Coming up, Mr. Ridge," said the bartender, stepping away toward the row of bottles on the wall.

"Pay the man, Cherzi," said Ridge, stepping away along the empty bar toward the rear tent fly. "I'm gone to hit *el fuera casa.*"

"Why do I pay for your bottle?" said the glassy-eyed Russian.

"That's for not seeing us," said Ridge. He grinned and slapped the bar top as he rounded the end of it toward the rear fly.

"Ridge!" said the Russian, loud enough that the former assassin stopped and looked at him from the end of the bar.

"I see you now," said Cherzi. The sawed-off shotgun exploded, sending a streak of fire along ten feet of plank bar top, raising a cloud of splinters and dust in its fiery wake.

The bartender's eyes widened as he froze, bottle in hand.

The half-breed had seen it coming, but his expression didn't change as Newton Ridge let out a sharp yelp and flew backward in a bloody mist, the load of steel nail heads shredding the canvas tent as the blast launched him through it. He landed sprawled on the ground outside the tent.

The bartender suddenly dropped out of sight. The half-breed calmly folded his arms across his chest and stared at Cherzi as the Russian clasped a hand around the smoking shotgun and swung it toward him, the second hammer still cocked and ready.

"Is problem with you?" Cherzi asked the half-breed, his eyes drooping, glassy.

The half-breed shook his head slowly.

"He came here to kill Hughes," he said, "probably you and Tiggs too if you tried to stop him."

"You were in on it?" said Cherzi.

The half-breed only shook his head.

"Then how you know this?" said the Russian.

"He told me I should borrow money from Hughes if I got the chance," said the half-breed.

"Oh, I see," said the Russian. He looked at the bloody torn-open canvas wall flapping idly on a breeze. "He is very funny man, eh?"

"Yes," said Cold Foot, "a very funny man." He gave a nod at the bar, toward the bottle standing near the Russian's elbow.

The Russian nodded, glassy-eyed.

"Burns, get for this man a glass," he called out to the hidden bartender.

Cold Foot stepped over to the bar.

"Why you did not back for him his play?" Cherzi asked Cold Foot as the bartender arose and began filling a shot glass for the half-breed.

"I didn't like him," said the half-breed. "Besides, I'm not going back to the mines. I quit working for the Pettigos. I think I will stay around here, see what Bob Hughes is going to do next."

"Why do you think he is going to do something next?" the Russian asked.

"Hombres like him always do *something next*," said the half-breed, tossing back a mouthful of rye.

"I think that you are right," said the Russian. He smiled knowingly. "You wait here with me until Hughes and the new deputy return."

Chapter 16

Before Bellibar, Siebert and Billy Boyle reached a point halfway up the rock-walled canyon leading to Lookout Hill, a band of riders seemed to appear from out of nowhere and close in tight around them. On a high ridge in the upward distance, a line of riflemen stared down at them. Siebert instinctively reached for his big Remington, but before he could raise it, Bellibar growled at him under his breath.

"Leave that gun where it is, Aces. Don't go showing these boys how stupid you are, first thing."

"I don't have to take that kind of talk from you," Siebert growled in reply. He started to grab the Remington anyway, but the cocking rifles and revolvers surrounding them caused his gun hand to freeze.

"Anybody makes a move for a gun is dead," said a strong, threatening voice. "You've got sand, Billy Boyle. I'll give you that. I had to ride down here myself and see just what the hell you were doing, bringing these strangers up to Lookout Hill."

"Don't kill me, Fletcher," Boyle said quickly. "These

two are Pettigo men, Sheriff Bob Hughes and his deputy . . ." His voice trailed as he looked at Siebert.

"Hot Aces Siebert, by God," Siebert said with a scorching stare, even as he raised his hand away from his gun.

"I've heard of you, Aces," said Fletcher Cady, his rifle barrel lowering a little. He eyed Bellibar up and down. "Sheriff Hughes, huh?" he said.

"Not really," Bellibar said coolly, looking Fletcher Cady up and down in return. "I'm Bobby Hugh Bellibar."

"I figured as much when I heard him say he's Aces Siebert," said Cady. "You two are known to ride together." His attitude mellowed some. "What brings you fellows up the trail to Lookout Hill?" He flashed a heated look at Boyle and added, "I mean, besides this *cucaracha.*"

"Fletcher, please," said Boyle, still fearing for his life under Cady's burning gaze. "I knew you and Bert would want to hear what these two are doing in Copper Gully. That's why I brought them."

"Why don't you ride on up, Billy Boyle?" Fletcher Cady said with a gesture of his head. "The longer I look at your face, the more I want to shoot holes in it."

Without another word, Boyle veered his horse away and rode up the hill at a gallop.

"Now, then, Bobby Hugh," Fletcher said to Bellibar, as Boyle's horse left dust swirling in the air above the trail, "you were saying?"

Siebert chuckled, seeing Boyle race away in fear.

"You're not all *that* mad at him, I can tell," he said to Cady.

Jesus . . . ! Bellibar just stared at him.

So did Fletcher Cady. He cocked his head a little to the side and turned back to Bellibar.

"Are you going to say why you're here?" he asked flatly.

"Yes, I am," Bellibar answered in a no-nonsense manner. "To be honest, we came up here from the lower hill country to see about riding for you Cadys. One thing led to another . . . I killed a couple of your men," he said, brushing past that part. "First thing I know, Dale Pettigo made me sheriff—put me in charge of watching over the town, making sure no more of your men tried to gather there to make a run at the mines."

"Hold it. Go back," said Cady.

"The part about us wanting to ride for you?" said Bellibar.

"Don't mess with me, Bobby Hugh," Fletcher Cady warned, leveling his rifle barrel on him again, the men gathered around him doing the same. "I mean about you killing a couple of my men."

"It was unfortunate," said Bellibar, "but Harvey Moran and Bad Sharlo Bering threw down on me—I had to lay them down." He looked saddened by the happening.

"You killed Bad Sharlo, with Moran backing his play?" asked Cady, unable to completely mask how impressed he was. The men looked at each, equally awed.

"They showed up in hell bloody and confused—didn't even know they were dead yet," Siebert said proudly, even though he hadn't even seen it.

Cady ignored Siebert. He stared at Bellibar.

"And that got you made sheriff of Copper Gully," he said.

"It did," said Bellibar. "I appointed my pard here and a dope-eating Russian outlaw as my deputies." He grinned. "My first official act is to ride up here and see if you'd like to partner up, rob the mine payroll with us."

Fletcher kept a poker face, wondering if these two hard cases knew anything at all about the gold hidden at Pettigo-American Mining Company. He had a hunch they didn't.

"That would all be fine, Bobby Hugh," he said, "except we're already set to rob the place ourselves. I don't see us needing a couple of partners." He considered it, then added, "Ride with us maybe, for a share, since you came all this way—"

"Huh-uh, Fletcher," said Bellibar, cutting him off. "I'm not going to spell out what we both know to be a fact. Unless you can gather your men at Copper Gully unbeknownst, and slip up that gully to the mines without being spotted, Pettigo's mercenaries will shoot you boys to pieces." He thumped himself on the chest. "That's where I come in. I can keep quiet, let you gather without any problem, or I can send a man to the Pettigos and have them waiting."

"You've put some thought into it, I see," said Cady. "But what if we shot you both down, right here, say?"

"Kill us and my dope-eating Russian will be up that gully and in Pettigo's lap the second you boys send a man into town." Bellibar grinned. He wasn't worried, noting the gunmen hadn't refocused their weapons on him and Siebert. Fletcher's was an empty threat, the kind you make right before giving up and going along with the game.

"All this for a mine payroll," said Cady.

"It must be a damn large payroll," Siebert put in, "as long as you boys have been out to get it."

"We've been after this payroll for a long time, that's a fact," said Fletcher Cady. "I must be out of my mind, getting it stuck in my craw so bad." He eyed both Bellibar and Siebert, convinced they didn't know a thing about the stolen Mexican gold sitting there, just waiting to be had by men bold enough to take it.

"So, what's it going to be?" Bellibar asked, looking all around at the faces of the gunmen, confident he knew Cady's answer. "Are you going to fire away or clear a spot for us?"

Before Fletcher Cady could reply, another man stepped his horse forward through the gunmen.

"Not so fast, Fletch," the man said. "I want to look these men in the eye first. We might want to shoot them, after all."

Seeing the look on Bellibar's and Siebert's faces, Fletcher Cady gave a jerk of his head toward the man.

"Meet my big brother, Bert," Fletcher Cady said with a dark smile. "If he says shoot you, I suppose that's how it'll go."

Now the gunmen did refocus on the two. Bellibar hadn't counted on this, but he held steady and gave Bert Cady a firm stare. So did Siebert.

Bert Cady stopped his horse beside his brother and looked Bellibar in the eye.

"We usually don't let anybody in our fold unless they're sent by our good friend Wilton Marrs. Were you sent here by Marrs?" he asked bluntly.

"I wish I could say we were—this fellow being a friend of yours," said Bellibar, remembering what Saginaw Sparks and Paco Reyes had said about all of them killing Marrs, that friends of Marrs wouldn't be welcome at Lookout Hill. This was nothing but a trap. "But I won't lie," he said, straight-faced. "We never heard of the man. We come here strictly on knowing the Cady reputation."

"That's too bad," said Bert Cady, still pressing, trying to run his trap. "We don't break our rules. If you don't know Marrs . . ."

"Wait a minute," said Siebert, in mock consideration. "That name does ring a bell."

Ignoring Siebert, Bellibar said bluntly to the Cadys, "I told you I won't lie about it."

"It's true. He won't lie at all. That's a fact," Siebert cut in, sounding shaky. "I've tried to get him to. He just won't lie—*hates a liar*, in fact—"

"Shut up, Aces," Bellibar said over his shoulder. To the Cadys he said, "I don't know your friend Martin. That's all I can say on the matter." He deliberately mispronounced Marrs' name for good measure.

"*Marrs*," Bert Cady said, correcting him. He turned

his eyes to his brother. "What do you think about it, Fletch? Maybe make an exception this one time?"

"This is a big job," Fletcher Cady said. "We could use more guns, losing Bad Sharlo and Moran."

"Yeah, not to mention Paco and Sparks being missing," said Bert Cady. He looked at Bellibar and Siebert and said, "Looks like you two are getting ready for the biggest payroll robbery of your lives. Welcome to Lookout Hill."

Easy John Lupo had heard the shotgun blast on his way into Copper Gully. He had exchanged his long black riding duster for a faded, striped poncho that covered the big Walker Colt holstered across his stomach. As he rode onto a nearly empty street, he saw three men carrying a body away from the rear side of the ripped, blood-splattered tent cantina. He reined his horse over and looked down and recognized the bloody face of Newton Ridge.

One more out of the way, he told himself. He had started to rein his horse away toward the front hitch rail when he heard the harsh voice of a man walking alongside the body.

"What are you looking at, Mex?" the man said in an unfriendly tone.

Mex? Here, in his own country?

The words took Lupo aback for a moment until he caught himself and realized he was not dressed in his usual Anglo-style border clothes. Strange how something as simple as a different outer garment changed a whole people's perception of the man wearing it.

Half bowing his head as if reminded of his lower place in the world, Lupo touched the brim of his black sombrero without making eye contact with the man.

"Nothing, señor," he said, giving his best attempt at a peasant accent.

"Damn Mexes," he heard the man say to the ones carrying Ridge's body, "they're always underfoot here."

As he reined his horse away and back toward the front hitch rail, he recognized the half-breed, Clayton "Cold Foot" Cain, standing by the tent fly staring at him.

"*Buenas tardes,*" he said, again touching the brim of his sombrero.

The half-breed didn't reply, but he grudgingly gave a slight nod of his head.

"I see that death has reared his ugly head on this beautiful day," Lupo said, spinning his reins around the hitch rail. "A terrible accident, no doubt?" He gave an affable smile without lifting his head to eye level.

"Careful you don't have a terrible *accident* yourself," the half-breed said menacingly.

Lupo raised a hand in a show of peace and walked past him inside the big tent. He stood at the nearly empty bar waiting for the bartender, who appeared agitated at the prospect of serving an unfamiliar Mexican. When the bartender did arrive, he gave Lupo a less than friendly stare.

"Mescal, *por favor,*" Lupo said.

The bartender left and came back with a wooden cup and a straw-wrapped bottle. He stared sharply at Easy John until the Mexican took a gold coin from inside his poncho and laid it on the bar top.

The bartender examined the coin closely, then stared at Lupo again before turning and walking away.

Lupo glanced along the bar and saw the glassy eyes of the Russian staring at him: another face he recognized from studying the gunmen through the powerful lens of his binoculars, back when the Pettigo mercenary force began growing in both size and fierceness.

Touching his sombrero again, Easy John turned away from the bar and had started to a small, out-of-the-way table when he almost ran into the half-breed, who had slipped inside behind him.

"I know you," the half-breed said.

Lupo recognized the same glassiness in Cold Foot's eyes that he saw in the Russian's.

"No, señor, I do not think so," Easy John said. He tried to sidestep him, but the half-breed blocked his way.

"You're Juan Lupo," said the half-breed. "I saw you once in Matamoros."

Easy John glanced around, saw the Russian stand up in interest and walk toward them.

"Aw, *gracias*, señor," he said. "I am familiar with this Juan Lupo. He is a very handsome hombre and I am honored you think I look like him." He shrugged. "But sadly—"

"I didn't say you look like him," said Cold Foot, "I said you *are* him." His hand fell onto the butt of his holstered gun.

Lupo was a second away from dropping his bottle and cup and reaching under his poncho for the big Walker, knowing he would have to step back to do so, as close as the Russian stood to him. But before he set himself to making his move, the Russian stopped a few feet away and stared at the half-breed.

"What is now the trouble?" he asked Cold Foot, sounding put out. "I told you it is not trouble I want to have here." He turned his glassy eyes to Lupo. "Who are you and what do you want here?"

Lupo put away the idea of going for the big Walker. He held up the bottle and cup.

"Only this," he said meekly, "and a chair on which to sit while I quench my thirst?"

"All right," said Cherzi, gesturing to the table where Lupo had been headed anyway. "Have your drink. This man will no longer bother you."

"I know him," Cold Foot insisted, both of them in a dope-induced stupor.

"Be a nice person," said Cherzi, raising a finger. "We are all three foreigners here."

Foreigners here?

Lupo looked at Cold Foot, a shoulder-length single braid of hair hanging beneath his hat, a Cheyenne beaded necklace around his neck. He glanced down at his own striped peasant poncho. *Thank the saints for good Mexican dope,* he told himself.

"But he's been called a bounty hunter," said Cold Foot.

"So what, are you wanted?" Cherzi asked. "I have been called a Bulgarian, but what does it matter?"

Cold Foot had to think about it.

"You asked what I am doing here," Lupo offered, lowering his tone, adjusting his meek countenance a little now that he saw what he was dealing with. "I'm here to meet Billy Boyle and ride with him and his amigos." He gestured his eyes in the direction of Lookout Hill. "We talked about robbing the mine payroll?" he whispered.

"I do not know what it is you speak of," the Russian said. But his glassy eyes couldn't hide the truth.

Lupo saw it. The time was here, just as he thought. Lookout Hill was ready to move against its neighbor, the Pettigo-American Mining Company.

"You must wait for the sheriff and his deputy to return," said Cherzi. "They are with Billy Boyle. I am not to tell anybody anything."

Bellibar and Siebert, the new sheriff and his deputy . . .

Lupo thought about it without letting the surprise show on his face. He held the empty wooden cup out to the half-breed just to see if he would take it. He did.

"Gracias," he said. "Maybe I should come back when the sheriff is here," he said to the Russian.

"What about your mescal?" asked Cherzi.

"I'll take it along with me," said Lupo, wanting out of there while both men still saw him through a fuzzy veil. He saw that Cold Foot was not as doped as the Russian—he might yet be a problem.

Walking out of the tent with both men shadowing him, Lupo stepped up into his saddle, touched his sombrero brim and rode away. But he only rode for a mile before veering his horse into a stand of scrub mesquite and fire bush, and stepped down from his saddle and hitched his horse out of sight. Climbing atop a large rock beside the trail, he slipped a Spanish-style dagger from his boot well, looked at it in his hand.

"*Mi puñal* . . . you must not fail me on this day," he whispered to the glittering blade. He touched his lips to the cold steel as if in a lover's kiss. He took off his poncho and his belly rig, but shoved his big Colt down behind his back just in case and pulled his shirttail out to cover it. He crouched atop the rock and waited.

Chapter 17

In his inebriated state, the half-breed rode along the narrow trail at a medium gallop, trying hard to clear his mind. He watched the rocky terrain for an ambush, but when Lupo made his move and leaped down from his position atop the rock, it caught Cold Foot by surprise. Even if he'd been expecting the attack, it would have done him little good, the weight of the Mexican coming down atop him unchecked.

Seeing the flash of steel in the Mexican's hand as they both flew from the saddle, Cold Foot instinctively grasped his wrist before Lupo's blade made its way into his chest. As the half breed managed to offer a defense for himself, the two rolled along the rocky trail, tumbling in a rising swirl of dust.

When they stopped rolling, the half-breed rose first to his knees, then to his feet, grabbing a knife he carried stuck down in his own boot well.

Lupo came to his feet ten feet farther along the trail as the half-breed's horse galloped on, spooked and whinnying loudly. He saw the flash of the half-breed's blade streak across the air between them just in time to keep him from rushing in. Crouched, the Mexican agent held himself back. The two men circled crablike. Lupo thought about the Colt behind his back beneath his poncho. He would use it as a last resort, but he wanted no noise. He needed to remain unseen and unheard, as he had been these past weeks while studying the comings and goings of the Pettigos and the Lookout Hill boys.

"I knew you were him," the half-breed growled, still winded from the hard fall. "You never fooled me for a minute."

"Yes, I am Juan Lupo," the Mexican said as the two continued their slow circling stance. "I saw in your eyes that you wanted to kill me as soon as we looked at each other, but I did not understand *why*. That is why I waited here for you. I knew you would come, and I wanted to know."

"It doesn't matter *why* I want to kill you, Easy John," said the half-breed. "I wanted to kill you when I first laid eyes on you in Matamoros. When I saw you ride into Copper Gully, I just wanted to kill you even worse than before." He tossed the knife back and forth from hand to hand as they circled.

"In that case, what better way to kill each other than with the bite of cold steel, eh?" Lupo said.

"I couldn't have said it better, Mex," the half-breed said.

"All right, then," said Lupo, crouching with even more deliberation, but he stopped short and straightened a little. "But as you see, I have only my dagger."

He gestured toward the Colt in the half-breed's holster, wanting to keep it silent too. "You have the advantage."

"Oh, the gun," said Cold Foot. "I almost forgot." His bloodshot eyes had cleared considerably. He raised his Colt from its holster, examined it and cocked it toward Lupo.

It took courage for Lupo to not draw the big Walker from behind his back and end things quickly. But he held on, even as the half-breed pointed the gun at him, taking aim.

"One shot and it's all over, Mex," the half-breed said. "I could quit hating myself for not killing you sooner."

Lupo felt his hand want to grab for the Walker; still, he kept held himself in control, fighting the urge.

"But I won't do that," said the half-breed, uncocking the gun and pitching it aside in the dirt. "I want to watch your face up close while you're wriggling and dying on the end of my—"

His words stopped as Lupo charged at him, but he retaliated fast, launching forward in a charge of his own. Stabbing and slashing wildly at each other, the two fought chest to chest for only a second. Yet at the end of that tense second, as they backed away from each other, both stood crouched and bleeding from stabs and slashes on their blocking hands, their defending forearms, their exposed sides, their faces, their abdomens.

Ignoring his own bleeding, the half-breed gazed upon Lupo's cuts and punctures with a gleam in his eyes.

"Yeah," he said in a dark tone, "this is what I wanted to see."

The two charged again. This time they didn't back away. Instead they fell to the ground, rolling, kicking, stabbing and cutting each other relentlessly until Lupo's dagger slipped free of his blood-slick hand. Before he could grab his dagger back from the ground, he felt the half-breed's blade go deep into his lower side and stop against solid bone.

The half-breed's knife stayed stuck in Juan Lupo as Lupo rolled away to once again reach for his own lost dagger. This time he closed his hand around his dagger's handle and felt a layer of dirt and grit that allowed him the traction he needed. He swung the knife hard as he rolled back to the half-breed and saw the blade open a deep, long gash on his shoulder.

But the half-breed wasn't finished. Even as blood spewed from his shoulder, he grabbed his knife and gave it a hard merciless rounding before jerking it from Lupo's bleeding side.

Lupo bellowed in pain and he flung himself atop the half-breed, pinning the man's knife hand to the dirt with his knee. He jabbed a bloody thumb deep into the half-breed's eye until he felt the eyeball pull loose and jump to one side. Still he pressed his thumb even deeper, to its hilt into warm, soft substance and membrane. Gripping his bloody head like a punctured melon, he held Cold Foot in place as he stabbed his blade deep into the exposed side of the half-breed's neck—once, twice, three times.

On the third vicious stab, he fell way on the ground

and stared up, blinking at the sky, feeling the earth sway beneath him like the deck of a troubled ship. The dagger fell from his hand onto the ground beside him. He felt for it and closed his hand back over it. He patted the bloody knife as if for a job well done. Beside him he watched blood fountain up from the half-breed's throat, three feet in the air, then fall away to nothing.

Turning onto his side, knife in hand, he crawled over and looked down at Cold Foot's grim bloody face. The half-breed's remaining eye stared straight up into the endless sky with a look of disbelief.

"It's all right . . ," Lupo gasped. He patted Cold Foot's bloody chest. "It's okay. . . ." He tugged at the half-breed's shirt, trying to close the wide slash in the material. "It's all right . . . ," he whispered again. He patted Cold Foot's dead chest one last time, then rested his head down on it and felt a warm darkness close in around him.

When the three hours it should have taken Lupo to ride to Copper Gully and back turned into five, the Ranger set out down the trail searching for him. At a turn in the trail, the Ranger saw a horse coming at him, no rider on its back. He fell in beside the trotting horse, caught it by its bridle and brought it to a halt.

He was glad to see that it wasn't Lupo's horse, yet he had a suspicion that the horse had something to do with Lupo's trip into Copper Gully, and that made him wish he'd waited for Lupo closer down the trail. But this was how Lupo had wanted it, he reminded himself, nudging the stallion on along the trail, leading the horse beside him.

Before he'd gone a mile farther, he saw Lupo riding his horse toward him at a walk. Sam let out a breath, rode closer and stopped again, this time seeing how Lupo sat bowed in his saddle. Looking past Lupo, he eyed the trail behind him closely. Then he moved forward again, seeing the drawn look on Lupo's face.

"What took you?" he asked, studying Lupo even closer, seeing something was wrong.

Lupo had washed the blood from his face and hands with canteen water and torn a shirt from his saddlebags into strips to dress the worst of his wounds as best he could.

"One of Pettigo's men followed me," he said, "a halfbreed Cheyenne named Clayton Cain. That's his horse you have there. I couldn't risk him getting on our trail, so I killed him."

Noting Lupo's hand clutching his lower side beneath his poncho, Sam asked, "Are you shot? I didn't hear any gunfire."

"No, I'm not shot," said Lupo. "It was a knife fight. I took some cutting before I finally pinned him down."

Sam looked at him closer, seeing a stark paleness to his face and hands.

"We'll make camp here. I'll take a look at those wounds," he said.

"No, not here," said Lupo. He nodded farther toward a turn in the trail. "Up there in the turn. From there we can see most of Copper Gully. I need to show it to you."

"Following you," Sam said, backing the stallion a step and letting Lupo pass him. As he fell in behind Lupo, leading the half-breed's horse behind him, he watched the wounded Mexican riding slightly hunched over but otherwise unimpaired by his wounds. When Lupo stopped at the turn thirty yards ahead, Sam watched him step down from the saddle stiffly.

Lupo gestured a hand out across a steep drop.

"We cannot be seen from this distance," he said, directing the Ranger's vision up along the jagged gully. It ran straight and deep, stretching up the side of a steep, rocky hill that dwarfed the hills surrounding it. From their position above the lower end of the gully, Lupo traced his gloved finger upward, following the gully into the far distance where it ended short beneath the crest of the hill.

"It looks as if some higher power sank a giant ax into the hillside, eh, Ranger?" he said. "Perhaps in a fit of rage against my people."

Sam only looked at him. He could see Lupo fighting against the pain of his wounds, trying not to give in to them.

"Not the kind of higher power we both know, of course," Lupo added, crossing himself idly as he spoke. The Ranger recognized a note of wry irony in his statement.

Sam looked up the deep-walled gully, and at the high walls of rock that terraced its sides at random intervals.

"I can see why this gully is the only access to the mines," he said. Then he looked at the roofline of the town below the deep gash in the hillside and spoke its name in Spanish.

"Barranca del Cobre," he said. "I can also see how nobody gets past the town in any great numbers without being seen. There's no other way up the gully except riding along the main street."

"This was the intentions of the early Spaniards," Lupo said. "They knew how to use the land itself to keep others out." He gazed at the up-reaching gully. "But there is more to the Pettigos' security than this alone," he added.

"I figured there might be," Sam said, staring into the distance where the eleven-mile gully ran out of sight.

"The Pettigos have so many gunmen they leave one posted as guard, stationed every few miles apart along the gully floor," said Lupo. "There are four in all. The one closest to Copper Gully listens for any unusual gunfire coming from town. If he hears anything, he fires warning shots for the next gunman, who passes along warning shots in return. Finally the warning makes its way up the gully to the mines."

Sam considered it.

"No wonder nobody ever makes it up to the mines and pulls a surprise attack on them," he said.

"*Sí*," said Lupo, "the Pettigos are not fools. They pay the peasants they employ to mine the copper so little that they can afford many guns to keep their world protected. The peasant miners are little more than slaves. Yet the Pettigos' gunmen live a good and prosperous life."

The Ranger thought it over as he surveyed the rugged, steep terrain.

"This is the perfect place to hide a wagonload of stolen golden ingots," he said. As he spoke, the two turned to their horses and swung up into their saddles, Lupo taking only a second longer, owing to his pain. Sam observed him in silence as they turned their horses and rode twenty yards deeper into the brush and rock cover above their trail.

This time when they stepped down from their saddles, Lupo held on to his saddle horn for a moment. Sam continued to keep a close eye him.

"Until I get my sights on Bellibar and Siebert, this is your show," he said, watching Lupo straighten up enough to walk over to a rock and sit down, clutching his lower side. "But I have to ask, are you going to be able to do this?"

"I *will* do this," Lupo said with determination. "You must believe me." He didn't mention Bellibar and Siebert just yet.

"All right," said Sam, "I do believe you."

"*Gracias*, Ranger," he said, keeping the pain out of his voice.

"But I will ask, how do you plan on us getting up the gully to the gold without the posted guards tipping off the mines?" He pulled down both of their bedrolls from behind their saddles and pitched them on the rocky ground.

Lupo gave a tight, forced smile as Sam gathered dried brush and kindling twigs into a circle for a fire.

"Sometimes to solve a problem in the present, one must look to the past," he said. "I could not imagine the Spaniards putting themselves on a hilltop which had only one trail in and out of their encampment. So I searched the other side of this hill for two weeks until I found an old, tunneled trail."

The Ranger listened as he stepped over a few feet and brought back dried scrub pine branches.

"I followed the trail until I could see a guarded building where the wagon sits," Lupo continued. "I could have taken it that very day, but I could never have gotten away without the mercenaries catching me. The wagon tracks would have led them to the hidden trail and all would be lost."

"What makes you think they don't already know about the tunnel and the hidden trail?" Sam asked, stooping, striking a wooden match and starting a low fire.

"The trail has not been used for a very long time," said Lupo. "There were no hoofprints or boot prints to be seen." He paused, then said, "Besides, it would no longer matter if they know or not. I have dynamite hidden halfway down the trail. As I go escape through the tunnel, I blow up the trail behind me."

"What will my part be in this?" Sam asked, bringing the fire to a working level for boiling water.

Lupo looked at the Ranger until Sam realized he could answer the question himself.

"You need somebody to help you take out the guards," Sam said. "Somebody with a rifle who can hold them back until you get started down the back of the hillside."

"If I am lucky, I can slip in and get the wagon and get out unseen while the Cadys are attacking the Pettigos from up the gully."

"But if you *are* seen," Sam said, "you're dead, and the gold is never recovered."

"I could never get down the back trail with horsemen riding after me," Lupo said.

"It's not going to be easy for your rifleman either," said Sam. "The mercenaries will be stirred up like hornets, with the outlaws from Lookout Hill coming up the gully at them and the backside of this hill blowing up at the same time."

As they talked, Sam had taken a small pot from inside his bedroll, poured water from his canteen into it and set it beside the growing campfire. Steam curled as the water bubbled on the fire side of the pot.

"I know it is a lot to ask, Ranger," Lupo finally said.

"Then don't ask," Sam replied before the Mexican agent could finish. "I'll give you the cover you need." He paused before saying, "How do you know Wilton Marrs was telling you the truth, that the Cadys will be attacking the mines this week?"

"He has not lied to me before—that is all I can go on in this line of work. He told me the Cadys know about the gold but they are keeping it a secret from their men. If they successfully raid the mines, the gold will be in their hands. This is my only chance to get the gold back to my government."

Sam heard urgency and stifled pain in his voice.

"I understand," he said. "I'm after Bellibar and Siebert. They'll be there. So will I." He picked up the pot of water and set it beside Lupo. "Now throw off the poncho. Let's see the damage."

Lupo lifted the faded poncho with the Ranger's help. Seeing the bloody shirt and the crimson bandages behind the opened bib, Sam kept the worst of his opinion to himself.

"He got you good, Easy John," he said.

"*Sí*, he got me good," Lupo replied, looking down at himself. "And now we clean the wounds and cover them"—he made a determined expression—"and back to work."

Chapter 18

———

In the middle of the night, Hodding Siebert felt himself being watched, hovered over by someone or *something* that had no business being there. Cautiously, he opened his eyes just enough to see the healing woman standing over him in her long black robe. *Uh-oh . . .* Above her he saw two small wispy birds circle and touch down lightly onto her shoulders. They stepped back and forth in place, as silent as death—no chirping, these birds, he noted.

No fluttering of wings, nothing. . . .

He felt a cold sweat form at the back of his hairline. There was something eerie and wrong about those quiet birds.

I—I killed you, he said to the hooded woman, or did he only think he said it aloud?

He batted his eyes, sitting up with his Remington drawn from under his saddle, cocked and aimed. Only now the healing woman was gone. He stared across the circle of low campfire light in time to see one of the silent little birds go skittering off into the darkness, vanishing into the brushy terrain.

"Damn!" he murmured, the Remington out at arm's length.

From across the campfire, standing guard with his trademark shotgun, Hayworth Benton had looked around at the sound of the gun hammer cocking. He swung around with his ten-gauge shotgun at port arms as Siebert rose from his blanket, the gun lowered now but only a little.

"What's going on over there?" Benton asked.

Siebert just started walking in the direction of the small fleeing bird, staring straight ahead as if in a trance.

"I know it's you!" he shouted. "You're dead! I killed you, remember?"

"What *the hell*?" said Benton. He raised his big ten-gauge instinctively.

The commotion caused the other men to spring up from their sleep; more gun hammers cocked.

"Don't shoot! I'll get him!" Bellibar shouted, up and running across the campsite just as Siebert left the circle of firelight and stepped away into the rock and high brush.

But as he hurried into the brush, he saw Siebert stop and look all around.

Jesus! Now what? Bellibar thought.

"Aces!" he called out. "It's me, Bobby Hugh."

But Siebert didn't reply. Instead he listened intently to the sound of deep chuffing and the stomp of a hoof. *Got you!*

He saw the black silhouette of the woman's big mare standing bareback in a pale glow of moonlight.

"Die, you ornery bitch!" he shouted, raising the Remington. But as he started firing wildly, he watched the black silhouette gallop away, out of sight into the greater blackness.

Twenty feet behind Siebert, Bellibar threw himself flat to the ground, seeing streaks of gunfire loosed in every direction.

"For God's sake, Aces, stop shooting that damn gun! You're going to hit somebody!" Bellibar shouted, drawing his Colt from force of habit, ready to kill Siebert if he had to, to keep Siebert from killing him.

"It's her, Bobby Hugh!" Siebert shouted back at him. "It's her and that blasted mare!"

"Oh, Jesus!" said Bellibar, rising, hurrying forward in a crouch, hoping to shut him up before the others heard his mad ramblings.

"It's her, that damned *witch* I killed!" Siebert said, turning toward him in a haze of burned powder. "Her and that ornery, hex-casting, evil-eyed mare, I swear to God it is!" the empty Remington hung smoking in his limp hand.

"Quiet, Aces!" Bellibar whispered harshly. "They'll all hear you."

"I don't give a damn who hears me! It's that dead *witch*!" Siebert shouted even louder. "I think I winged the mare, which I'm thinking is really a demon up from hell! I'm going after them both! I'm not stopping until—"

Behind them at the edge of the clearing, the men

looked at each other when they heard Siebert fall silent beneath the thump of gunmetal against skull bone. A moment passed as they listened to the struggling sound of Bellibar dragging his knocked-out partner through the dried brush.

"He's a sleepwalker, that's all," Bellibar said, trying to play the situation down.

"Sleepwalker, my ass," said Fletcher. "I know a straight-up idiot when I see one—he needn't slobber on his saddle horn to prove it."

On the ground, Siebert came around with a groan, raising his hand to the side of his head. Bellibar had taken his smoking Remington and carried it stuck down behind his belt.

"Boss, I never seen nothing like it," said Benton. "He come up from his blanket with the strangest look I ever saw . . . except *once*, that is," he added with hesitance.

"Except *once* . . . ?" said Fletcher Cady.

He and all the men looked at Hayworth Benton as Siebert tried to sit up in the dirt.

"Back in Tennessee, when I was a boy," Benton said, "there was a man who was known to be possessed by the devil."

Fletcher Cady just stared at him with a raised hand, stopping him.

"All right, everybody back to sleep," he said. "We're getting up and riding out in two hours."

Two of the men grumbled and looked all around; one man crossed himself. Fletcher Cady and his brother, Bert, started to turn and walk away. But Fletcher stopped and looked at Bellibar.

"I heard him ranting about witches, demons," he said.

"Sleepwalker," Bellibar insisted. "He'll be all right, though. I'll see to it."

"Damn right you will," said Fletcher Cady. "We've got a busy night tonight and a busier day tomorrow." He pointed a finger at Bellibar. "If he's not *all right*, you're going to walk the idiot off into the rocks and clean his ears out with Benton's ten-gauge." He walked away, grumbling to his brother, "I expect everybody in the hill country heard all that shooting—*sleepwalker*, my ass."

"You said you were done with it, Aces," Bellibar hissed down at his partner, who sat slumped with a hand to the side of his head.

"I was—I mean, *I am*, Bobby Hugh," said Siebert. "But this was her—her and the blasted Belleza. It was no dream."

"Belleza?" said Bellibar.

"It means 'beauty,' " said Siebert.

"I know what it means," said Bellibar. "You named this mare?"

"No, it was already her name. She hated me right off, Bobby Hugh," he added, shaking his throbbing head. "Maybe she saw something evil in me, like Benton saw in that fellow back in Tennessee."

"Stop it," said Bellibar. "It's gone far enough. You're not possessed, leastwise no more than the rest of us. She saw how much you hate animals, that's all." He reached a hand down to help Siebert to his feet.

"It's not that I hate animals, Bobby Hugh," Siebert said, rising. "It's just that . . . well, maybe I do hate them at that," he admitted after a short consideration of the matter. "But that's not it. . . ."

"Whatever it is, keep it to yourself," said Bellibar. "You got everybody wanting to kill you."

The two started walking back to their bedrolls; the other gunmen were already settled back down. Hayworth Benton had sat back down by the campfire where he'd been seated before.

"When I get the chance, I'm going to talk to that fellow, Benson," said Siebert. "He seems to know about things like this—" He stopped short and looked around when he realized Bellibar was no longer beside him. His partner stood back, staring at him in the flicker of firelight.

"Are you done with it, Aces?" he asked in a stern tone of voice.

Siebert squeezed his eyes shut and clenched his fists tight, as if struggling to wrench something loose from deep inside his brain. After a moment he let out a long, strained breath.

"I'm done with it," he said. "Give me back my gun."

"I'll give it back to you when we get to Copper Gully," Bellibar said with resolve. "You won't be needing it before then."

Siebert seethed but said nothing. He had the small Colt Pocket, but it only had one shot left in it. If he really needed to, he could shoot somebody in the head and take his gun. That would have to do for now.

A sprawling hacienda that had been built for Edgar Randolph "E. R." Pettigo sat far back behind the

Pettigo-American Mining facilities, away from the noise and the smell of the copper-smelting furnaces. The large house had been built atop the interlocking stone and mortar foundations and breastworks of an ancient Spanish fortress. The stone windowsill where E.R. set his mug of coffee measured a full two feet thick. He stood bowed slightly, his palms spread atop the windowsill supporting him, looking out through the darkness in the direction of the plank and stone building where the wagon sat under guard.

"Damn it, Jennings," he said, "there could be no worse time for this to happen." He raised a palm, made a fist and pounded it solidly on the sill. Ash broke and fell from the cigar in his mouth. "What the devil was he thinking? Can this be what they teach these young men in their fine Eastern universities?"

"In all fairness to young Mr. Pettigo, sir," said Denver Jennings, "Dale doesn't know about the gold. I'm certain if he did he wouldn't have made that fool sheriff. He doesn't take losing a payroll as serious as losing all that Mexican gold . . . if you don't mind me saying so, sir."

Jennings sat in a pinto-hide-covered chair, a glass of bourbon in his hand, a cigar hanging between his fingers.

E. R. Pettigo slumped a little and shook his head. Then he stood up, picked up his coffee mug and faced Jennings.

"I never wanted him to have to see this side of me. My fortune has been untarnished for many years. I wanted him to see me as a completely honest baron of commerce and industry."

"Begging your pardon, sir," said Jennings, "with all respect, is there really such a thing as a *completely* honest baron of industry? Has there ever been?" He offered a knowing half grin and stuck the cigar into his mouth.

E. R. Pettigo sighed and gave a tired smile.

"I wanted there to be, someday," he said. "Back when I was a young man starting out . . . I always hoped that someday after my fortune was secure, I could turn my business interests completely legitimate, clean it up, keep it upstanding." He wagged a finger. "That was what I wanted to bequeath my son. Something he could be proud of." He paused for a moment. "But when you brought this Mexican gold deal to me, how could I say no?"

"You would have been a fool to turn it down, sir," said Jennings.

"Oh, would I?" said Pettigo, a little ice in his tone.

"You know how I mean it, sir," said Jennings, sipping his bourbon.

"Yes, I do," said Pettigo. "The fact is, I saw this big opportunity lying in wait and I could not turn it down. A man never turns down free money, I don't give a damn how rich he's got." He gave a dark little chuckle and tipped his coffee mug as if in a toast to greed.

Denver Jennings joined in, raising his bourbon glass in the salute. They both drank, completing their toast.

"If I might say so, sir," said Jennings, "I wouldn't worry too much about what young Mr. Pettigo thinks about your stolen gold deal. From what I've seen of Dale, he has an itch for adventure, along with his thirst for making a fortune. Most likely he would think no less of you. To be honest, I don't understand how you've kept him from knowing about it."

"He trusts me, Denver," said Pettigo. "I told him the wagon is loaded with crates of ancient Mexican artifacts. Many of the crates near the tailgate actually are loaded on top with some old broken pottery, beads and such"—he shrugged—"things that he thinks are priceless to me, but not particularly so to anyone else."

"The same thing I tell the men I have guarding it," Jennings said. "I called it Mexican junk." He gave a chuckle. "I have checked the load after every guard detail. No one has tampered with the crates since Junior Baugh tried to."

"Yes, poor Junior Baugh," said Pettigo, "a classic case of curiosity killing the cat."

"Yep, it was too bad to have to kill him, sir, but we couldn't have him finding out, spreading the news all over the place." He paused, then said, "As for Dale knowing about it, sir, I don't think he would ever—"

"He's to never know, Denver," said E.R., cutting him off, "and I mean that most adamantly."

"Of course, sir, I understand," said Jennings. He set the glass of bourbon down on a side table and leaned forward, getting down to business.

"Talk to me, Denver," Pettigo said, stepping closer, sensing something more was on his mind.

"Here's the way I look at it," said Jennings. "At first I was worried about Dale making this saddle tramp sheriff. But gold aside, it's like Dale said: it's better having somebody between us and the Lookout Hill boys. Besides, we've got Tiggs and the Russian watching over him, and I even sent Ridge and the half-breed down to check on them. I let Ridge know he'd get a hundred-dollar bonus if Hughes ended up dead without anybody knowing who did it."

"Wise thinking, Denver," said Pettigo. "Dale would never have to know we had anything to do with it." He nodded, then stopped and said with concern, "Are you sure Ridge can handle it?"

"Newton Ridge is an old hand at secret assassins," said Jennings. "I have faith in his work." He shrugged. "Something happens he doesn't get it done, you give me the word, I'll ride down and stick a bullet in Hughes' head myself—two or three if it suits you."

"That may well be the remedy, Denver, if Ridge doesn't satisfy our request," said Pettigo, folding his hands behind his back in contemplation. "But for now I am more interested in getting the gold off this hilltop without the Cadys knowing about it than I am in killing this saddle tramp sheriff."

"Of course, I understand, sir," said Jennings.

"I'm thinking about moving the wagon out of here, making a night move straight down the gully," said Pettigo. "What do you think of the idea?"

Jennings considered it for a moment, puffing his cigar. "We've got guards posted all along the gully, sir," he said, "so we'd get word the second they see any sign of the Cadys." He nodded. "There's no reason why it shouldn't work. The gully trail is dangerous traveling of a night. But with good mounted guards accompanying the load, a good man at the reins, I see no great problem in doing it."

"I'm glad to hear that you agree, Denver," said Pettigo, "because I would like for you to be the man at the reins."

"Me, sir?" Jennings looked surprised.

"Yes, you. Why not you?" said Pettigo. "I trust you more than any mercenary I have working for me."

"I'm honored, sir, and of course I'm glad to do it," Jennings said. "I just thought you might want me in a saddle, keeping the other mounted guards on alert."

Pettigo smiled, his hands still folded behind his back like some general at parade rest.

"That would be me leading the mounted guards, Denver," he said.

"Sir . . ." Jennings shook his head slowly. "With all respect, is that a good idea, you leading the guards?"

"Why not?" said Pettigo. "I've led men all my life—men of commerce, businessmen. Some of them pretty rough characters, I can tell you."

"I have no doubts about you, sir," said Jennings. "But this is not the sort of thing you're used to being involved in."

"You'd be greatly surprised at what I've been involved in, years ago," said Pettigo.

"*Years ago*, sir," said Jennings, still trying to make him see good reasoning. "Again, with all due respect, this is the sort of thing a man needs to be doing all the time to stay game-sharp and gun-ready. You'll get no second chance with this should you happen to run into the Cadys along the way—"

"I will be leading the mounted guards, Denver," Pettigo said more firmly. "That's my decision. With no further discussion on the matter, let's lay our plans and get cracking, shall we?"

No further discussion . . .

Jennings looked at him, realizing as he should have realized all along where Dale Pettigo got his hard-headedness, his arrogance. *It must be a Pettigo family trait,* he told himself. But seeing there was no point in arguing with the old man, he took a breath, calmed himself and said, "Yes, sir, let's get cracking."

Chapter 19

The Ranger and Juan Lupo had both their eyes fixed in the direction of the single pistol firing in the distance. But when the gunfire ended, the two only looked at each other knowingly and turned back to the matter at hand.

In the campfire light, Sam had taken strips of fresh cloth torn from a spare shirt and washed them in hot water. He'd hung them to dry near the fire while he'd washed Lupo's wounds, stitched the deeper gashes together with needle and thread from a small sewing tin he carried in his saddlebags. Lupo sucked in a breath of pain but made no complaint as the Ranger stuck the needle through his flesh.

"I wish I had some whiskey for you, Easy John," Sam offered, drawing the thread snug, watching the deep crimson gash close beneath his hands.

"Whiskey is for happy occasions," John replied, watching him intently. "I would not waste it at a time like this."

Sam nodded absently and continued tacking the

open wounds together. When he finished, he covered the barely seeping wounds with dried strips of clean cloth and wrapped longer strips around the Mexican's abdomen to hold the bandages in place.

"That's as good as you'll get from me," he said, picking up Lupo's poncho and placing it on the blanket beside him. "It'll have to do until we get you somewhere and have you looked at proper."

"I have no time to leave Copper Gully and get looked at proper, Ranger," Lupo said. "I rest tonight. Tomorrow we ride into the edge of the gully and watch for the Cadys. Do you see any reason why I cannot?"

"You've got some deep wounds, Easy John. That's all I'll say on the matter," Sam replied. "If you ride tomorrow, I ride beside you. If you need to heal a day or two, I'll go along with that too."

"Oh? But what about Siebert and Bellibar, and all the people they have killed?" said Lupo. "Would you let them slip away, after hunting them all this time?"

"I'll get them, Lupo," said Sam, "but if it means getting you killed . . . they'll keep."

"I will rest tonight and ride tomorrow," Lupo said with determination, as if closing discussion on the matter.

"That's what I figured," Sam said, turning to the pot of coffee he'd set to boil on the small fire.

He poured two cups of coffee and set Lupo's at his side. He picked up a tin plate he'd filled with warm beans and elk jerky and placed it on Lupo's lap.

"Eat this," he said, "start getting your strength back."

"*Gracias,*" said Lupo. He lifted the tin plate stiffly and ate.

"Now that you're cleaned up and sewn back together, what did you find out in town?" Sam asked.

Lupo swallowed a bite of beans and elk and sipped hot coffee.

"I must tell you about Bellibar and Siebert," Lupo said. "They are now the new sheriff and deputy in Copper Gully." He stared at Sam waiting for his response.

Sam looked taken aback, but only for a moment. Finally he shook his head and let out a breath.

"Nothing those two do should surprise me anymore," he said, "but how did it happen?"

Lupo chewed beans, swallowed and sipped coffee.

"The Pettigos control everything in Copper Gully," he said. "So it must have been by their authority."

"Nobody in their right mind would pin badges on those two wild-eyed squirrels," Sam said.

"Somebody *has*," said Lupo. "If I were to guess, I would say it was Dale Pettigo who did it. But it doesn't matter which one. Bellibar and Siebert were riding to Lookout Hill. My hunch is that they could not wait to betray the Pettigos and join the Cadys."

"I'd say your hunch is right," Sam replied.

"I have observed Pettigo-American Mining Company very closely these past weeks, Ranger," said Lupo. "Every month when it is time for them to pay their miners, the Cadys begin sending men around looking for a weakness to exploit. With Bellibar and Siebert watching over the town and allying with the Cadys, this month will be the perfect time for them to strike."

Sam nodded, considering it, and sipped his coffee.

"This is why we ride into the gully tomorrow," he said.

"Then finish eating, and get rested," Sam said. "I'll put out this fire so we won't announce ourselves."

"You can put it out now," said Lupo. "I am like a wolf. I am used to eating by the light of the moon."

"So am I," Sam said. "It looks like we've both come to the right place." He scraped his boot back and forth across the small campfire until it turned from a glowing light to blackness on the ground. In the darkness, Lupo finished eating in silence and lay down on his blanket for the night.

The Ranger—with his bedroll facing out over the remaining lights of town—leaned back onto his saddle watching the distant darkness that lay along the trail leading down from Lookout Hill. When the moon moved on across the sky, he continued to watch, half dozing, until deep in the night he saw the flash of a match flare up and fall away in the darkness, leaving in its wake the glow of a burning cigar.

There it is, someone on the far trail. . . .

He homed in on the faint light of the cigar like a nighthawk, seeing it move steadily and silently along the trail as if floating freely in the black night air. When he'd convinced himself that nothing would disappear if he turned his eyes away from the light for a second, he stood up and stepped close enough to bat the side of his boot lightly against Lupo's leg.

"Easy John, wake up," he whispered, even though the distance between them and the burning cigar was great.

To his surprise, Lupo was not asleep.

"I see it," he said in the same lowered tone. He reached a hand up to the Ranger. Sam took it and helped him rise stiffly to his feet.

When Lupo leaned to pick up his saddle, Sam stooped down and picked it up for him.

"I am able to carry my end of things, Ranger," Lupo said.

"I know you are," Sam said, "but it's quicker for me to do it right now." He took up both of their saddles and carried them to the horses. "You wait here and keep an eye on our smoker," he added over his shoulder. "I'll get the horses ready."

Lupo nodded to himself, seeing the Ranger's reasoning. He picked up his rifle in the darkness and stood watching the burning red glow move along the far trail. When the Ranger returned a few minutes later, leading their horses behind him, he also looked over at the burning cigar.

"You know these high trails, Easy John," he said. "Get us up in front of them."

"We are headed there now, Ranger," he said, shoving his rifle down into its boot. "The longer this hombre smokes his cigar, the better for us," he added. "But it does not matter. We know they are there. We will find them along these hill trails, eh?"

Grabbing his saddle horn, Lupo swung himself up stiffly onto his horse. Once Sam saw Lupo was successfully atop his ride, Sam swung up into his own saddle and turned the big stallion to the trail. Lupo turned his horse and rode beside him.

At the head of a group of riders, Bert Cady turned in his saddle and looked back along the men moving forward quietly, single file on the narrow trail. Beside Bert, his brother, Fletcher, heard him growl and curse under his breath.

"This son of a bitch!" Bert hissed.

Fletcher turned quickly in his saddle and batted his eyes as if trying to believe them. As the long line of riders rounded a turn in the trail, Fletcher and Bert both saw the red glow of a cigar moving along behind the last men.

"I'm going to kill this idiot!" Bert growled, yanking his Colt from his holster.

Fletcher caught his brother's horse by its bridle and stopped him from storming toward the guilty man.

"Damn it, Bertrim, hold on," said Fletcher, keeping a firm grip as Bert Cady yanked on the reins. The horse neighed in protest. "Those two are our ticket up through Copper Gully."

"Not that cigar-smoking bastard," said Bert. He started to yank harder on his horse's reins, but he stopped as Fletcher sidled his horse over against his.

"Listen to me, Bertrim," Fletcher said in a firm, lowered tone, seeing that the men behind them were beginning to bunch up. "Kill them both if you want to. I'll even help you—"

"I don't need no help," Bert growled.

"I'm just saying," said Fletcher, "kill them both, only not now. Wait until we're divvying up Mexican gold ingots. Do you hear what I'm saying? First the gold, then the idiot. Don't let nothing keep us from getting that gold, not when we're this close." He paused, watched his brother settle down a little.

"Damn it, I know you're right," said Bert, cooling off. He looked Fletcher up and down in the moonlight and took a deep breath. "Let go of my cayuse, Fletch. I won't kill him."

"Are you sure, Bert?" Fletched asked.

"I've got it under control," Bert assured him. "Ride back with me if you'll feel better."

Fletcher raised a hand to the men nearest behind them.

"Everybody hold up right here," he said, turning behind his brother and riding back past the single line of men.

Seeing the Cady brothers riding quickly back toward him, Bobby Hugh Bellibar instinctively dropped a hand onto the butt of his holstered Colt. When they moved past him, he let out a breath of relief. But his relief ended when he saw Bert Cady snatch the cigar stub from Siebert's mouth, grind it to dry rubble between his gloved hands and let it fall to the ground.

"Hey, hombre, what the hell do you think you're doing?" said Siebert. "That was my only cigar!" He started to nudge his horse forward, but beside Bert Cady, Fletcher's Colt came up quick, cocked and pointed from less than four feet away.

"One more step, Siebert, and I'll burn you and your horse down right here and now," said Fletcher Cady, aiming down the length of his gun barrel.

Siebert stopped, but he didn't look concerned. A strange grin came to his face.

"Would you really, now?" he said.

"Bet on it," Fletcher said in a sharp tone. His finger was wrapped around the trigger; his thumb held the cocked hammer.

One quick raise of his thumb would do it. Yet Siebert seemed as if he couldn't care less.

"I'm not *betting* on it," he said. "In fact, if I were to bet, I'd say you're not about to let fly." He gave a dark chuckle. "If you get that upset about one damned cigar, imagine what a gunshot would do this close to Copper Gully. Hell, you'd start up a whole string of gunshots running straight up the Pettigos' front door."

Bert Cady couldn't stand it any longer. He jerked his own gun from his holster.

"I'm killing him—that's all there is to it!" he said.

"Don't do it, Bertrim. Damn it, we went through all this!" said Fletcher.

"The gold?" said Bert. "To hell with the gold! I'll take my chances on nobody hearing it. Plus, it's worth giving up the gold to get to kill this son of a bitch."

"*Gold?*" said Bellibar, staring at Fletcher and Bert in the moonlight.

Fletcher realized his brother's slip up and tried to fix it.

"Yeah, the *payroll* gold," he said. Reaching his free hand over and shoving Bert's gun barrel down. "Pettigo-American always pays its help in gold. Everybody knows that. Right, Bertrim?"

Some of the men had drifted back to watch; they looked at one another.

Bert caught himself and once again calmed down. He looked back and forth as he slid his Colt back into his holster.

"That's right. They pay in gold coin. I'm talking about the payroll gold," he said. "What the hell other gold would I be talking about?"

"None," Fletcher offered. "That's all the gold we're talking about."

But it was too late to straighten out what he'd said. The more they tried to cover it, the worse it was going to sound. Bellibar listened and watched, as did Siebert and the rest of the men.

Bert turned his horse toward Bellibar, who sat staring at him.

"Keep this monkey under control," he said, gesturing toward Siebert. Turning to Siebert, he said, "One more shine out of you, I won't even use a gun. I'll cut your damned heart out and feed it to you."

Siebert sat slouched in his saddle, his wrists crossed on his saddle horn. He waited until the Cadys rode away and the rest of the men fell back into line.

"Ouch...," he said quietly to Dellibar. "Maybe you best give me my gun back now, Bobby Hugh. The crowd's starting to get a little cross and edgy with me."

Jesus.... Bellibar shook his head in disgust, starting to wish he'd made sure Aces Siebert was dead the day he'd left him floating downstream.

"I told you, Copper Gully," Bellibar replied. "You'll get it then, and not a minute before."

They rode on in silence for the next hour and a half

until the line of riders stepped their horses onto Copper Gully's main street. Bellibar rode up ahead of the men and the Cady brothers and met the Russian as he stepped out of the adobe building, stuffing his shirttail into his trousers. His gun belt hung over his shoulder. Behind him, a plump, naked young woman ran out onto the boardwalk. She slowed long enough to wiggle into her thin gingham dress and raced away in the dark toward the tent cantina.

"Who you are, and why do you come here?" Cherzi called out before recognizing Bellibar in the grainy darkness.

"It's me, the sheriff," Belliber replied, riding in closer, seeing the shotgun waving back and forth in the Russian's hands. "Don't shoot," Bellibar added, raising his hands chest high. "These men are all with me . . . with *us*, that is."

"Oh," said Cherzi, looking back and forth among the faces of the Cadys and their men.

Bellibar stepped down from his saddle, walked up to the Russian and reached out for the shotgun.

"I'll take that, for safekeeping," he said.

Cherzi handed it over.

Seeing Bellibar had the shotgun and had things under control, Fletcher Cady stepped his horse forward and looked down at him.

"We'll water our horses and rest them for an hour," he said. He added in a lowered voice, "Then we're pushing straight up the gully to the far end."

Cherzi grinned watching the Cadys and their men turn their horses toward the livery barn.

When they were gone, Cherzi turned quickly to Bellibar.

"Newton Ridge and the half-red Indian fellow rode down to check on us," he said, sounding almost worried about it.

"Did they suspect anything?" Bellibar asked.

"I do not know," said Cherzi. "But I killed Ridge. Cold Foot is with us. He says he wants to ride with you, but I told him to see you about it."

"And where is he?" Bellibar asked, looking around the darkness.

"I don't know," said the Russian. "He's been gone since this afternoon."

"All right, then, forget him for now," Bellibar said, needing answers in a hurry before the Cadys returned. "Tell me about the mining yard and the buildings— how everything looks at Pettigo-American."

"Is big dirty place," Cherzi said. He shrugged. "There is livery barn, blacksmith shop, supply buildings—"

"Hold it," said Bellibar. "What's in the supply buildings?"

"Supplies," Cherzi said flatly

"I mean is there anything of importance? Have you been inside them?" Bellibar asked.

"Just tools, equipment," said Cherzi. "I have been in all except the one by the house, the one that is guarded."

Guarded! All right!

Bellibar stared at him for a moment, then said, "This guarded one you can't go in?"

"Nobody can except the guards and Denver Jennings," said Cherzi.

"So you have no idea what's inside it?" Bellibar asked.

"Is wagon filled with relics," said Cherzi. "Is no secret. Old man Pettigo tells everybody that's what's in there."

"I bet he does." Bellibar grinned, getting suspicious. He wasn't certain what this all meant, but ever since Bert had made his slip of the tongue, everything Bellibar thought of now had a shiny yellow sparkle to it.

"Relics," said Cherzi. He shook his head in disgust. "Who cares about old relics? The Mexican miners don't care. None of us mercenaries care."

"That's what I say, who cares about relics?" Bellibar repeated. *And yet here's a man, Edgar Pettigo, who keeps a wagonload of them under guard,* he thought to himself.

He held the shotgun out to Cherzi.

"Are you sober enough to ride and handle a gun?" he asked.

"Russian always sober enough to ride and handle gun," Cherzi said with an uptilt of his chin.

"Then get your horse and get ready to ride, Cherzi," Bellibar said. "We're hitting Pettigo-American."

"Ah, the big payroll!" Cherzi said, a gleam coming into his eyes.

"Yeah, the big payroll," said Bellibar, "maybe even bigger than we think."

"What?" Cherzi asked.

"Never mind," said Bellibar. "When we get inside there, make sure you stick close to me." Bellibar wasn't sure what to expect, but if it was worth Pettigo guarding, it was worth *him* stealing.

"I will. You got it, boss," said the excited Russian.

Chapter 20

———

In the grainy, moonlit darkness, the Ranger and Juan Lupo skirted the outer edge of Copper Gully and looked onto the main street from a dark alley. Having arrived shortly after the Cadys and their men, the two watched the stable boy hurry from the livery barn leading four freshly attended horses and deliver the animals back to their owners. Collecting his fee, the boy grabbed the reins to four more horses and hurried back to the barn to water and grain them.

Meanwhile, the gunmen sat sprawled along the boardwalk out in front of the new sheriff's office. At one end, the Cady bothers stood on the street leaning against a hitch rail. Beside them stood one of their top gunmen, a Montana outlaw named Sonny White, who, along with two other outlaws, had met them along the trail from Lookout Hill.

When the gunmen had arrived moments earlier, a few townsfolk had poked their heads out of doorways, and lamplight had swelled behind closed windows. But upon seeing the size of the group and the demeanor of its members, the townsfolk quickly ducked back inside, and windows once again turned dark.

"How many do you make it to be, Ranger?" Lupo asked, his voice lowered, unable to mask the pain radiating from his knife wounds.

"Upwards of twenty men," Sam replied in the same lowered voice beneath a gust of dusty night wind. As he spoke, his gaze shifted away from the moonlit street to something shadowy he thought he'd seen move farther back across the alley behind them.

"*Sí*, twenty sounds right," Lupo said. His eyes also went to the rear of the alley, but only for a moment.

"Did you see something back there, Easy John?" the Ranger asked him quietly.

"I thought I did," Lupo replied. "But the moonlight and wind plays tricks on the eye."

"Maybe," Sam said with little conviction, eyeing the darkness closer. His eyes were not in the habit of falling for tricks of moonlight or wind.

Even as they spoke, another gust of wind bellowed and fell, stirring dust, leaving it looming midair at the rear of the alley. Between flanking black shadows, the two saw a number of small winged creatures cut sharply through the slanted purple moonlight and career away on the night wind.

"Birds . . . bats perhaps," Lupo offered.

"Perhaps," Sam agreed, willing to let it go at that for the time being.

With no more on the matter, they turned back to the men and the horses on the dirt street.

"They could never have gathered here in this great

number without Bellibar being in with them," Lupo whispered. "If they could, they would have done so and robbed Pettigo-American long before now."

"Why would the Pettigos make a man like Bellibar sheriff, knowing they have so much riding on this place?"

"Even smart men do stupid things," Lupo said. "I have learned to not question *why* when opportunity presents itself, only to take advantage—to strike before anyone realizes they have made a mistake and they hurry to correct it."

"It never hurts to wonder why," said Sam.

"*Sí*, you are right," said Lupo, "unless wondering gets in the way of doing what must be done."

Sam gazed out onto the street and looked back and forth, seeing two of the Cadys' men step out and take up their horses' reins while the others remained resting along the boardwalk. One of the men carried a railroad lantern in his hand. The lantern had been fitted with a tin blackout shield that blocked half of the lantern's light, allowing it to only be seen clearly from one side at any great distance.

"These two are getting ready to ride on ahead," said Sam in a whisper.

"*Sí*, they are the ones who will silence the guards for the others, and for us as well," Lupo replied. "They are our key to getting inside. Let us hope they do a good job."

Sam and Lupo turned to their horses as the two men on the street mounted and rode off along the main street at a gallop.

"While they ride up the gully taking care of the

guards, we will flank them along the edge of the rocks," said Lupo, the two of them leading their horses quietly to the rear of the alley.

When they were out of the alley, they stepped up into their saddles in another gust of night wind. Sam drew his rifle from its boot and laid it across his lap. He watched Lupo climb stiffly up into his saddle and adjust himself as a thin dust devil rose and swirled and danced alongside them.

"The wind will help cover our sound," Lupo said, "even if it does keep the guards alert."

The two turned their horses to the same back trail they'd come in on, and rode away in silence as the dust devil loomed and swirled in place, as if watching them go.

On the street, Sonny White straightened quickly from against the hitch rail and turned toward the dark alley, his gun coming up hand, cocked, ready to fire.

"Who the hell's there?" he called out toward the alley. Wind kicking up dust and a scrap of debris at the alley's edge.

Beside him the Cady brothers turned as well, following his lead, their hands going to their gun butts, without drawing.

"Whoa, now, Sonny," said Fletcher Cady beside him. "Don't be firing that six-shooter."

"One shot and this all falls apart on us," Bert Cady joined in, standing on the other side of his brother.

"I heard a horse's hoof," said Sonny White, still staring into the blackness.

"Lower the gun, Sonny," said Fletcher. "You heard Bert. One damn gunshot and you'll hear a lot of horses' hooves—it'll be ours, taking us home empty handed."

"Sorry," said Sonny, lowering his gun, letting the hammer down, but keeping it in hand. "I know I heard a hoof back in there somewhere," he added.

"You might've heard this wind," said Fletcher Cady. "These Mexican west winds sound like all sorts of things."

"Fletcher, you're the boss," Sonny White said, "but I've heard Mexican *wind*, and I've heard *hooves*. I know the difference."

Fletcher just stared at him in the moonlight until White let out a breath, lowered his gun into his holster and leaned back against the hitch rail.

"Mexican west wind it is," he said in submission. In a lowered voice he said, "Now, you were talking about these saddle tramps you want me to kill . . . ?"

"That's them down there," Fletcher said, nodding without pointing toward Bellibar and Siebert, who sat on the far end of the row of gunmen. "Keep it to yourself. As soon as we get inside Pettigo-American Mining, kill them both."

"Will do," said White. "Mind if I tell Matt and Jarvis about it, though?"

"Why's that?" Fletcher Cady said bluntly. "Can't you do it by yourself?"

"I can do it by myself well enough," said White. "But you know us three always do everything like that together." He shrugged. "Hell, they don't call us the three musketeers for nothing."

"I never heard anybody call the three of you that," said Fletcher.

"Well, they do," said White, a little edginess coming into his voice. "Anyway, that's the way the three of us work."

Fletcher let out a patient breath, looked at his brother, then back at Sonny White.

"All right, tell Matt and Jarvis," he said, "but make sure none of yas tell anybody else."

"We won't," said White, "you've got my word." He paused, then asked, "Who are these two? What'd they do to get your bark on so tight?"

"Bobby Hugh Bellibar and Hot Aces Siebert," said Fletcher Cady.

"I've heard of them." White nodded. "Some awfully bad hombres as I recollect."

"Any problem killing these *awfully bad hombres* for me?" Fletcher asked.

"No, not at all," said White. "You can count them dead and done with, soon as we get inside the mines."

The Ranger and Lupo caught up to the two riders easily, but instead of getting too close, they pulled away from them. Riding a hundred yards up to their left, they flanked the gunmen from along a narrow game path that wound its way through rock along the steep, jagged slope. Beneath them, the two forward riders kept out of the pale moonlight and moved along quietly in the black shadows below the hill line.

At a point on the game path that Lupo seemed to recognize even in the darkness, he brought his horse to a halt and held a hand back toward the Ranger to stop him.

"Out there is the first guard outpost," he whispered. "The forward riders will slip out and kill the guard. Watch for the lantern signaling back to the Cadys when they are finished. By now the rest of the gunmen are moving forward through the gully."

The two waited in silence, staring into the darkness below. After a tense moment they both saw a light that appeared to rise from the ground and make one single streak across the dark like a small comet, then disappear.

"Cadys' men have just shed the first blood of Pettigo's mercenaries," Lupo said with a breath of relief. "One guard post down, three more to go," he added. "Let us hope the next three will go as smoothly as this one."

"The Cadys put some thought into this," Sam noted, knowing that below them the two gunmen had just killed a man, maybe two, and were now slipping back across the gully floor, back out of the moonlight to the cover of the black hill line shadows below.

"As have I, Ranger," Lupo assured him.

The two turned their horses in the dark and rode on.

When Lupo stopped again, the Ranger stopped with him. They both turned in their saddles without either of them saying a word and watched in silence until once again the streak of the lantern announced its blood success.

As soon as the glowing signal lantern made its arch, Lupo held up two gloved fingers in the darkness for the Ranger to see.

"Two down . . . two to go," he said.

In the rising wind, they nudged their horses forward and rode on. But this time, Sam noted that Lupo began to lead them gradually higher up the gully wall. An hour later when they once again stopped at a point Lupo had plotted out beforehand, they waited until they saw the arch of the signal lantern for the third time.

"Three down . . . one to go," Lupo said.

This time, before the Mexican agent had time to turn his horse and ride on, he saw Sam sitting atop his stallion staring squarely at him, his rifle up from his lap, pointed loosely in Lupo's direction.

"Want to tell me why we've been headed up farther from the gully the past hour or so?" he said coolly.

"Ah," said Lupo, as if to keep the conversation casual, "I knew this change in direction would not go unnoticed by you. I knew you would be asking before long."

Sam could tell Lupo was stalling, wanting to put him off.

"I *am* asking," Sam said bluntly, cocking the rifle, making sure Lupo heard it. "Now start answering."

"It is not what you think, Ranger," Lupo said. "It is not some sort of double cross."

"Then what is it?" Sam asked, flatly.

"It is . . . a change of plans," Lupo said after a moment of hesitance.

"A change in plans, this late in the game?" Sam said.

"*Sí*," Lupo said, "I'm afraid so. I knew that two men could not get inside Pettigo-American from the gully floor. It will take a force the size of the Cadys', and even they will have a hard fight. Do you understand?"

Sam didn't answer; he only stared.

"So I planned on us going around to a spot on the hillside that I scouted out long ago. While the Pettigos prepare to be attacked from the valley floor, we will be taking the gold and slipping out with it right under their noses."

"While the Pettigos are preparing for an attack?" Sam said. "So far they haven't heard a sound. They have no idea anybody's coming."

"I know," said Lupo. His hand came up from his lap, holding his Big Walker Colt in the air. Sam almost shot him before he saw the gun was not meant for him. Lupo fired the gun three times, shattering the quietness of the night. "Now they do," he added.

Even as Lupo lowered the Colt, they saw three rifle shots streak upward from the gully floor. A second passed, and then streaks of gunfire from the Cadys' forward riders erupted in the darkness. The fight had started. Sam knew it would prove to be a long and bloody one if the Cadys were intent on robbing Pettigo-America Mining.

"Come on," said Lupo, nudging his horse forward, "we don't want to get hit by a stray bullet. There is still much to do tonight."

Sam nudged Black Pot along behind him, but he kept his rifle ready as they headed farther upward away from the gully floor.

"Keep talking," he said to Lupo. "If I don't like what I hear, I'll turn around and ride out. I can take up Bellibar and Siebert's trail when the dust settles, if they're still alive."

"You would leave me," said Lupo, "after agreeing to help me recover my country's gold?"

"As far as I'm concerned, when you changed the plan without telling me, I stopped owing you a thing," Sam said.

"Ah, but I did not change the plan, Ranger," Lupo said. "This was my plan all along."

"You know what I mean, Easy John," said Sam. "Don't mince words with me, or I'll cut out this minute."

"All right, Ranger," said Lupo, "you must forgive me. In my business, trust is a hard thing to establish. I could not tell you my entire plan until I knew things were under way—until I saw I could trust you completely."

"Or until I saw you were misleading me," Sam added.

"Okay, this is true, Ranger," Lupo admitted. "But what is done is done. Now we must go on with our mission."

"Tell me about this spot you scouted out on the hillside," Sam said. "How do we get in from there?"

"Instead of trying to breech the big iron gates that protect the front of Pettigo-American Mining," Lupo said, "I have arranged for us to have ropes waiting for us. We will climb up and—"

"Hold it," said Sam, cutting him off. "You've *arranged*? Arranged how?"

"All right . . ." Lupo took a breath. "I have taken one of the mercenaries into my confidence," he said. "He will be watching for us. He will drop ropes for us. Once we are inside, everything else will go as planned.

While the Pettigos and the Cadys fight it out, we will take the wagon down the hidden tunnel back trail and disappear with it." He paused, then said, "Are you still with me, Ranger?"

Sam looked back at the gunfire streaking back and forth along the gully floor. The fighting would grow far worse before it was over. He knew he was straying far from his job of tracking down Bellibar and Siebert. But this was where the trail had led him.

"Is there anything else you haven't told me?" he asked, still staring down at the streaks of gunfire.

"No," said Lupo in a sincere voice, "there is nothing else. You must believe me. My intent is the same as before. I am only out to recapture my nation's stolen gold. Anyway, I did not lie to you. I only withheld part of the truth." He offered an apologetic smile. "You must forgive me. Sometimes I do it for good reason. Other times I do it only out of habit, eh?"

Sam considered it for a moment longer, his eyes studying the gun battle below, knowing that farther up the gully the alarm had been sounded. The men at Pettigo-American Mining would be armed and ready by now.

"No more tricks, no more *withholding the truth*, Easy John," he warned, turning his eyes form the gully floor and facing Lupo in the grainy darkness.

"I am not keeping anything else from you, Ranger, I swear to it on my nation's honor," said Lupo.

Sam looked at him for a moment, and then the two turned their horses together and rode away, upward along the thin, rocky game path.

Chapter 21

The gunfire on the gully floor had grown more intense by the time the Ranger and Lupo reached a high cliff on the left of the hilltop where Pettigo-American Mining stood. A half dozen of Pettigo's mercenaries camped at the first guard post had ridden out to meet the attackers head-on, while higher up inside the compound the other men steadied themselves for battle.

Along the high hillside, Sam and Lupo saw the streaks of gunfire split back and forth through the night like mad fireflies. When the two stopped at a dark point on the thin path, they looked up in time to see a rope flop down against the side of the rocky face of the cliff. As they stepped down from their horses, another rope flopped down and dangled in the darkness.

"I know what you are thinking," Lupo said. "You wonder how I knew to have two ropes waiting."

Sam didn't reply.

"I prepared for having someone to help me. Had I not met you along the trail, I would have recruited one of *Capitán* Fernando Goochero's *rurales.*" He paused, then added, "But I am glad it is you, a man I know I can depend on."

Sam gave no response. Instead he removed his sombrero and hooked its string around his saddle horn.

"What about our animals? Will they be safe here?" he said, watching the night wind lift strands of the horses' mane and tails.

"*Sí*, this is a good place for them," Lupo said. "The tunnel trail comes down not far from here. When we come down, we will get our horses and tie them behind the wagon." As he spoke, he took off his sombrero and hung it over his saddle horn. He busily rummaged among the rocks at the base of the cliff and pulled up a large canvas shoulder pack with PETTIGO-AMERICAN stenciled on it.

The dynamite, Sam told himself.

As if hearing the Ranger's thoughts, Lupo hefted the pack in his hands and ginned in the darkness.

"Enough *explosivos* to close the trail behind us forever if we wanted to," he said. He slipped his arms through the pack's shoulder straps and adjusted it up onto his back. He started to say more, but a strange-sounding birdcall from the darkness above them stopped him.

They both looked up two hundred feet where the blackness met the purple moonlight along the jagged upper edge of the cliff. A silhouette figure waved an arm back and forth at them.

"It is my inside man," Lupo said. He grabbed one of

the ropes and shook it hard in response to the man above them.

Sam looked down at his rifle in his hands.

"Don't worry, Ranger," said Lupo. "I have rifles and ammunition waiting for us up there."

Sam stepped over and shoved his rifle down into his saddle boot. He looped Black Pot's reins around a spur of rock and ran a hand down the stallion's side.

"I'll be back for you," he said under his breath. Then he turned to Lupo, who stood with rope in hand.

"Ready?" Lupo said.

Taking the rope dangling next to him, Sam said, "Let's go."

The two began their climb upward, hand over hand, each step searching for a toehold in the darkness. Off to their right on the gully floor, gunfire exploded as the Cadys' gunmen pushed hard through the rock and brush toward the heavy iron gates protecting the mining company. While the battle raged, wind gusted and swirled and tugged at the Ranger and Lupo as if to remind them that they had entered a place where no men should be, there in the dark, clinging by rope to an unyielding terrain otherwise reserved for bats, nighthawks and lesser creatures of the night.

But as the gun battle continued, the two slowly, gradually forced themselves upward against heavy gravity to the cliff's edge and in turn fell over onto the ground. Being the first to reach the top, the Ranger scooted around quickly on his stomach, reached over the edge, grabbed Lupo by his shoulder pack and pulled him up.

"Gracias," Lupo gasped, throwing the pack straps off his shoulders and lying collapsed beside the cumbersome load.

"Who the hell is this?" someone standing above them demanded from Lupo.

Sam looked up the grainy moonlight and made out a silhouette pointing a rifle in his direction. But before Sam could even reply, Lupo reached out and shoved the rifle barrel away.

"It's none of your concern, Foley," Lupo growled. "He's with me. That is all you need to know."

"You're right, hombre," the man said. "It's none of my concern. I don't give a damn who he is, so long as you brought me the money you promised."

Lupo produced a leather pouch from inside his shirt and shook it. The muffled sound of large gold coins caused the gunman to smile in the darkness.

"Ah, that sounds sweeter than a maiden's whisper," the gunman said, reaching out for the pouch.

But Lupo pulled it back.

"Not so fast, my greedy amigo," he said. "Where are the rifles and the ammunition you promised?"

"Got them right here," the man said. "Winchester repeaters, fully loaded—bandoliers of ammunition in case you accidently left something standing." He gestured toward a bundle on the ground as he stepped over to it. Sam and Lupo followed close beside him.

"Check it out," Lupo said, picking up a rifle and handing it to the Ranger.

Sam levered a round into the rifle chamber and

hefted the gun, judging by the weight that it was fully loaded.

"This one's good," he said.

"Yes, sir, good as gold," said the gunman. He looked at Lupo and threw back a canvas cover on the ground. "Look what a few more gold coins can buy for you."

Lupo and the Ranger looked down in the pale moonlight at a row of French hand grenades. Lupo picked one up and turned in his hand.

"If I do not buy these, what will you do with them?" Lupo asked. Sam listened, knowing it to be a strategic question.

The gunman shrugged and said, "Then I'll have to slip them back into the arsenal shed before I leave."

"And if I purchase these," Lupo said, "exactly how many does that leave for the Pettigos to use against us?"

Even more strategic, Sam thought.

The gunman gave a dark chuckle and said, "Exactly *none.*"

"I see," said Lupo. He reached back inside his shirt and brought out more gold coins.

"You are damn wise for a Mexican," the man said, taking a stack of gold coins from Lupo and dropping them into the pouch in his hand.

Lupo let the slur pass him by.

"Here's a cigar for the both of yas, to light them with," the man said.

Lupo took the cigars, passed one to Sam and stuck the other in his shirt pocket. He began handing the grenades to Sam, who stuffed them into Lupo's shoulder pack.

"Tell me, how is it you were able to get these grenades out of the arsenal?" Lupo asked. "Does Pettigo trust you that much?"

"Damned right he trusts me," said the gunman. "He knows I would never betray him. I gave him my word," he chuckled. "Leastwise, I never betrayed him until the right price came along."

"I understand," Lupo said, standing, dusting his hands together.

"Now, if we're all finished, gentlemen," the gunman said, "I'll just bid you both adieu, shimmy down one of these ropes, grab one of your horses and cut out." He tipped a battered derby hat.

Sam gave Lupo a look.

"Be careful you do not take the Appaloosa," Lupo said.

"No problem, you have my word," he said, still with a dark chuckle in his voice. He approached the dangling ropes.

Sam didn't trust him; he started forward to stop him. He wasn't going to take a chance on this man riding off on Black Pot. But before he could make a move, Lupo's left arm reached around the gunman's face from behind. The man let out a muffled cry as he suddenly rose onto his toes, his head trapped in the crook of Lupo's forearm.

Lupo jerked back hard on the gunman. The man's hands clutched Lupo's forearm, but only for a second. Then he turned loose, his arms flailing uselessly at his sides as Lupo sank his big boot knife deeper into his back, the tip of it slicing through his heart.

Sam watched as Lupo rounded the blade, making sure the gunman was dead.

Finally Lupo gave the man a shove off the big blade and let him topple to the ground. He stooped and wiped the blade back and forth, cleaning off the blood on the man's shirt.

"Do not think harshly of me, Ranger," he said, taking back the leather pouch of gold. "After all, he was going to take your stallion."

"We don't know that for a fact," Sam said, even though the man had given every reason not to trust him.

"*Sí*, I think we *do* know that," said Lupo. He stepped over to the ropes with the big knife in hand and sliced each rope, making sure every trace of them fell away into the darkness. "He betrayed Pettigo, the man he gave his word to. Then he gave us his word. So what is his word good for?" Lupo shrugged. "He would have stolen your stallion just to show you he could."

Sam didn't reply, although he had to admit, Lupo was most likely correct.

"Anyway, he is dead," said Lupo philosophically. "There is nothing to be said or done about it now." He saw Sam look toward the place where he'd cut the two ropes. "We no longer needed them," Lupo said as if to still any questions Sam might have about his cutting the ropes. "With the ropes gone, we know our animals are safe, and nobody knows we are here."

From the direction of the gully floor, the gunfire had grown louder, closer. Return gunfire from the front wall and the iron gates of the mining compound had also intensified. So had the Mexican west wind.

Lupo stooped, picked up the shoulder pack and swung it up onto his shoulder.

"Come with me, Ranger. Let us complete this mission," he said quietly. "First to the livery barn for the strongest horses we can find. Then on to the gold."

Inside the Pettigo hacienda, Edgar Randolph Pettigo and his son, Dale, stood watching the darkness through the front window while Denver Jennings and three other mercenaries busily reloaded rifles from an open crate of ammunition sitting on the floor behind them. They saw flashes of gunfire outside coming from the wall and front gates, which sat on a lower terrace than their sprawling home.

"If I find out that idiot Hughes has fallen in with the Cadys, I'll kill him with my bare hands, so help me God!" said Dale, pounding a fist into the palm of his hand.

Pettigo looked at his son as he levered a bullet into his rifle chamber.

"Hell yes, he fell in with them!" he exclaimed. "If he wasn't already with them to start. Instead of warning you they were coming, he let them slip right through."

"I'll kill him— I'll kill him— I'll *kill him!*" Dale Pettigo ranted.

"Save all that anger for the gunmen at the front gates," said his father. "There's plenty of killing to be done."

"I'll do my share, Father," said Dale. "You can rest assured. It's just that I feel like such a fool, making that saddle tramp a sheriff, putting our interests into his hands."

"None of this comes as a surprise," said E. R. Pettigo. "The Cadys have been out to rob us ever since they took over Lookout Hill. You said this would round the Cadys' gunmen all together instead of us hunting them down every month. You were right in that regard." He gestured toward the darkness, the streaks of gunfire coming from the long, wide gully.

"Yes, in that regard I was right," said Dale, "but I take little comfort in that fact alone—"

Edgar Pettigo cut his son short, turning to Denver Jennings and the other mercenaries.

"Men," he said, "here is what you've been getting paid for all these weeks. From the sound of it, all the Lookout Hill boys are gathered here. Go to the wall and pass the word along—*kill them all and be done with it.*"

"You heard E.R.," Denver Jennings said to the men, throwing a bandolier of bullets over his shoulder. "Let's go kill these sons a' bitches."

He turned and fell in beside Edgar Pettigo and his son as the two walked across the tile floor, through the hacienda and out the front door.

"How many men are guarding my artifacts, Denver?" the senior Pettigo asked, glancing toward the guarded barn as they walked along across the yard toward the fighting on the terraced level below.

"Six, sir," said Denver, "same as always." He gave Dale Pettigo a passing glance, knowing he had no idea there was gold in the wide building so close to the house. "Should I double the guards?" he asked quietly.

Not wanting to raise suspicion, Edgar Pettigo replied

without hesitancy, "No, Denver, on the contrary. Pull away four of the guards and bring them to the front wall where they're needed. If they don't make it inside the compound, they can't possibly threaten my Indian artifacts, now, can they?"

"No, sir, you are absolutely right—they can't. I'll go bring four of the guards along," said Denver Jennings, cutting away from the Pettigos and hurrying over to the building housing the gold.

When Jennings pounded on the door, a guard opened it and looked beyond Jennings toward the front of the compound where the gunfire roared.

"Have they broken through yet?" asked rough-faced Dodge Peterson.

"What? No!" said Jennings, sounding agitated. "And they're not going to, not as long as we're here." He stepped around Peterson and saw the other five men spread out around the wagon. The guards took a step closer, rifles in hand.

"I don't feel right standing here guarding a damn wagonload of beads and broken bowls, Denver," said Gus Quinn. "All the fighting's going on out front."

"This is your lucky day, Gus," said Jennings. "E.R. just sent me to get four of yas and get to the front wall." He looked at the other men. "Tuell and Cravens, you both stay here, keep guarding. The rest of yas follow me." He turned and walked out of the building at a brisk pace. The men looked at one another, then fell in and hurried along behind him.

Gus Quinn looked back to the remaining guards with

a smug grin and called back, "Don't worry, fellows. We'll keep these bad ol' Lookout Hill boys from getting in here, scaring the two of you."

"Son of a bitch," Cravens said under his breath as the door closed behind the hurrying men. "I could've stayed in Missouri and been a *guard* if I felt like it."

"I hear you. I didn't turn mercenary just to hide from a fight," said Tuell.

The two looked at each other, and then Tuell let out a breath and said, "What's these Indian artifacts look like anyways?"

"I don't know," said Cravens. "Pettigo keeps six men here so they'll all keep one another out, same as they guard against outside thieves. That's why nobody's ever seen this junk."

Tuell gave a sneaky grin.

"Until *now*," he said. "Are you with me?"

Cravens looked all around, as if making sure they weren't being watched.

"Hell yes," he said. "Why not? It beats standing here squeezing a rifle all night." He spit and said, "Anybody ever finds out, we'll know for sure who told."

"Yeah, well, you go watch out front, in case anybody comes along," said Tuell, reaching for a burning lantern hanging on the wall. "I'll pull us out a crate and open it."

Chapter 22

As Cravens stood staring out through the narrowly cracked front door, Tuell dropped the freight wagon's tailgate and set the glowing lantern on it. He grabbed a crate and dragged it back and dropped it onto the gate. With a pry bar he'd picked up from a tool table, he loosened the plank top and slid it aside. He picked up the lantern, held it in closer and stared down blankly into the crate.

"Talk to me, Tuell," Cravens called out in a lowered voice. "What have we got in there?" He half turned and looked back from his spot at the door.

"Just what we expected," said Tuell, sounding disappointed, "a bunch of beads, some arrowheads, a couple of tomahawks. . . ." He slid the lid back on the crate and shook his head. "This was nothing but a waste of time."

"Try another one," Cravens called back to him. "Maybe you'll find a dried squaw or something."

"A dried squaw . . . ?" Tuell gave him a glance around the back corner of the wagon.

"Yeah," said Cravens, "the Spaniards used to tan Injuns just like tanning a hawk or a bear."

"Where'd you hear something like that?" Tuell asked.

"I didn't have to *hear* it anywhere," Cravens whispered in a sharp tone. "It's a fact."

"A fact . . ." Tuell shook his head with disgust, reached in and dragged another crate back to the tailgate. This one had been lying beneath the first one on the wagon bed. "Keep an eye out there," he added, hearing all the shooting coming from the front wall overlooking the gully.

With the pry bar, Tuell loosened the nails on the second crate and slid it to the side. He held the lantern in closer, looked inside.

"It's the same as the other one," he called out without looking around toward Cravens. He grinned wryly. "No sign of any dried squaw for you."

Cravens didn't answer. Tuell reached out to pull the lid back in place, but he stopped when he saw the lantern glow set something aglitter down in the packing straw beneath the artifacts.

"Whoa, wait a minute, now," he said more to himself than to Cravens. "What have we here?" He hurriedly pushed the packing straw aside with his fingertips and picked up a one-by-two-inch gold ingot from a whole deep stack.

"Holy Toledo! Get back here and look at this, Cravens!" He turned the ingot in his hand, holding it close to the lantern light. "Dried squaw, my ass! This crate's full of gold."

Staring down wide-eyed at the ingot, he heard footsteps hurrying toward him. As he turned around grinning, he held the ingot in one hand and the lantern in his other. "This whole damn wagon might be full of go—!"

His words stopped short with a jolt as Lupo's knife sank into his heart.

"*Fácil, fácil, hombre,*" Lupo whispered, taking the lantern by its handle just as Tuell turned it loose and gasped for a breath that would never come to him. Using the knife as a guide, Lupo directed the dying man backward and seated him on the wagon tailgate for a moment. He looked around at the front door, where he had left Craven's body lying slumped against the wall. Sliding his knife from Tuell's chest, he wiped the blade on the dead man's shoulder. He walked to the rear of the building, unlocked the doors and threw them open.

Without a word, Sam led two teams of wagon horses inside and straight to the front of the wagon. Lupo walked back to the wagon's tailgate and gave Tuell's body a shove. As Tuell hit the dirt floor, Lupo picked up the ingot and pitched it back into the crate. He gave the crate a quick glance. Seeing the stacks of ingots beneath the straw, he slid the lid on and hammered it down with the handle end of his big knife.

As Lupo restacked the two crates and closed the tailgate, Sam busily hitched the horses to the wagon.

"Ready when you are," Sam called out in a hushed tone.

Lupo took a deep breath in preparation. He walked alongside the wagon and looked up at the Ranger.

Sam sat in the driver's seat ready to go, the thick sets of reins in hand, both his rifles and Lupo's leaning in the wagon beside him.

"Throw the doors open and climb on," Sam said down to him.

"In a moment, Ranger," Lupo said with calm deliberation. "First, please hand me my rifle." He reached a hand up.

Sam started to reach for the rifle to hand it down to him, but he caught himself.

"Why?" he asked pointedly.

Lupo lowered his hand and said, "Because I have something that I must say."

"And you'll need your rifle to say it?" Sam deftly moved all the reins to his left hand; his right hand drifted down to the Colt on his hip.

"I hope I will not need it," said Lupo.

"I hope you won't either." Sam stared at him

"I'm afraid I have lied to you, Ranger," said Lupo. Then he corrected himself quickly. "Well, not exactly *lied*. But not exactly been *honest* either."

"Out with it, Easy John," Sam said. "We don't have all night, if you want to get down the hidden back trail."

From the front wall the gun battle raged.

"There is no hidden back trail, Ranger," Lupo said, spilling it all at once as if spitting something foul from his mouth. "That is what I lied about."

"All right. . . ." Sam nodded slightly. He raised his hand from his Colt and took the reins in both hands. "I was wondering when you were going to tell me."

"You—you knew there's no hidden trail down the back of the hillside?" said Lupo.

"I had a pretty good hunch there wasn't," Sam said, "leastwise not one built by the Spaniards that you could still run a wagon on. If there was, the Pettigos would most certainly know about it."

Lupo considered it in earnest.

"You knew, yet you climbed up here with me anyway?" Lupo said, surprised. "Even after I promised no more tricks or lies?"

"I figured if I didn't come with you, you'd try riding the wagon down alone, as determined as you are." Sam looked him up and down and added, "I couldn't see letting you get yourself killed."

"But it is for my country, Ranger," Lupo said. "You did not have to get involved."

"I am involved," said Sam.

"But the Matamoros Agreement says—"

Sam cut him off.

"I know what it says, but that's on paper, for the benefit of those in armchairs and oaken desks," Sam said. "The fact is, anything that happens to your country or mine, either one, affects us both. Whether we like each other or not, we're neighbors—our people better stand together if we all plan to stick here the next few hundred years."

"I don't know what to say, Ranger," said Lupo.

"I've said enough for the both of us," Sam replied wryly. "So, why don't you go blow that front gate and let's skin out of here?"

"The front gate?" said Lupo.

"That's what you had in mind, isn't it?" Sam asked. "Since you don't have a back trail down?"

"Ah!" Lupo said, raising a finger. "I lied about the back trail, but there is a side trail that will be much safer to ride down, at least to the gully floor." As he spoke the battle raged.

"Where is it?" Sam asked.

"It is a hundred yards west of the main gates." He picked up the shoulder pack that he had dropped onto the floor before killing Tuell, and swung it up onto his shoulder. "You will have no trouble finding it. Wait for my explosion, then follow the smoke. I will jump on as you come through." He reached his hand up again and asked, "Now, may I *please* have my rifle? There will be shooting. . . ."

"I don't see why not," Sam said, picking up the rifle and pitching it down to him. "*Buena suerte,*" he said.

"*Sí,* good luck to you as well," said Lupo, catching the rifle, heading for the rear door.

Sam hitched the reins around the long brake handle and stepped down from the wagon. Winchester in hand, he walked to the wide front doors and waited for Lupo's explosion before he would throw the doors open.

As soon as the Lookout Hill boys had fought their way up the gully and taken cover from Pettigo's riflemen above the wall and behind the iron gates, Bobby Hugh Bellibar turned to Hodding Siebert, who was lying on the ground beside him. Behind them they had hidden their horses inside the rocky wall of the gully and crawled forward on their bellies.

"Stealing is never supposed to be this hard," Bellibar commented in a serious tone, reloading his rifle. "If it was, nobody would go into it. I sure as hell wouldn't."

"You're speaking for me too," said Siebert. "What kind of rotten son of a bitch kills a man to keep him from stealing his money?"

"Only the very worst kind," said Bellibar, shaking his lowered head.

The two outlaws had fired along with the other gunmen until both of their rifles turned hot to the touch. A cloud of gray smoke loomed above them. As gunfire from the mining compound lulled for a moment and the Cady brothers signaled the Lookout Hill boys forward, Siebert let out a breath.

"Here we go. . . ." He sighed heavily. He started forward on his belly. But Bellibar stopped him, grabbing the back of his belt.

"What the hell are you doing?" Siebert said, looking around at Bellibar as he stopped. "Everybody's moving in. I don't want us to miss our cut."

"Settle down, Aces," said Bellibar. "The only cut we're apt to get from the Cadys is one across our throats. Now that we got them past Copper Gully, they're through with us, don't you know?"

"Oh? What are you saying?" said Siebert, looking at him in the darkness as the others moved forward taking new positions.

"What am I *saying*? Jesus, Aces, I just said it,"

Bellibar said, sounding a little put out with him. "They're going to let us fight as long as we can hold a gun. But the minute the smoke clears and it's time to split the take, they'll kill us deader than hell. Wouldn't *you* if you were the Cadys?" He stared away at the fighting a hundred yards in front of them.

Siebert shrugged and said, "Sure, why not?" after giving minimal thought to the matter.

Bellibar stared at him. All right, he decided, that was as much of an answer as he'd likely get.

"I think there's more to this than a payroll robbery," he said to Siebert. "I've thought it ever since Bert Cady mentioned gold."

"I wondered that myself," said Siebert. "Fletcher tried too hard to cover it up."

"Yes, right, exactly," said Bellibar, impressed that Siebert had read everything the same as he had. "So, here's what I think. While these men are rushing the place, getting shot to pieces for a damn payroll, you and I need to see if there's gold hidden somewhere—"

His words stopped short as they heard someone crawling toward them across the rough, rocky ground.

The two turned their guns toward the sound.

"Do not shoot at me," Cherzi whispered hoarsely, coming into sight.

"Damn it, Cherzi, where have you been?" Bellibar whispered. "We thought you'd gotten yourself killed back there!"

"No, not me," Cherzi said. "You said stick close to you, so I am doing that."

"I was getting ready to tell Aces here about the

wagon you said the Pettigos keep in a building beside their house."

"Yes, it is full of Indian things," said the Russian. Renewed gunfire arose at the iron gates and below the stone front wall.

"Right, *Indian things*," Bellibar repeated to Siebert with a sly grin. "I expect everybody far and wide these days is looking for *Indian things*." It didn't hurt to be friendly, he thought. He knew he would still most likely kill Siebert before all this was over—the Russian too for that matter. But for now he needed all the help he could get. If there was a wagonload of gold in there, he wanted it. If it turned out there was no gold . . . well, adios, *compañeros*. . . . *Estos tontos,* he told himself, looking back and forth between the two of them, still grinning.

"Then I say let's go get ourselves some *Indian things*," said Siebert. He rolled up onto his knees as gunfire streaked back and forth at the front wall of Pettigo-American Mining.

"Wait. Listen to me, Aces," said Bellibar. "We are going to get closer to the wall and lie low until the Cadys and their Lookout Hill boys blow open the gates. Once they do, we'll slip inside and go into business for ourselves."

"Sounds good," said Siebert.

"Me too," said the Russian.

The three of them rose, turning away from the fighting and moving at a crouch. They hurried to where their nervous horses stood waiting. Unhitching the animals, the three mounted and rode west of the fighting to lie low. But as they started diagonally toward the wall of the compound, a blast of dynamite lifted and twisted the large iron front gates off their hinges and sent metal and chunks of stone flying in every direction. They felt the heat of the blast and the sting of dirt and chipped stone from a hundred yards away. Their horses reared in panic. But the three held them in check.

"Good Lord!" Bellibar shouted as his horse touched back down beneath him. "There goes the gates!"

"What are we waiting for?" Siebert shouted. "Let's get through them—"

His words fell short beneath another blast, this far to their west along the wall. The spooked horses reared again.

"What the hell are these Cadys doing, blowing the whole damn place up?" shouted Siebert.

"I've got a feeling this is not the Cadys," said Bellibar, staring toward the second explosion as the dust and smoke loomed in a large jagged opening in the stone wall at the top of the gully.

"Then who the hell is it?" shouted Siebert as gunfire erupted at the iron gates.

Staring toward the gaping hole in the stone wall left by the second explosion, Bellibar saw a freight wagon roll out of the mining compound through flickering brush fire and settling debris and turn west sharply.

"I don't know, but we're going to find out," said Bellibar, nudging his horse forward as they watched the big wagon bounce along over blown-out chunks of stone and upturned dirt. "Cherzi," he called out to the Russian, "is that the wagon they keep under guard?"

Cherzi booted his horse up beside Bellibar and stared hard through windblown dust as the wagon rolled along, its canvas cargo cover flapping on the wind.

"I don't know . . . maybe," he said. "It's big like that wagon. It has a canvas cover—"

"Good enough, that's our huckleberry," Bellibar said. "Let's go. If it's *not* the wagon we want, whoever's driving will be more than happy to tell us where it is."

The three booted their horses and rode upward onto the steep rocky side of the gully, in pursuit, while at the destroyed iron gates, the gun battle raged.

Chapter 23

Even as Denver Jennings and the mercenaries fell back from the iron gates under heavy gunfire, they heard and saw the second explosion farther to the west. When Jennings spotted the big freight wagon going through the open wall, he looked all around for the Pettigos and cursed under his breath when he didn't see them. Bullets sliced through the air around Jennings, who grabbed Dodge Peterson by his shoulder as the gunman hurried by.

"Where're E.R. and Dale?" he shouted in Peterson's face above the fray.

"Over by the mine shack," Peterson shouted in reply. "E.R. took a bullet. They carried him there out of the fight."

"Jesus," said Jennings. He looked all around quickly. "Take some men. Get to the barn and get us some horses," he demanded.

"Horses? How many?" said Peterson.

"As many as you can get saddled and ready by the

time I get back," said Jennings. "I'm going to see about E.R. Then we're going after that wagon."

"After all that Indian junk?" Peterson asked, giving him a bemused look.

"E. R. Pettigo loves that *Indian junk*," Dodge said. "He's the boss. We're paid to do what suits him."

"All right," said Peterson, "I'm gone." The two turned and raced away in opposite directions. Dodge Peterson ran in a crouch toward the livery barn as bullets flew past him. He passed three mercenaries huddled down behind stacks of wooden ore crates and called out to them, "You three, come with me. Hurry it up."

In the opposite direction, Denver Jennings ran across a bullet-raked yard toward the mine shack Peterson had told him about, seeing an oil lamp glowing in a single rear window. As he drew near, he saw two men step out from around a corner of the shack with rifles up and pointed.

"It's me, Jennings. Don't shoot," he called out.

"Denver . . . ?" said the familiar voice of a mercenary named Herman Waite.

"Yeah, it's me, Herman," Jennings called out. "I heard E. R. got shot. How's he doing?"

"Not worth a damn," the second man cut in, a former Wyoming regulator named Sal Tucci.

Jennings slowed to a halt and looked at them.

"Sal's right," said Waite. "You want to see old man Pettigo with air in his chest, you best hurry."

Jennings turned, bounded across the low plank porch and flung open the front door. Two more gunmen moved toward him in the light of the oil lamp, their Colts coming up cocked and pointed at his chest.

"Lower them," Jennings demanded, hurrying on across the floor to a battered desk where Dale Pettigo had laid his father. The two mercenaries, Randall Blaine and Jake Jenner, followed suit and stepped back.

"Sorry, Denver," Blaine murmured, stepping over and closing the front door.

But Jennings didn't seem to hear him as he came to a halt and saw Dale look up at him, dropping a blood-soaked cloth he'd held pressed to his father's chest.

"He's—he's gone, Denver," Dale said in a broken voice. He patted his dead father's shoulder. "I know he would have wanted you here. He always thought of you like a part of our family."

"I always thought of him the same way, Dale," said Jennings, shaking his head slowly, looking down at E.R.'s blood-streaked face, his closed eyes, his parchmentlike forehead. "You too, Dale, as far as that goes."

Outside at the front wall and the destroyed gates, the battle continued in full rage.

"A time like this, we're going to stick together like family too, Denver," Dale Pettigo said. He lifted an arm and looped it over Jennings' shoulder. "This is not the time to mention it, but I'm going to see to it you don't get left out when it comes time to settle up his estate. He told me right before he died to make sure you get that favorite saddle of his."

A saddle . . . Jennings just looked at him. *A fucking saddle . . . ?*

He took a deep breath and calmed himself.

"Did he mention anything about the wagon, by any chance, his artifacts?" he said.

"He rambled something about it," Dale said, shaking his bowed head. "But nothing that made sense, I'm afraid. He seemed to think the wagon is made of stolen Mexican gold, or full of stolen Mexican gold, something like that. . . ."

"You don't say," Jennings said quietly, Dale Pettigo's arm up over his shoulder, making him steadily more uncomfortable. "The reason I mention it is that that wagon is headed out a hole in the wall right now, onto the side trail around the edge of the gully."

"No!" said Dale, dropping his arm from Jennings' shoulder. "Then we must get right after it! I won't have my father's artifacts stolen! I know how much they meant to him. He kept them guarded night and day."

This stupid son of a bitch. . . .

Jennings just stared at him again.

"I sent some men to the barn for horses," he said. "They'll be coming any minute." He took a step back. "What if there really was stolen Mexican gold on the wagon?"

"What do you mean *if there really was*?" Dale asked, giving him a curious downward look. "If it's *stolen* Mexican gold, I would be obligated to turn it over to the Mexican government, of course, wouldn't I, then?"

"Yes, I couldn't agree more," said Jennings.

"As it is, once we recover the artifacts, I'll see to it they go to some university museum, some historical trust perhaps."

"That's the spirit," said Jennings.

At the door, Randall Blaine and Jake Jenner stepped forward.

"Couldn't help overhearing you, Denver," said Blaine. "Want us to take the other two and go meet those horses, make sure they get here? It's gotten hot and heavy out there." He jerked a thumb toward the sound of the melee.

"Yes, do that, the both of you," said Jennings.

"And make sure they don't bring my roan," said Dale Pettigo. "I'll not risk getting that horse marked up. Just bring me one of the men's horses. Any one at all will do."

The two men looked at Dale Pettigo.

"You heard him," said Jennings, "get going. I want that wagon back worse than you can know."

As soon as the men were out of sight, Dale took out a handkerchief, blew his nose and collected himself in his grief.

"I'm going to be strong though this, Denver," he said. "And I'm asking you to be strong with me." He paused, took a breath and held his chest out. "Are you with me, Denver?"

"Without a doubt, I'm with you," Jennings said. Taking Dale by his forearms, he added, "Do me a favor, step over here by your father?"

"Of course," said Dale, letting the gunman usher him to his dead father's side. When he stopped, he faced Denver and said, "How's that?"

"That's fine," said Denver. "Now if you'll turn toward your father . . ."

"Certainly," said Dale, turning, taking a deep breath

and staring straight across his father's body at the rough plank wall. "This is sort of like taking a tintype, except we have no camera, of course "

His words were silenced by the explosion of Jennings' big Colt as it bucked in the gunman's hand. The bullet bored through the back of Dale Pettigo's head and splattered blood and brain on the wall. Dale fell across his father's chest, his arms swinging back and forth down the desk until they slowed gradually to a halt. Outside, the battle continued with fury.

Jennings stepped in closer; he looked down at the smoking bullet hole in the back of Dale's head as he opened his Colt and replaced the smoking empty cartridge shell with one from his gun belt. His eyes went from Dale's shattered skull to the lifeless face of Edgar Randolph Pettigo. He leaned in slightly closer to the dead man.

"A fucking saddle?" he said aloud.

When the wagon came bouncing and swaying through the gaping hole in the stone wall, the Ranger stood half-crouched at the driver's seat, the reins in his hands. Dust and debris still swirling and settling around him. He hadn't stopped the wagon, only slowed it enough for Lupo to throw his shoulder pack over onto the seat and jump up beside it. He clenched a lit cigar between his teeth.

"Keep rolling, Ranger!" he'd said, already picking up his rifle from the floorboard. He'd searched the darkness behind him while brush fire danced here and there from the dynamite blast.

Beside him, Sam glanced down, seeing him clutching his side wound with his free hand.

"How are you holding up?" he'd asked above the sound of the four horses and the bumping, squeaking wagon.

"I'm good . . . Keep rolling!" Lupo said firmly, struggling with pain in his lower side.

The Ranger nodded, slapped the long end of the reins to the rear horses' rumps and they rolled on.

When they'd gone three hundred yards flanking around the gully just beneath the rim, they came to a slender, steep trail that cut downhill long and winding until it spilled onto a narrow stretch of flatlands.

"Stop here," Lupo said suddenly, looking all around in the moonlight.

Sam leaned back, the reins in one hand; at the same time he pulled back hard on the long wooden brake lever.

As the wagon bumped and groaned to a halt, Lupo jumped down from the seat and reached for the shoulder pack. He looked around at a huge, land-stuck boulder surrounded by smaller boulders and rock, which held back a sloping hillside of dirt and scrub pine.

"This is where I blow the trail," he said, puffing on the cigar, stoking up the fire on its tip. He gestured a nod, directing the Ranger farther down around a turn in the trail. "I will do nothing until you are around the turn and out of range. Then I will light a long fuse. Wait for me there. I will have to climb around the side and down to you."

"I'll be there waiting," Sam said. Before reining the

wagon horses forward, he stood still, listened closely for a moment and said, "Riders coming. I hear their hoofbeats."

"*Sí*, then hurry, Ranger. Get around that turn," said Lupo. "I must get a long fuse prepared." He reached out and slapped a hand on the wagon horse's rump just as the Ranger gave them the end of the reins and sent them forward with a jolt.

As he watched the Ranger and wagon speed away down the rocky trail, Lupo gripped his wounded side with his free hand for a moment and squeezed his eyes shut against the pain. He felt warm blood seep from the sticky bandage and run between his fingers. Running his hand down the front of his thigh, he felt where the warm blood had turned clammy cold in the night air. He started to sway but stopped himself.

You have no time to die, Easy John, he told himself. He adjusted the pack on his right shoulder and walked up into the rocks. He circled around the gigantic land-stuck boulder, dropped his pack at his feet, then kneeled and scraped out a hole in the dirt between the large monolith and another massive boulder leaning over against it. As he pulled bundle after bundle of tri-sticks of dynamite from the pack and burrowed them deep back into the hole, he heard the beat of horses' hooves grow more distinct, coming down the trail behind him.

With his smoking cigar between his teeth and a thick coil of fuse in his hand, he hefted the shoulder pack onto his back. He walked backward, stooped, uncoiling the long fuse, laying it out around the large boulder until he reached the top, and dropped flat as the riders came into sight in the pale moonlight. From atop the huge boulder, he looked down on the trail below. Three riders moved their horses along the trail at a walk, one of them leaning deep, staring intently at the wagon tracks in the dirt.

These were not the riders he heard, Lupo told himself. The sound he heard was still coming—many horses, farther back on the trail, coming at a thundering pace. He watched the dark silhouettes below come to a halt and look back along the trail as if hearing the same thing he heard. He had to hurry! Everything depended on him blowing up the trail, putting thousands of tons of rock and dirt between these men and his nation's gold.

"*Sante Madre,*" he whispered, crossing himself for the first time in as long as he could remember. He glanced around as if to make sure no one had seen him. Then he puffed his cigar up into a fiery glow. Sticking the end of his cigar to the end of the long fuse, he dropped the fuze sizzling onto the boulder, backed away and disappeared onto the rock gully wall.

Chapter 24

On the narrow trail beneath the boulder, Hodding Siebert turned to Bellibar and the Russian with a curious look on his face. He'd caught a glimpse of a small black shadow streak across the purple sky above the trail and career away. From the nearby rock and a stand of scrub cedar came a faint chirping sound that died away as quickly as it had started.

"Did you see that?" he said.

Bellibar and Cherzi Persocovich gave each other a look. Bellibar turned a concerned glance back toward the sound of horses' hooves.

"We didn't see nothing, Aces," said Bellibar. "What was it?"

Siebert sounded agitated.

"If I knew what it was I wouldn't ask if you saw it," he said in a short tone, looking all around in the dark. "Did you hear it, then? It sounded like birds, or bats—hell, I don't know what it sounded like," he added, even more agitated.

"Settle down, Aces," Bellibar cautioned him. "You

starting to get spooked again. All we hear are horses, and they'll ride right down our shirts if we don't get out of here." He gathered his horse and booted it up into a fast pace down the rocky trail.

"Damn it to hell!" said Siebert, turning to the Russian as Bellibar rode away. "What Bobby Hugh can't understand is that I've been hexed."

"Hacked?" said Cherzi. He made a slight chopping gesture with his hand.

"No, damn it, *hexed*! You illiterate no-English-speaking son of a bitch!" Siebert shouted. "I've been hexed by both a witch and her demon mare. I can't shake myself loose of them!"

Cherzi stared blankly at him.

"Yes, is horses I hear too," he said in conclusion, turning his horse behind Bellibar and booting it into a run.

"Damn you and your Belleza *negra demonio* to hell, *bruja*!" Siebert shouted at the rock and scrub cedar. As his words echoed away across the yawning gully below, he stared at the rock and scrub with his hand on his Remington. But when no reply came, he cursed under his breath, feeling the ground beneath him tremble with the beat of horses' hooves.

"We're going to finish this thing! Mark my word, *bruja*!" he shouted, a raving madman railing mindlessly against the night. He saw the dark silhouettes of riders come into sight as he jerked his horse around and booted it into a hard run.

But down the trail, hearing Siebert bellow like a

lunatic, Bellibar had slid his horse to a sudden halt and jerked it around on the trail.

"For the love of God, what's that idiot doing now?" he'd said, looking wide-eyed and sidelong at the Russian, who'd slid his horse to a halt beside him.

"He is hacked," Cherzi said. He shrugged one shoulder. "A witch has hacked him . . . or her horse hacked him. I don't know." He shrugged again and shook his head.

Bellibar took a deep breath; he collected his restless horse beneath him.

"He's gone off again," he said, hearing the horses' hooves thundering closer down the trail. "Let's get him, Cherzi. Knock his head off with your rifle barrel if you have to."

The two raced back up the trail toward the land-stuck boulder, but halfway there, they met Siebert heading toward them at a run. As the three slid their horses to a halt and gathered in the middle of the trail, Siebert shouted, "Get going. They're right behind me!"

The Russian took a hard swipe at Siebert's head with his rifle barrel but missed. Siebert jerked his horse back and reached for his Remington. *What the hell?*

"Don't shoot, Aces!" shouted Bellibar. "I told him to do that if he had to. He misunderstood!"

But Siebert brought the Remington up anyway, cocked, leveled out at arm's length.

"Misunderstand *this*, you potato-wine-drinking son of a bitch!" he growled. His horse reared as he took aim. But before he could get a shot fired, the trail seemed to lift beneath them as the night turned a bright glowing orange-blue.

The trail hung suspended in air just long enough for men and horses to succumb to a feeling of weightlessness. Then, when it appeared gravity had given in to the earth's whim of rising skyward, the trail slammed back down, hard, as a scalding, debris-filled wind sent men and horses flipping, rolling, kicking and scrambling, sliding farther down the rocky trail.

Bellibar rolled over the side of the trail, but he managed to hold on to a jagged rock spur with both hands, knowing without looking that nothing lay beneath him but a two-hundred-foot fall into rock and spike-hard cedar tops.

Still on the trail, forty feet farther down it than where he'd been, Siebert stood up stunned and charred, smoke curling from his shoulders.

"That was jarring," he said to himself, dazed. He reached down near his feet, picked up his hat, slapped out flames licking atop the crown and placed it, still smoking, back on his head. Seeing Bellibar's hand clutching the rock spur, he walked over like a man in a trance, stooped down and dragged him up.

Farther down the trail, all three horses had risen from the dirt and stood shaking themselves off, smoke and dust looming about them. Higher up on the side of the gully, Cherzi staggered forward and wandered out of sight into a maze of rock.

Bellibar caught his breath, wiped a hand over his mouth and looked back and forth, badly rattled by the blast.

"Where's . . . the Russian?" he said.

"Howdy to you too," said Siebert, both men's hearing muffled beneath a loud deep ringing in their heads.

"Damn it, Aces, we've no time for mannerisms," said Bellibar. "Whoever blew this trail thinks we're on the other side of it. We've got to ride the freight wagon down, strike while they think we're dead."

"Suits me," said Siebert, rising to his feet, not completely sure what Bellibar had said. "I saw the Russian walking off up there." He gestured upward farther onto the gully wall.

"Help me up, let's get going," Bellibar said loudly, unable to gauge the volume of his voice.

Siebert reached down and pulled him to his feet. Turning, they staggered down the trail toward the three horses.

From atop a broad, flat-top rock above the trail, higher on the gully wall, Lupo lay staring down at the two ragged gunmen as they staggered off toward their horses. One hand gripping his bleeding side, his rifle lying close beside him, he let out a breath and shook his head. Somehow these two and another one had managed to get past the big boulder before the blast sent it tumbling down, tons of pent-up dirt and rock spilling, closing the trail behind it.

Lupo looked off to his left beyond the looming veil of dust and smoke and saw the bodies of man and horse strewn out along the other side of the closed trail. Clearly the Pettigos' mercenaries had caught the brunt of the blast head-on in their attempt to ride down the wagon of gold.

Greedy fools and gold. What can one say?

He still had no time to lose, he cautioned himself, puffing on the cigar still burning in his lips. With luck, he and the Ranger would ride down and through the long gully before the Lookout Hill boys or anyone else following them could circle around the mining compound and get back on their trail. There were dozens of smaller trails to choose from leading in every direction.

Rising onto his knees, he gave a last glance toward the dead, made the sign of the cross again—thanking a God in whom he had long since stopped believing? *Perhaps . . .* , he thought, offering no further apology on the matter.

His was not a life of perfection, nor was he a man afforded by his nature to admit to any divine intervention, for the good or the bad. He rode as bold men ride . . . on whatever luck the saints abide.

The Ranger would understand that, he thought with a thin smile, feeling woozy from his loss of blood. Gripping his wet side, the pack weighing heavy on his shoulder, he whispered, "Someday, faith. For now, only the promise of it. . . ."

He rose to his feet, adjusted the shoulder pack and readied to leave. But as he turned, he jolted to a halt as a smell of burned hair filled his nostrils and two vise-like hands clutched his throat in a death grip. Lupo's cigar fell from his lips and landed at his feet.

"Why you try to kill this poor boy?" Cherzi said, his clothes smoking, some parts of it rekindling into small flames on the gusting wind. His eyebrows, lashes and hair were blackened curly stubs; his ears resembled crisp, overfried pork rinds. The whites of his wide eyes shone bloodred.

Lupo thrashed, trying to fight but weakened by his wounds. His heavy pack fell from his shoulder and spilled onto the rock. Hand grenades rolled out like lopsided apples. A small oak-handled pickax was among the strewn contents. Lupo caught a watery glimpse of the pick handle as he sank to the ground. He pounded both fists against the Russian, but did no good for himself. He struggled for his gun across his belly, but Cherzi turned one hand loose from his throat and knocked the gun down from his hand. It hit the rock and fired a wild shot that echoed across the gully floor.

"Now you die, Mexican," Cherzi said in his face.

The Russian put his hands back around Lupo's throat for a tight, finishing squeeze. Lupo felt the world blackening around him. The Russian raised him from the ground with both hands and slammed him down on his back atop the flat rock surface. Lupo's cigar flew from his mouth. He lay stretched out in a way that made it impossible to grab his boot knife, and his rifle was out of reach. His hand swept among the spilled contents of the shoulder pack, searching frantically for the pick handle, for his big Colt. *Anything!* But instead he grasped one of the round iron French grenades. It would have to do.

He made a wide swing and struck the Russian full on his jaw, sending him sprawling backward on the flat rock. Gasping for breath, Lupo struggled to rise onto his feet, knowing the Russian would be back upon him any second. But he only made it onto his knees, his hand reaching for his boot knife as the Russian shook off the blow to his jaw, staggered upward and lunged back toward him.

No time to grab the knife from his boot, Lupo threw his empty hand up to protect himself. But as he did so he fell back beneath the strong Russian. He glimpsed the burning cigar on the ground beside him. Without even thinking, he made one desperate stab at the tip of the glowing cigar with the short fuse sticking out of the hand grenade.

To his amazement he heard the sputter and sizzle of the fuse catching fire. So did Cherzi.

"Huh?" The Russian, crouched atop him, looked at the sizzling grenade in Lupo's hand. What was this?

Lupo wasted no time. His free hand reached out, grabbed the waist of Cherzi's trousers and yanked them forward. The Russian's wide suspenders stretched out, allowing the Mexican to drop the grenade down Cherzi's trousers and turn the suspenders loose. Cherzi grabbed himself and let out the bellow of a wild and tortured bull, the fuse sizzling and burning in the center of his crotch. The smell of more burned hair filled the air—this time bellowing up out of the Russian's buttoned trouser fly.

Cherzi gripped the smoking crotch of his trousers and ran screaming, zigzagging, unable to turn the grenade loose long enough to reach down in his trousers and remove it. The smell of burning flesh wafted with that of burning hair.

Lupo took the opportunity to grab the big Walker Colt lying beside him. Still gasping for breath, blood pouring down his wounded side, he needed both hands to raise, cock and aim the heavy revolver. But it made no difference; before he could fire at his wild, screaming target, Cherzi ran in a frenzy straight off the flat top of the rock, his legs still pumping as if running on air.

The grenade exploded in a large shower of fire and white-hot shrapnel just as the airborne gunman began his downward plunge. A black mist of blood, flesh and fragmented bone matter showered in every direction and rained down in the purple moonlight. Lupo shook his head as if to clear it. Using the tip of his gun barrel to help raise himself to his feet, he stood up and searched for his rifle and pack.

That was close.

Staggering in place, he rubbed his throat. Feeling the blood once again running down his leg from the knife wound in his side, he managed to pick up the rifle, stuff the scattered contents back into the shoulder pack and begin to drag it across the boulder. He couldn't stop now. There was still much to be done, he thought, even as he felt himself sink farther down with each attempted step. Wait. He wasn't going anywhere, he realized. . . .

He felt his hand release the rifle and the shoulder pack, and he found himself once again stretched out on the hard surface, flat on his back, staring up at an endless starlit heaven.

Chapter 25

—◆—

Silver morning wreathed the horizon as the Ranger stepped down from the large bareback horse he'd unhitched from the freight wagon and ridden back around the long turn in the trail. He'd waited as long as his lawman's dark curiosity would allow before turning back to investigate the single gunshot and see what was taking Lupo so long to meet him. He suspected the two particulars were closely related.

When he reached a spot where he noted the bloody mess, bits of cloth, torn flesh, half of a shredded boot lying scattered midtrail, he looked all around, then up the front of the blood-splattered rock. Having no idea who the gory mess had been, he turned the big horse by the single rope lead of a makeshift hackamore he'd fashioned around its muzzle and nudged the animal up a path around the side of the large rock.

A few yards up the steepening path, he stepped down quietly from the horse and led it the last few yards up around the base of the rock. He tied the animal's lead rope to a wiry sprig of scrub juniper and climbed up around the short back end of the rock, rifle in hand. Before pulling himself up the last few feet to the top of the rock, he stopped and listened intently for any sound above him. Hearing none, he climbed upward the few remaining feet. As soon as he stood up he tensed and raised his rifle, seeing Bobby Hugh Bellibar standing thirty feet across the rock in front of him, facing away, staring down at Juan Lupo, who lay unconscious at his feet.

Without turning to face the Ranger, Bellibar stood with his big Colt in his hand, hanging down at his side, his thumb over the hammer, ready to cock it.

"Howdy-do, lawman," he said almost amiably. "Glad you could make it. I'm just getting ready to turn your *compañero* here into Mexican stew." Smoke wafted around his head and shoulders from the same cigar Lupo had been smoking earlier.

Sam leaned to the side enough to see the French grenades lined up along both of Lupo's sides. A small pool of blood lay beneath his wound. He moved forward, one deliberate step at a time, until he'd closed the gap to fifteen feet between them.

"Where's Hodding Siebert?" he asked, coming right to the point.

"He's all over your horse's hooves," said Bellibar with a dark chuckle. "You just rode through his brains and belly down there."

Sam glanced all around, knowing better than to believe anything Bellibar told him.

"You're lying," said the Ranger, playing a hunch.

"Damn, you're good!" Bellibar said. He chuffed and

shook his head. "All right, I'm not going to lie. That's not Hot Aces all over the trail," he said. "But for your information, that puddle of coyote food down there was a poor Russian immigrant, and a damn good friend of mine named Cherzi Perso—covet . . . or *Perso-covich*." He shrugged, giving up. "Hell, something like that. Anyway, this damn Mex killed him."

"A good friend, huh?" Sam said, his rifle leveled at the center of Bellibar's back. He glanced around as he spoke, watching, listening, searching, getting his best feel of things.

"That's right, a damn good friend," said Bellibar, puffing Lupo's cigar. Sam saw smoke rise above his head and drift away on the dissipating west wind. "Look down from the front edge there. You can see most of his head and some strings of guts." He gestured a sidelong nod toward the front edge of the big rock. "Want to see?"

"Not particularly," said Sam, keeping his eyes on Bellibar, knowing how unpredictable he could be. "If he was your *good friend*, how come I never saw him all the time I was tracking you and Hodding Siebert?"

"Would you recognize him now if you had?" Bellibar said.

"I expect not," said Sam.

Bellibar paused and let out a breath. "All right, I'm not going to lie," he repeated. "He was no friend of mine. He was riding mercenary with the Pettigos until we came along—showed him the light, so to speak." He paused and then said, "That was you, then,

dogging us all that time. I knew there was somebody
back there . . . There most always is."

"Where's Hodding Siebert?" Sam asked again, more
firmly, staying on course.

"I expect he's right behind you, lawman," Bellibar
said, still without turning to face him. "Aces, what say
you?" he called out louder. "Have you got this law dog
collared and heeled?"

"You bet I do," said Siebert, standing behind the
Ranger at the edge of the rock, having climbed up
silently right behind him. "I'll go ahead and kill him
right now," he added, sounding anxious. He started to
cock his rifle hammer; Sam started to swing around
and fire. But Bellibar halted everything.

"Whoa, Aces!" he said. "Don't pull that trigger until
he tells us where he's hidden that wagon! What the hell
is wrong with you anyway?"

"You know damn well what's wrong with me!" said
Siebert. "I've got a lot on my mind." He looked all
around wide-eyed, fearfully. "I'm troubled by things!
Dark, ugly things, damn it! Things nobody understands unless they happen to you!"

"Jesus, Aces, don't start!" Bellibar warned him.
"Everybody behind us is either dead or too far away to
catch us. Don't go nuts on me now—we've about got
this thing done."

The Ranger listened closely; was this his opening?
He held the rifle up, ready to swing it in either direction,
and edged inches back, putting himself in a straighter
line between the two of them.

Bellibar half turned, facing Sam, the cigar glowing good and ready in his mouth. "You did hide that wagon somewhere down the trail, didn't you?"

"You know I did," said Sam, bluffing. "Blow up Juan Lupo there and you'll never see that wagon, leastwise not what was in it." He turned his next words to Siebert. "What kind of *dark, ugly things*?" he asked.

"None of your business, lawman," said Bellibar, trying to stop it, knowing how stone-crazy Siebert could get, left unchecked.

"I've had a hex put on me," said Siebert, ignoring Bellibar, his voice sounding shaky. "I'm hexed by both a *bruja* and her damn demon mare—"

"Shut up, Aces!" shouted Bellibar. "It's not his damn business! He's the law, remember? Shake it off! Get done with it."

"All right!" Siebert shouted. He shook his head in an attempt to clear it. Then he took a deep, calming breath and let it out.

"That's the way. That'll do it," said Bellibar, having been through this many times before. "Are you done with it?"

"Yeah, I'm done with it," Siebert said, his rifle still leveled at the Ranger in spite of his mental difficulty.

Sam watched, waited, ready to strike at just the right second.

Aces Siebert looked calmer now, more intent on killing him, Sam thought.

But just as it appeared that Aces Siebert had collected his mind and nerves and gotten them back under control, two small birds swooped down out of the morning haze and circled around him. The birds cheeped and screeched as if scolding him; and zipped in and out angrily, trying to light atop his singed and blackened hat.

"Get away from me!" Siebert screamed at the birds. His voice turned high-pitched, hysterical. Taking his left hand away from his rifle, he snatched his hat off and slapped wildly at the little birds.

Here it comes. . . .

Sam readied himself.

"Stop it, you idiot!" shouted Bellibar.

Seeing his chance, Sam took it as the two birds were suddenly joined by a third, a fourth.

Siebert screamed and slapped at them tearfully, breaking down, losing any concentration on what was at hand.

"Damn it to hell, Aces!" shouted Bellibar. He looked both stunned and enthralled as he witnessed some insane dance of man and bird atop a broad flat rock standing in the breaking sunlight on the morning sky. "Forget the damned bir—"

Instead of finishing his words, Bellibar jackknifed forward, bowed at the waist. He staggered back brokenly, his Colt clasped against his stomach with both hands as the Ranger's rifle shot resounded out across the gully below.

Sam levered another round into his rifle chamber and waited for only a split second to see if he would need it. He did.

Bellibar straightened enough to raise his Colt and cock it just as the second bullet from Sam's rifle tore through the center of his chest and sent a spray of blood and heart tissue streaking out across the flat rock behind him.

"Son of a . . . ," said Bellibar through a mouthful of warm, surging blood, dropping to his knees. He swayed for a second, then fell face-forward, his Colt flying from his hand.

Convinced that Bellibar was dead, Sam swung toward the screaming, hat-waving gunman. Siebert had dropped his rifle and begun running back and forth, swatting at what had grown to be a half dozen circling, careening, angry sparrows.

"I didn't kill her! I didn't kill her!" Siebert screamed. As Sam raised the rifle and took aim, Siebert tripped and tumbled off the rear edge of the rock and landed ten feet below on the path leading upward around the rock. Hearing him screaming as he hit the ground, Sam didn't go to the rear of the rock. Instead he ran to the front edge, raised his rifle to his shoulder and waited.

Siebert's screams resounded down around the rock to the trail below, mixed with the sound of the heated birds. He ran away along the rocky trail, still swatting, still screaming and cursing the birds. The screaming only stopped when the sound of the Ranger's rifle barked sharply and echoed along the gully walls.

Sam lowered his rifle a few inches, enough to see Siebert crawling along the middle of the trail, a gaping hole in the center of his back, a dark trail of blood smearing the ground behind him. Above Siebert, the birds still circled and chirped, only calmer now, seeming appeased—yet not completely.

Sam levered a fresh round into the rifle chamber, took aim and squeezed the trigger. Siebert's body flopped an inch off the ground, then settled into death, as still as the rocks around him.

Sam watched the covey of small birds zip away into the brush and rock and scrub growth on the gully walls. Somewhere down there he thought he saw something move, something large and black streaking among the rocks in the fresh morning light. Strange, he thought, but had he heard a horse down there, right after he'd put the kill shot through Siebert's back? He couldn't say for sure, but he thought he'd heard a long nickering sound, like laughter of some sort?

"Whoa, hold on," he murmured, cautioning himself.

Turning, he walked across the rock to Lupo, whose senses had been brought around by the chaos.

"I—I thought I heard . . . a horse down there," Lupo said, weak, half-conscious. Even as he spoke, he reached a hand up for the Ranger to help him to his feet.

But Sam took his hand and laid it back onto his chest.

"Lie still, Easy John," he said. "Let me get these grenades away from you." He took the grenades and stuffed them back into Lupo's shoulder pack.

"Is everybody dead . . . who should be dead?" Lupo asked.

"That depends on how you look at it," said the Ranger.

Lupo put a hand to the side of his head as if doing so would clear things up for him.

"I—I could have sworn . . . I heard a horse," he said

haltingly. "It made the strangest sound. Did you hear it, Ranger?"

Sam looked at him for a moment, debating with himself.

"Yes, I heard it too, Easy John," he said finally. He wasn't going to mention the birds. That was a little more than he would expect anybody to believe, especially a seasoned lawman like Juan Lupo, a man like himself. Everything had a reasonable explanation if you searched for it long enough. He waited and considered it for a moment. Well . . . most everything, he decided, and he put the matter away and stood and lifted Lupo to his feet.

"Speaking of horses," he said, "I've got Black Pot waiting down the cliff behind the mining company. I'll get you patched up and on your way. Then I'll get him and come back." He hefted the pack onto his shoulder.

Lupo looked troubled as they crossed the flat rock, his arm looped across the Ranger's other shoulder for support.

"I know I heard the strangest sound," he said.

But before he spoke any more on the matter, the Ranger cut him off, saying, "Forget it, Easy John. The shape you're in, you were apt to hear anything." He smiled wryly to himself and stared straight ahead, seeing morning sunlight break sharp and slantwise across the high, rugged land.

Arizona Ranger Sam Burrack is back!
Don't miss a page of
action from America's most
exciting Western author,
Ralph Cotton.

VALLEY OF THE GUN

Whiskey Bend
The Badlands, Arizona Territory

Afternoon shadows stretched long across the rocky
land as Arizona Ranger Sam Burrack walked into
Whiskey Bend from the south, dust-covered, leading
his copper black point dun by its slack reins. When he
saw the tall figure wearing a black duster step out into
the empty street forty yards in front of him, he knew
what to expect. He stopped for only a second, long
enough to flip the reins up over the dun's saddle and
give the tired horse a push, sending it out of the way.

Staring straight ahead, he slowly drew his big Colt
from its holster and walked on, his thumb over the
gun's hammer. He didn't stop again until he stood
thirty feet from the gunman facing him. He took note
of the man's riding duster gathered back behind the
long custom-made Simpson-Barre .45-caliber pistol holstered on his right hip.

The gunman, Lighting Wade Hornady, had stayed behind while the other five riders left Whiskey Bend only a moment earlier. The dust of the five riders still loomed in the air on the far end of the wide street. Seeing the gunman reach for something in his vest pocket, Sam tightened his thumb over the gun hammer, ready to cock it on the upswing. Yet he held back because the man raised a gold watch by its braided horsehair fob and held it in his right hand.

"Pardon me, young man, whilst I wind my watch," Hornady said, cool, confident, opening the lid on the shiny timepiece and glancing down at it. "If I don't wind it while I'm thinking about it, I fear I'll spend the entire evening under an air of uncertainty." He grinned around a long cigar clamped between his teeth. Smoke wafted from beneath his thick mustache. "I hope you don't mind, *Marshal* . . . ?"

"I'm in no hurry," the Ranger said flatly. If this cordial manner was the way Lightning Hornady wanted to play it, he would accommodate him—*but only up to a point*, Sam cautioned himself. Correcting the gunman he said, "It's *Ranger* . . . Arizona Territory Ranger Samuel Burrack."

The gunman looked bemused; he stopped winding the watch, his left thumb and finger still clutching its stem.

"Oh, I see . . . ," he said. "Then you would be the young fellow who caused such a stir, killing Junior Lake and his whole gang back in—"

"I would be," Sam said, cutting Hornady short,

staring into his eyes, yet managing to pay attention to the gunman's hands.

"I have to say, I am taken aback, Ranger," Hornady said, his left hand taking the watch now, his right hand dropping easily down his side, hanging near the big custom Simpson-Barre revolver. "When they asked me to stay behind and kill you, I didn't realize what an important fellow you are."

Sam didn't reply right away. Instead, he watched the gunman's left hand closely as it slipped the watch back into his vest and lingered there. The Ranger found it interesting that the gunman had held the watch in his right hand and used his left hand to wind it.

Wade Hornady opened and closed his right fingers near his gun butt, his left hand clasping the lapel on his duster. He chuckled behind his long cigar.

"Why have you been dogging our trail so fiercely, Ranger?" he asked. "Don't you have plenty of other innocent citizens to harass and aggravate?"

"You and your pals robbed the bank in Goble day before yesterday," said the Ranger. "That's why I'm dogging you."

Hornady's right hand appeared ready to grab for his holstered revolver. But Sam had already seen enough to know the move wasn't coming from the right hand. Lightning Hornady was only drawing his attention to the custom revolver.

Watch for the left . . . Sam cautioned himself.

Hornady shrugged, gave his confident grin.

"It was only a small pissant of a bank, nothing

worth getting excited over—certainly not worth getting yourself killed over, is it?"

This journeyman gunman played his part well, Sam noted, so well that the Ranger decided if he waited long enough and gave this gunman enough room, the odds were good that Lightning Hornady might get an edge and kill him right here where he stood.

Sam continued to stare at him, revealing nothing.

"Well, *is it*?" Hornady asked again.

Without reply, without warning, the Ranger cocked the big Colt on the upswing, just like he'd planned to all along, and put a bullet through the unprepared gunman's chest. The Colt bucked in the Ranger's hand; the single explosion resounded along the street and out across the hill line.

Wade Hornady flew backward, his cigar abandoned in midair, appearing suspended there for a moment as he slid on the rough dirt street behind a settling mist of blood. As the cigar fell to the ground and the downed gunslinger came to a halt, Sam turned from side to side, crouched, fanning the smoking Colt toward any window or darkened doorway that could offer cover for any of Hornady's cohorts.

Once satisfied that Hornady had truly been left alone to kill him, Sam lowered the big Colt an inch and walked forward toward the prone gunman. Hornady struggled for the belly gun inside his duster as his bootheels scooted him backward in the bloodsplattered dirt. He stopped and stared up as Sam loomed over him.

Sam reached down, brushed Hornady's bloody

hand aside and jerked a smaller custom Simpson-Barre revolver from a belly rig. He looked it over, admiring the ornate engraving covering its entire barrel and frame. Evening sunlight glinted soft on the gun's ivory grips.

"Some gun . . . ," Sam said quietly. He shoved the adorned revolver into his gun belt, then drew his long-barreled revolver from its holster and let it hang from his left hand. He stared down at the bleeding gunman as townsfolk began easing back into sight and gathering a few safe yards away.

"We—we were still talking," Hornady said in a strained voice. He stared up at Sam in disbelief.

"You were," Sam said quietly. "I was all through."

Hornady looked at the gaping hole in his chest; blood surged.

"You shoot a man down . . . just like that?" Hornady rasped in an air of moral outrage, a stunned expression on his pale, tortured face.

"Yep, just like that," Sam said matter-of-factly. He stooped beside the bleeding gunman and studied the wound closely. "Dad Orwick must think highly of you, leaving you all by yourself here."

"I always work . . . better alone," the outlaw said, gasping for breath. "Until now, that is," he added, looked down at his bloody wound. "Looks like you've done me in. . . ."

"My bullet missed your heart, Lightning," Sam said. "You've got a good chance of living though this."

Hornady looked surprised at hearing the Ranger call him by his trail name.

"You—you know who I am?" he said.

"Yep, everybody's heard of Lightning Wade Hornady," Sam replied.

"Let me get this straight," Hornady rasped and coughed, raising a bloody finger. "You know who I am. Still, you just . . . walk up and shoot me . . . ?" He appeared to have a hard time making sense of it.

"You want a doctor?" Sam asked without replying. "There's a good one here, if we can catch him sober this hour of the day." He untied a bandanna from around Hornady's neck, wadded it, laid it on his bloody chest and placed the gunman's hand on it.

"Catch him *sober* . . . ?" Hornady coughed and shook his head. "No, thanks. If the drunken son of a bitch don't kill me . . . I'll go off to rot in Yuma prison. Huh-uh . . . not for me."

"Suit yourself," said the Ranger. "Thought I'd ask." He reached into Hornady's boot well and pulled out a large knife in a rawhide sheath, with knuckle dusters shielding its handle. He looked the knife over, shook his head and shoved both it and Hornady's big custom revolver down in his gun belt beside the gunslinger's smaller revolver before turning to walk away.

Hornady glowered, looking at his two custom revolvers and his big boot knife wedged behind the ranger's gun belt.

"Wait. . . . I changed my mind," he said, seeing the gathered townsfolk moving in closer. "I do want a doctor . . . drunk or sober. I don't want to die . . . not until I see you lying dead somewhere, Ranger . . . buzzards scooping out your brains." His words ended in a bloody cough.

"That's the spirit," Sam said flatly. He turned to an older man wearing a long gray beard who had walked up and looked down at Hornady's wound. Seeing a tin star on the bearded man's chest, Sam asked, "Are you the sheriff?"

"Yes, I am," the man said, turning a glance on the Ranger, then back to the wounded gunman. "I'm Grayson DeShay, volunteer sheriff, for the time being anyway." He shook his head slowly and added, "And I know who the two of you are. This one with his belly bleeding is Lightning Wade Hornady. You're Samuel Burrack, the ranger who passes through here now and again, I'm told."

"You're right on both counts," Sam said. "I apologize for not coming to find you first, Sheriff. But this man was gunning for me as soon as I walked into town."

"I understand, Ranger," said Sherrif DeShay. "Anyway, I wasn't sheriff here your last time through. I decided it wise to hang back out of the way, for fear of you shooting me, thinking I was one of his pards."

"I understand, Sheriff," Sam said. "That was wise thinking."

Hornady had a sour expression on his face. "Well, ain't this just wonderful . . . ? The two of you *understands* each other so well," he said in his cynical, pain-filled voice.

"Lightning here wants a doctor," Sam said to the sheriff, ignoring the bitter wounded outlaw's remark.

"An undertaker might serve him better," the volunteer sheriff replied. "What do you want me to do with him if he lives?" he asked. "What'd he do, anyhow?"

"Bank robbery," Sam said.

"Him and the bunch he rode in with?" DeShay asked.

"Yep," said the Ranger. "He's with Fannin Orwick's Redemption Riders. Ever heard of them?"

"*Dad* Orwick? You bet I have," said DeShay. "I saw him once in Carson. That was years ago, though. The old bull's got more wives and kids scattered across these badland hills than you could squeeze into two freight cars. Calls his whole brood the Family of the Lord—which reveals how highly he thinks of himself, I expect."

"That's him all right," Sam said. "He robs banks to support his *family*. I need to get on their trail while it's still warm. I'd like you to hold him until a posse gets here from Goble. If the posse doesn't make it, turn him over to the circuit jail wagon when it makes its rounds."

"I'll do that, Ranger," said DeShay, "only I didn't see Dad Orwick riding with the bunch who came through here."

"You wouldn't if Orwick played it right," Sam said. "I saw where three horses split off the trail a mile out. I expect he and a couple of his gunmen circled town. They'll take up with the others farther along." He nodded toward a line of hills in the distance.

"Shit," Hornady grumbled to himself with contempt. "These two peckerheads wouldn't recognize Dad if he walked up and kicked them in the sack."

DeShay ignored Hornady's grumbling and gazed

out with the Ranger. "It makes sense he'd do that," he replied.

Sam turned to DeShay, lifted the two Simpson-Barre revolvers from behind his gun belt and handed them to him. "You can sell these guns to help pay for this one's keep here."

"You can't sell my guns," Hornady shouted in spite of his pain. "I've got money. . . . I'll pay for my jailing. . . . I can afford my keep."

"Do what best suits you, Sheriff," Sam said. "Any money he has on him is most likely stolen."

"Obliged, Ranger," said DeShay. He hefted the two custom-made revolvers in his hands and looked them over closely. "I might want to keep these for myself." He gave Hornady a flat grin.

"What about my knife, Ranger?" Hornady asked with a scornful tone. "I expect you thieving sons-abitches will steal it too, huh?"

"Shut up," Sheriff DeShay warned, giving Hornady a stiff kick in his side. Hornady let out a deep, painful moan and grasped his chest.

Sam pulled Hornady's knife and its rawhide sheath from behind his belt and handed it to the sheriff.

"If you'd waited a second longer, you'd see me give it to him, and save yourself a kick in the ribs," Sam said.

"I'll see you in hell, Ranger—*in hell*, I tell you!"

"Another word out of you and I'll tell Dr. Lanahan to stitch your mouth shut," DeShay said to Hornady. "If he's drunk enough, he'll likely do it and have himself a good laugh about it."

Hornady coughed blood and closed his eyes as the Ranger walked away. When Sam picked up the reins to the black point dun, he turned to the sheriff and said, "If you need me, I'll be at the livery barn getting this dun fed and tended before I move on."

"Obliged, Ranger," said DeShay. "I'll be along and let you know how he's doing, if Doc doesn't miss a lick and cut him in half." He grinned fiercely down at Hornady, then turned to two townsmen standing nearby and gestured down at the hapless outlaw. "You fellows get him up and carry him over to Doc Lanahan's for me." He turned to another townsman and said, "Gainer, go fetch the doc from the saloon. Tell him to sit his bottle down. He's got a patient needing him."

"This is his drinking time. What if he won't come?" asked Ted Gainer, a tall, serious-looking man with a thick, wide mustache and watery eyes.

"He'll come. He heard the gunshot," DeShay said confidently. "He always comes, even if his path ain't in a straight line."

Ted Gainer turned toward the saloon a block away, where a crowd of onlookers jammed the open batwing doors, some of the more curious of them already stepping down from the boardwalk and walking forward.

"Tell him I'll get some coffee boiling," DeShay called out in afterthought. He grinned down at Hornady as the two townsmen stooped to pick him up. "That'll help him clear away some of the dancing squirrels and pin whistles before he goes to cutting and stitching on Lightning Wade here."

Hornady moaned at the prospect and closed his eyes.

The two townsmen laughed as they raised Hornady by his shoulders and bootheels and walked away along the dirt street with him hanging limp between them. But Hornady saw nothing funny about it. He cursed to himself and let his mind drift away into a dark tunnel of unconsciousness, blood dripping steadily from his wound.

"That blasted Ranger," he murmured in a weak voice. "Just when everything's going my way . . ."

Ready to find
your next great read?

Let us help.

Visit prh.com/nextread